Manas' Quest

KARAN'S KAVACH KUNDAL

AMAN SHEKHAR

notionpress
.com

INDIA · SINGAPORE · MALAYSIA

ISBN
Paperback 979-8-89588-976-3
Hardcase 979-8-89610-988-4

Disclaimer

This work is a piece of fiction. The characters, events, and places described in this book are products of the author's imagination and are not intended to represent any real individuals, occurrences, or locations. Any resemblance to actual persons, living or deceased, events, or locales is purely coincidental.

The author wants to clarify that this work is not intended to hurt or offend anyone's feelings. It is a work of creativity and storytelling, meant solely for the purpose of entertainment and artistic expression. The author does not endorse or condone any of the actions, beliefs, or behaviours depicted in this book.

Readers are encouraged to interpret the content with an open mind and in the spirit of fiction. The author's intention is to create a unique and imaginative narrative that explores the boundaries of storytelling.

The author would like to express gratitude to readers for their interest in this work and hopes that it provides an enjoyable and thought-provoking reading experience.

PREFACE

In the eternal dance between light and darkness, there are moments when the shadows stretch long, threatening to consume all. This is a story born from such a moment, a mythic tale that winds its way through the lost pages of time, where gods and mortals, the undying and the doomed, stand on the precipice of fate itself.

Thousands of years have passed since the great wars of the Ramayana and the Mahabharata, where divine forces clashed, and the destinies of men were forever rewritten. The sacred relics from these epic battles—relics forged in the fires of celestial ambition and touched by the hands of gods—have long been hidden away, scattered across the realms. But their power remains, undiminished and undying, waiting for the day when they would be found again.

Now, in the twilight of this age, the balance of the world hangs perilously. The ancient armor of Karna—the indestructible Kavach Kundal—rumored to grant its bearer invincibility, is lost to legend. Protected by divine forces, this armor is more than a simple relic; it is the key to a greater power that could alter the very course of time and existence itself.

From the snow-covered peaks of the Himalayas to the shadowy forests of Lanka, a new generation rises to seek this lost power. Manas, a descendant of an ancient warrior line, joins forces with Parashurama, the immortal sage, and Ananya, a fierce and determined guardian, on a perilous journey to recover the pieces of the divine armor. But they are not alone in this quest. On the other side lurks Shukracharya, the master of dark arts, Ashwatthama, the ageless warrior with vengeance burning in his heart, and Raghav, a fallen comrade reborn with newfound strength and ambition. Their paths converge in a battle that is as old as time itself.

What follows is a tale of courage and betrayal, of ancient secrets and eternal truths, where every shadow hides a threat, and every step could be their last. As the forces of light and darkness collide, they must navigate a world where gods still whisper in the wind and ancient mantras hold the power to reshape reality.

This is a journey into the mystical realms of Indian mythology, where legends breathe, and the echoes of ancient battles resound in the hearts of those who dare to challenge their fate. It is a tribute to the heroes who live on, not in the pages of history, but in the eternal spirit of those who believe in something greater than themselves.

Prepare yourself to step into a world where time bends, where the divine and the mortal are but two sides of the same coin, and where the quest for immortality could either save or doom us all. The battle is not just for an ancient relic—it is for the very soul of existence.

Let the journey begin…

PROLOGUE

The sky above Kurukshetra was aflame with the hues of twilight, the very air thick with the echoes of a war that had shaped the fate of ages. As the last of the dust settled on this blood-soaked land, the gods themselves seemed to hold their breath, watching the mortals below. Among the fallen warriors and shattered chariots lay the remnants of a battle that would be sung for eons—a battle where the bravest of souls had bled and where legends had been forged and broken.

In a secluded corner, untouched by the eyes of men, an ancient sage stood alone. Shukracharya, the master of dark knowledge, gazed at the distant battlefield with eyes that seemed to pierce through the veils of time itself. His face, aged and worn by the millennia, bore a look of grim determination. For Shukracharya knew that this was but a fleeting victory in an unending war. He could sense the cosmic balance teetering, threatened by forces unseen, yet ever present.

Nearby, the immortal Ashwathama wandered aimlessly, his spirit tortured, his forehead bearing the curse that would never allow him peace. He had seen his father, Dronacharya, fall; he had felt the sting of betrayal and the weight of an eternal life marked by suffering. But he was not done. Not yet. The fires of vengeance still smoldered in his eyes, and his restless heart craved a different kind of resolution—a resolution that lay beyond the ordinary bounds of time and space.

In another realm, deep within the sacred groves of the Himalayas, the sage Parashurama meditated. His eyes were closed, but his mind was sharp, aware. The whispers of the past reached him even in the stillness of his sanctuary. He knew that something was stirring—something that had been set in motion long before the first arrow flew in Kurukshetra. The divine relics—Karna's Kavach Kundal, forged by Surya and lost in the ashes of time—were calling out. These relics, imbued with the power to change the very fabric of destiny, had lain dormant for ages, waiting for a worthy hand to claim them.

Far to the south, in the dense forests of Lanka, a tribe guarded its most prized possession, a secret known only to the chosen few. The tribe, blessed by Hanuman himself, lived in shadows, whispering of an "energy" that kept their hearts beating and their spirits unbreakable. But this energy was more than mere folklore—it was a piece of a celestial puzzle, one that many would kill to possess.

And then there was Manas, a descendant of ancient warriors, who knew little of his fate. Guided by a destiny written in the stars, his path would soon cross with the great and the malevolent, the divine and the cursed. Unbeknownst to him, his blood carried a secret—a secret that would make him the key to a battle beyond battles.

As the old order began to crumble, a new quest was set in motion—a quest for the lost armor of Karna, a quest that would see gods and mortals, demons and sages clash in a conflict that could alter the fate of the world. Some sought it for power; others, for vengeance. But the Kavach Kundal was no ordinary treasure. It was a gift from the heavens, a test from the gods, and it could grant invincibility to its bearer. Whoever held it could command the elements themselves, bring back the Saraswati River, change the course of time, and even defy death.

But the armor had a will of its own. It would not yield to just any hand. It waited, watched, and chose. And now, as forces ancient and new converged, the world braced for a reckoning.

And so, the journey begins—through shadows and light, through treachery and loyalty, through the corridors of time itself. For in the search for the divine armor, one would find not only the secrets of the past but the keys to the future.

The stage is set, the players are in place, and the winds of fate have begun to howl once more.

Let the quest for the Kavach Kundal commence.

CHAPTER 1

The towering peaks of the Mahendragiri Mountain loomed large against the twilight sky, their jagged silhouettes etched by centuries of relentless winds and harsh winters. The mountains, ancient and imposing, stood as silent sentinels to the passage of time, their secrets buried deep within icy, unyielding hearts. The fall seemed to stretch into eternity itself. He now lay battered and broken, his formidable form reduced to little more than a shadow of his former self. Each unforgiving impact against the rock face tore at his flesh, cracked his bones, and left him teetering on the edge of consciousness. Yet, death, that merciful escape, remained forever out of reach—an ever-present reminder of the curse that bound him.

When at last his descent ended, he lay twisted and still at the base of the mountain, the snow beneath him rapidly turning crimson with his blood. The cold wind wailed through the valley, a mournful dirge for the fallen warrior, while the stark, desolate landscape offered neither comfort nor solace to the agony that wracked his immortal frame. Hours passed, the fading light of day surrendering to the deepening shadows of night, before the first signs of life stirred in this remote wilderness.

A group of villagers, weary from their day's toil of gathering firewood, stumbled upon the scene. Simple folk, their lives shaped by the rhythms of the mountains and far removed from the complexities of the outside world, they halted in their tracks, startled by the sight of the fallen man. They exchanged nervous glances, each uncertain of what lay before them. One of the men, a middle-aged villager with a weathered face but kind eyes, took a hesitant step forward and knelt beside his motionless form. His breath caught in his throat as he reached out, his hand trembling as he sought a pulse.

"He's alive," the man whispered, his voice tinged with a mixture of relief and trepidation. "We must take him to the village. He needs help—urgently."

A sense of urgency gripped the group, and they quickly fashioned a makeshift stretcher from the branches they had collected. Lifting his limp body onto it with care, they began the slow, arduous journey back to their village. The path was treacherous, made all the more perilous by the gathering darkness, yet they pressed on, driven by a deep-seated compassion that outweighed their fear of the unknown.

Their village, a small, secluded settlement nestled in a sheltered valley far from the reach of the modern world, was a place where time seemed to stand still. The villagers lived simple, peaceful lives, tending to their animals, cultivating small patches of land, and preserving the ancient traditions handed down through countless generations. Here, the past lingered in every breath, a constant, unseen presence.

At the heart of this village stood the humble dwelling of the *Vaidya*, an elderly healer whose knowledge of the ancient medicinal arts was unmatched. Known affectionately as *Baba*, the *Vaidya* had dedicated his life to the service of others, his wisdom sought after by those near and far. His small hut, constructed of stone and wood, was filled with the rich, earthy scent of drying herbs, a quiet sanctuary where life and healing coexisted in harmony.

When the villagers arrived with the body, the Vaidya was busy in his daily prayers. His advanced years had not dulled the sharpness of his mind, nor the clarity of his gaze. His long white beard flowed down to his chest, and though his eyes were softened by age, they still sparkled with the keen intellect of a man who had seen much and understood more.

"Bring him inside," *Vaidya* commanded, his voice steady, authoritative.

The villagers obeyed without question, carrying Ashwatthama into the warm, dimly lit interior of the hut. The Vaidya's practiced eyes quickly assessed his broken form, taking in the extent of his injuries with a critical eye. The deep gashes and shattered bones were evident, but it was a wound on the stranger's forehead that truly caught the *Vaidya's* attention—a deep, angry scar, old and ragged, as though it had never fully healed. The *Vaidya's* brow furrowed in concern.

"This man has suffered greatly," he murmured, his voice barely audible as he spoke more to himself than to the others.

"His wounds from the fall will heal with time, but this wound on his forehead… it is different."

The villagers, sensing the gravity of his words, watched in silence as the Vaidya continued his examination. After a moment, he turned to the villagers and instructed them to fetch specific herbs from the nearby forest—rare plants that grew only in the shadowed corners of the mountains, their healing properties known to few. Though weary from their journey, the villagers did not hesitate. They set off into the night with torches to light their way, driven by the same unwavering trust they had in the *Vaidya's* abilities.

While the villagers were away, the *Vaidya* set to work on treating his more immediate injuries. His hands, steady and skilled from decades of experience, moved with the precision of a master healer. He applied poultices to the wounds, set broken bones, and murmured ancient prayers of healing, his voice a low, comforting hum that filled the small hut. Yet, even as he worked, his gaze kept returning to the wound on the man's forehead—a wound that seemed to pulse with an energy of its own, an energy that filled the *Vaidya* with a deep sense of unease.

As the night deepened, the villagers returned, their arms laden with the herbs the *Vaidya* had requested. The potent fragrances of rare roots and leaves filled the hut as the *Vaidya* prepared them with meticulous care. He ground the herbs into a fine paste, mixing them with oils and other ingredients from his stores, creating a salve designed to draw out infection and promote healing.

The *Vaidya* worked in silence, applying the salve to the person's wounds with gentle precision. But when he came to the wound on the forehead, he hesitated. The scar seemed almost malevolent, as if it were not merely a physical injury but something far more sinister. The *Vaidya* applied the salve with the utmost care, his hands steady but his heart heavy with the weight of his thoughts. Deep down, he knew that this wound was beyond his ability to heal.

"This wound," the *Vaidya* said quietly, his voice thick with apprehension, "is no ordinary injury. It carries a curse within it, a mark of something ancient and powerful. I can treat his other wounds, but this… this is beyond my skill."

The villagers, who had gathered around the cot, exchanged uneasy glances, their faces etched with concern and curiosity. They could sense the *Vaidya's* unease, though they did not fully understand its source. It was then that a small voice broke the tense silence.

In the corner of the room, a young boy, no more than ten years old, had been watching intently, his wide eyes fixed on the stranger lying on the cot. The boy, known for his love of stories and insatiable curiosity, had spent many hours listening to the elders' tales and reading the few old books the village possessed. He hesitated for a moment, unsure if he should speak, but the gravity of the situation compelled him to share what he knew.

"I've read about a warrior with a wound like that," the boy said, his voice trembling slightly.

The villagers turned to look at him, their expressions a mixture of surprise and curiosity. Encouraged, the boy continued,

"In one of the old stories… from the Mahabharata. They say there was a warrior, a great and powerful one, who had a wound on his forehead that never healed. He was cursed, cursed to live forever, because of what he did during the war."

Vaidya's heart skipped a beat. The boy's words resonated deeply with him, confirming the suspicions that had been slowly forming in his mind. He had heard the stories too—stories of a warrior cursed to eternal life, doomed to wander the earth in torment, unable to escape the consequences of his actions.

"That warrior," the *Vaidya* said slowly, his voice tinged with a mixture of awe and dread, "was Ashwatthama, the son of Dronacharya, the great teacher of the Pandavas and Kauravas. He was cursed to live forever, to bear the weight of his deeds for all eternity." He paused, letting his words sink in. "If this man is truly Ashwatthama… then we are in the presence of one of the most feared and powerful beings in all of history."

A collective gasp escaped the villagers, their faces paling with fear and astonishment. The stories of Ashwatthama were known to them all, but they had never imagined that such a figure could be real—let alone that he could be lying in their midst. The implications of the *Vaidya's* words were staggering, and the atmosphere in the small hut grew heavy with the weight of revelation.

"What do we do, *Baba*?" one of the villagers asked, his voice trembling with uncertainty. "If he is truly Ashwatthama, how can we help him?"

The Vaidya remained silent for a long moment, his mind racing as he considered their options. He knew that Ashwatthama was not a man to be taken lightly, and that his presence in the village could indeed bring great peril. But he also knew that the warrior was in a weakened state, and that they could not simply turn him away.

"We must continue to care for him," *Vaidya* finally said, his voice resolute.

"But we must also be vigilant. We do not know why he has come to us, nor what fate has in store for him—or for us. Until he recovers, we must treat him with respect, but we must also be prepared for whatever may come."

The villagers nodded slowly, their hearts heavy with unease. As the night wore on, the villagers slowly dispersed, returning to their homes with heavy hearts and troubled minds. The *Vaidya* remained by Ashwatthama's side, his thoughts a whirlwind of concern and contemplation.

As the Vaidya kept watch, Ashwatthama drifted deeper into a fevered sleep, his mind consumed by visions from a past that refused to let him go. In the dream, he was on the battlefield once more, surrounded by the chaos of war. The clang of steel against steel rang in his ears, the shouts of warriors and the screams of the dying echoing in the background. Ashwatthama fought fiercely, but the weight of the battle bore down on him, his strength waning.

Suddenly, he felt a sharp pain—a spear had found its mark, piercing his side. He staggered, the world spinning around him, but before he could fall, a hand caught him. Ashwatthama looked up to see Karna, his friend and ally, steadying him. "You must hold on, Ashwatthama," Karna urged, his voice strong and filled with urgency. "We cannot falter now."

But even as Karna spoke, Ashwatthama's vision began to blur, the pain overwhelming him. His strength ebbed away, and the world around him began to fade. It was then that a voice, loud and commanding, cut through the haze. "There is no time to rest!" Dronacharya's voice boomed, filled with a fury that shook Ashwatthama to his core. "Wake up! We must finish what we started!"

The force of his father's words was like a shockwave, ripping Ashwatthama from the clutches of his dream and thrusting him back into the waking world. He jolted awake, his eyes wide with alarm, his breath coming in ragged gasps. For a moment, he was disoriented, his mind struggling to reconcile the dream with the reality around him.

The dim light of the hut, the concerned faces of the villagers, the unfamiliar surroundings—all of it felt alien and threatening. Panic set in as Ashwatthama's hand instinctively went to the wound on his side, but instead, he felt the bandages and the tender flesh beneath. The confusion and anger swelled within him as he sat up abruptly, his eyes narrowing in suspicion as he took in his surroundings. The *Vaidya*, seeing the warrior's distress, stepped forward, his voice calm and soothing.

"You are safe here," he said gently. "You are in a village far from the battle. Please, rest and allow yourself to heal."

But Ashwatthama's anger flared at the words, his memories of the dream still vivid in his mind.

"Move," he snarled, his voice filled with a mix of anger and fear. "I must get back. There is no time to waste!"

He pushed the Vaidya aside with a force that belied his weakened state, the desperation in his voice clear. The villagers recoiled in fear, unsure of what to do. But the Vaidya, though startled, remained calm.

"You are not well enough to leave," he insisted, his tone firm. "Please, rest.

Ashwatthama's eyes blazed with frustration, his hand clenching into a fist as he struggled to rise from the cot. But even as he tried to stand, his body betrayed him, the strength sapped from his limbs.

He stumbled, and the Vaidya quickly moved to support him, guiding him back to the cot with gentle hands.

"You must regain your strength," *Vaidya* said softly, his voice filled with empathy."

Ashwatthama, though seething with frustration, knew the truth in the Vaidya's words. His body was broken, and his mind was still clouded with the remnants of the dream. For now, he had no choice but to relent. He sank back onto the cot, his breath coming in heavy, ragged gasps as the reality of his situation set in. The *Vaidya* watched as Ashwatthama's anger slowly gave way to exhaustion, the warrior's eyelids growing heavy once more.

"Rest now," *Vaidya* urged, his voice a quiet command."

As Ashwatthama's eyes closed, the *Vaidya* glanced at the villagers, their fear still palpable in the small hut. He gave them a reassuring nod, though his own heart was filled with unease. In the silence that followed, Ashwatthama drifted back into a restless sleep, his dreams still haunted by the ghosts of his past.

CHAPTER 2

The early morning light filtered through the dense canopy of the ancient forest, casting long shadows on the ground as the sounds of Manas and Ananya's training echoed through the clearing. Under the watchful eye of Lord Parashurama, they moved through rigorous drills, their bodies pushing against the limits of their endurance. Each strike, each defensive maneuver, was a testament to their growing strength and skill, honed by months of relentless practice. Lord Parashurama, standing with arms crossed, observed them with an intensity that only a master could possess. His presence alone was enough to keep them focused, knowing that any mistake would be met with stern correction. But today, there was a different kind of focus in his gaze, something deeper, as if his mind was occupied with thoughts from a distant past.

After a particularly demanding sequence, Lord Parashurama raised his hand, signaling them to stop. The two warriors, breathing heavily, looked to their master, awaiting his next instruction.

"Manas," Lord Parashurama began, his voice breaking the silence with its usual authority, "do you know the story of Karna's *Kavach Kundal*? Is there anything written about it in the biographies you've read in your ancestors' library?"

Manas, still catching his breath, took a moment to respond. He had spent countless hours poring over the ancient texts in his family's library, uncovering the secrets and histories of his lineage.

Yet, when it came to Karna's legendary armor, the details were surprisingly sparse.

"No, Guruji," Manas replied, shaking his head slightly. "Nothing important. There are mentions of it, but nothing that tells the full story."

Lord Parashurama's sharp gaze softened for a moment, recognizing the young man's hunger for knowledge. He knew that Manas had barely scratched the surface of the ancient tales that shaped their world.

"But Guruji," Manas continued, curiosity getting the better of him, "is the *Kavach Kundal* really necessary? And who made it? Can we find the one who made it and ask them to forge it again?"

A deep, resonant chuckle escaped Lord Parashurama's lips, a sound that seemed to carry with it the weight of countless ages.

"Do you wish to know the source of this *Kavach*?" he asked, his tone both amused and instructive.

Manas and Ananya exchanged curious glances. Lord Parashurama rarely spoke of such things, and when he did, it was always with a purpose. Sensing an important lesson in the offing, they both nodded eagerly.

"Yes, Guruji," Manas replied earnestly. "I want to know."

Lord Parashurama settled himself on a nearby rock, his gaze distant as he prepared to recount a tale that was as old as the mountains themselves.

"Very well," he said, his voice lowering to a more somber tone. "I will tell you the story of Dambodhaya."

"Long ago," Lord Parashurama began, "in an age forgotten by most, there was a king named Dambodhaya. He ruled over a vast kingdom, wealthy beyond measure, and powerful enough that his name struck fear into the hearts of many. Yet, for all his power

and wealth, Dambodhaya was not satisfied. Ambition burned within him—a desire to achieve what no mortal had ever achieved: immortality."

Manas and Ananya leaned in closer, captivated by the gravity of the tale.

"Dambodhaya performed severe penances, invoking the favor of the gods, seeking the ultimate boon. After many years of intense austerity, his devotion caught the attention of Lord Surya, the Sun God, who appeared before him in a blaze of radiant light."

"'What do you seek, Dambodhaya?' Lord Surya asked, his voice as warm and powerful as the sun itself."

"'I seek immortality,' Dambodhaya replied without hesitation. 'Grant me a life that will never end, so that I may rule for eternity, unchallenged and unrivaled.'"

Lord Parashurama paused, letting the weight of the request sink in.

"But Lord Surya, though compassionate, was bound by the laws of the universe. He shook his head and said, 'Immortality is not within my power to grant, Dambodhaya. All beings must face death, even the gods. Ask for another boon, one that I can grant.'"

"Dambodhaya, though disappointed, was not deterred. His mind worked quickly, searching for another way to achieve the invincibility he craved. 'Then grant me a thousand Kavach,' he demanded, 'armors that no weapon on earth can penetrate. And let it be so that only one who has performed a thousand years of penance can break even one of these Kavach. And when such a person does break it, may their life be forfeit as a result.'"

Lord Parashurama's voice took on a grave tone. "This was no small request. Dambodhaya was asking for near invincibility, a power that would make him almost untouchable by any living being. But the gods are bound by their word, and Lord Surya, seeing the intensity of Dambodhaya's desire, granted him the boon."

"'So be it,' Lord Surya declared. 'You shall have your thousand Kavach Kundal. But remember, abuse it, and the consequences will be dire.'"

Lord Parashurama's expression darkened as he continued.

"But Dambodhaya was too consumed by his lust for power to heed the warning. Clad in his thousand Kavach Kundal, he believed himself invincible and soon began to terrorize the world. He waged war on kingdoms, destroyed cities, and challenged even the gods themselves. His arrogance knew no bounds, for he believed that no one could ever perform the thousand years of penance needed to defeat him."

"Years passed," Lord Parashurama continued, "and Dambodhaya's reign of terror spread far and wide. No one dared to stand against him, for who could match the strength of a man protected by a thousand divine armors?"

"But as always, there are forces at work that even the mightiest cannot foresee. One day, a poor Brahmin, weary of the endless suffering brought by Dambodhaya's tyranny, approached him. The Brahmin, his voice trembling with both fear and anger, said, 'If you think you are so powerful, O mighty king, then why not challenge the two brothers who dwell in the forest? They are said to be invincible, even greater than you.'"

Lord Parashurama's eyes gleamed as he described the fateful encounter.

"Intrigued and eager to prove his dominance, Dambodhaya set out to find these brothers. He wandered through forests and mountains, his anger growing as he searched for them. Finally, deep within a sacred grove, he found them—**Nar** and **Narayan**, two sages whose names were whispered with reverence and awe."

"*The brothers were meditating when Dambodhaya's roar shattered the peace of the forest. He challenged them to a battle, his voice booming with confidence. 'Come forth and face me!' he demanded. 'Let us see who truly is invincible!'*"

"*At first, Nar and Narayan, embodying the spirit of peace and wisdom, tried to calm the furious king. They spoke of the futility of violence, of the need for harmony and balance. But Dambodhaya, blinded by his arrogance, would not listen. His desire for victory, for proving his strength, had consumed him.*"

"*So Nar, seeing that there was no reasoning with the king, stood to face him in battle. But before they engaged, Narayan, the wiser of the two, began a thousand-year meditation, calling upon Lord Shiva.*"

Lord Parashurama's voice grew more intense as he described the battle.

"*The fight that ensued was nothing short of legendary. For a thousand years, Nar and Dambodhaya clashed, their blows shaking the very earth beneath them. Nar fought with the strength and skill that only a divine warrior could possess, but despite his best efforts, Dambodhaya's Kavach remained unscathed.*"

"*But as the thousand years came to an end, Nar finally struck a blow that shattered one of the Kavach. Dambodhaya staggered, shocked by the realization that his protection was not absolute. Yet, with the breaking of the Kavach, the curse took hold, and Nar fell, his life force drained by the power of the boon.*"

Lord Parashurama paused, allowing the gravity of Nar's sacrifice to settle in.

"*As Dambodhaya reveled in his survival, he looked up to see Narayan rising from his meditation. With the power gathered from a thousand years of penance, Narayan chanted ancient mantras and brought his brother back to life, restoring him as if he had never fallen.*"

"Dambodhaya was stunned, his confidence shaken for the first time. But there was no time to recover, for now, Narayan stood ready to fight, and Nar took his place in meditation."

"The battle resumed, fierce and unrelenting, as Narayan fought with the same determination that Nar had shown. For another thousand years, they fought, and in the end, Narayan too broke one of the Kavach, only to fall as Nar had done. But once again, Nar, now empowered by his own meditation, brought his brother back to life."

Lord Parashurama's voice was a low rumble as he described the cycle that followed.

"This pattern continued, over and over again, with each brother taking turns to fight and meditate. With every thousand years, another Kavach was shattered, and another life was sacrificed and restored. Until, finally, only one Kavach remained."

"By this time, Dambodhaya was a shadow of his former self. The realization that he was not invincible had taken its toll, and he knew that the end was near. Desperate, he fled, seeking refuge with the very god who had granted him the boon—Lord Surya." "Dambodhaya threw himself at Lord Surya's feet, begging for protection, knowing that Nar and Narayan were close behind. When the brothers arrived, Surya stood between them and Dambodhaya. 'He is under my protection,'

Lord Surya declared. 'I cannot let you kill him.'"

The tension in Lord Parashurama's voice was palpable as he recounted the final moments.

"Narayan, filled with righteous fury, cursed Lord Surya. 'In Dambodhaya's next birth, he shall be born with the Kavach itself, and we will be reborn as well. When that time comes, it will be Nar who destroys the Kavach and ends the cycle.'"

"And so, bound by the curse, the saga of the Kavach Kundal was set to repeat itself, this time with new players, but the same inexorable fate."

Manas quickly grasped the storyline, and he connected the dots, realizing the profound significance of the events that had unfolded.

He understood that in the previous birth, his forefather, Karna, was born with the divine Kavach, a celestial armor gifted by his father, Lord Surya, which rendered him invincible, the same last Kavach which was left with Dambodhaya. Meanwhile, Nar and Narayan, who had been incarnated as sages in their past lives, were reborn as Arjuna and Lord Krishna, destined to play pivotal roles in the Mahabharata. As the great war of Mahabharata loomed closer, Lord Krishna, aware of the impending battle's complexities, foresaw the challenge that Karna's invincibility would pose to Arjuna. Understanding the gravity of the situation, Krishna devised a plan to protect Arjuna. On the twelfth day of the Kurukshetra war, Indra, the king of gods and Arjuna's father, descended to the mortal realm, disguised as a humble Brahmin. He approached Karna with the intention of asking for his Kavach and Kundal, knowing that Karna, renowned for his unwavering generosity, would not refuse a request made by a Brahmin, even if it meant sacrificing his own protection.

Indra's visit was a critical moment, for it marked the turning point in Karna's destiny. As the disguised Brahmin, Indra humbly requested Karna's Kavach and Kundal as alms. True to his reputation, Karna did not hesitate. Despite knowing that giving away his armor would leave him vulnerable in the battlefield, Karna honored the Brahmin's request, cutting away the Kavach and Kundal from his body and handing them over to the disguised Indra. This act of selflessness sealed Karna's fate, as he was left without the divine protection that had made him nearly invincible. It was a sacrifice that exemplified Karna's magnanimity, but it also served Krishna's purpose. Without the Kavach to protect him, Karna became vulnerable in the war, paving the way for Arjuna to fulfill his destiny. Manas realized that this event was not just a simple act of charity but a deeply strategic move orchestrated by Lord Krishna to ensure Arjuna's safety and success in the war. The removal of the Kavach was a critical maneuver that would eventually lead to the fall of Karna, despite his unparalleled prowess on the battlefield. This revelation underscored the intricate interplay of fate, strategy, and divine will in the epic saga of the Mahabharata.

Lord Parashurama fell silent, the weight of the story hanging in the air like a thick mist. Manas and Ananya, who had been riveted by every word, felt the enormity of the tale settle upon their shoulders.

Manas concluded, his voice low and thoughtful.

"So the *Kavach Kundal* that Karna wore... they are the same ones, passed down through the ages."

Lord Parashurama nodded solemnly.

"Yes. They are the remnants of a divine conflict, a battle that transcends time itself. And now, you must find them, for the consequences of their power falling into the wrong hands are beyond imagining."

Manas felt the burden of destiny pressing down on him, but there was also a sense of purpose. The path ahead was fraught with danger, but he knew now more than ever that he could not turn back. Lord Parashurama stood, his commanding presence once again filling the clearing.

"Enough talk. We have much to prepare for. The time for stories is over; now, you must be ready for what is to come."

With a nod, Manas and Ananya resumed their training, the story of Dambodhaya and the *Kavach Kundal* echoing in their minds.

CHAPTER 3

High in the remote Himalayan mountains, where the peaks kissed the heavens and the earth was blanketed in an eternal shroud of snow, a solitary figure emerged from the stillness of a long meditation. The sage, Shukracharya, draped in a simple *angavastram* that barely protected him from the freezing cold, stepped forward, his eyes gleaming with the wisdom of ages. His mind, however, was troubled, for he had sensed a disturbance in the delicate balance of power that governed the world—a disturbance that had drawn him from his deep meditation.

The landscape around him was serene, untouched by time, but Shukracharya's purpose was anything but peaceful. As he descended from his mountain retreat, the sage found himself walking through the undulating snow-covered paths, his breath visible in the cold air. His journey was solitary, his thoughts introspective, until he encountered a group of travelers—men who had wandered into these remote lands with no understanding of the sanctity they were disturbing. Upon spotting the sage, these men—rough, uncouth, and ignorant of the power that walked among them—saw an opportunity to amuse themselves. With grins that spoke of mischief and arrogance, they encircled Shukracharya, blocking his path and hurling taunts at the old man who dared to walk alone in such desolation.

The sage's tranquility began to waver under the relentless provocation, his inner peace disrupted by a growing frustration.

Anger, a force he had long mastered, now began to surface. The ancient power within him stirred, a power that had remained dormant for centuries, until now.

With a sigh that seemed to carry the weight of the world, Shukracharya dropped his staff into the snow and reached out, his fingers brushing against the forehead of the nearest mocker. His lips moved in a barely audible chant, reciting ancient mantras known only to those who had studied the deepest mysteries of the universe. The effect was immediate and terrifying: the man crumpled to the ground, his life force extinguished in an instant, his eyes staring blankly into the void.

The rest of the group froze in horror, the laughter dying in their throats as they watched their companion fall. They could not comprehend the power they had just witnessed. Before they could react, Shukracharya raised his hand again, and an invisible force rippled through the air, freezing the men where they stood. They were immobilized, their bodies rigid, their eyes wide with terror.

The leader of the group, his voice trembling, managed to stammer, "Who are you?"

Shukracharya, his expression unreadable, responded in a tone as cold as the air around them. "My name is Shukracharya, and I am searching for my book."

The words hung in the air, heavy with foreboding, as the men remained paralyzed, held by the sage's unseen power. Without another word, Shukracharya moved to the side of the path and, with a grace that belied his age, sat cross-legged on the ground, his staff lying beside him. The fallen traveler's lifeless body lay nearby, a silent testament to the sage's power, while the others stood rooted in place, unable to move or speak.

Shukracharya closed his eyes and began to meditate, his consciousness expanding as he reached out with his mind, probing the fabric of time and space. He sought answers, to understand what had transpired in the world during his years of meditation, and more importantly, to locate the book that had been lost to him.

As his mind journeyed through the ether, he saw visions—fleeting images of events that had unfolded in the last 2000 years. The world had changed, but not for the better. The balance of power had shifted, and darkness had begun to creep into places once protected by the light. Shukracharya's thoughts narrowed as he searched for a specific thread in the vast tapestry of time—the whereabouts of his book, *the Mrityormukti: Rahashyam*.

His meditative trance deepened, and the visions grew clearer. He saw the birth of a child, a descendant of Karna, marked by the same divine heritage. The boy had grown into a man, a warrior named Manas, who had become entangled in a battle with an ancient enemy—Ashwatthama. Shukracharya watched as their paths crossed, as destinies intertwined, and as the ancient conflict was rekindled in the modern age.

He saw Manas, desperate and determined, consuming Somras, the elixir of the gods, in a bid to gain the strength needed to face his adversaries. But it was not this that drew Shukracharya's attention. It was the image of Ashwatthama, holding in his hands the very book that Shukracharya sought. *The Mrityormukti: Rahashyam* had found its way into the hands of a warrior driven by vengeance, a man whose soul was as cursed as the book itself.

A sigh escaped Shukracharya's lips, a sound that echoed with both relief and resignation.

"So, finally," he murmured to himself, "a worthy keeper of my book has emerged. But he is alone in this world, struggling against forces that seek to destroy him."

Shukracharya's mind continued to explore the threads of fate, delving deeper into the events that were yet to come. He saw Manas, guided by his master Lord Parashurama, on a quest to find Karna's Kavach Kundal, the divine armor that had once made his ancestor invincible. But the sage knew that this was a futile mission, a wild chase after an artifact that had long been hidden from the world's eyes. A low, humorless chuckle escaped Shukracharya's lips.

"Fools," he thought, "they chase after shadows.

The Kavach Kundal cannot be found, for it is hidden beyond the reach of mortal men. And as for Lord Indra... he is nowhere to be found."

The sage's thoughts shifted back to Ashwatthama, the keeper of his book. Shukracharya could sense the immortal warrior's pain, his suffering. He was gravely injured, his strength diminished, yet his spirit was unbroken.

"I must help him," Shukracharya decided, his voice resolute in the stillness of his mind.

"Ashwatthama has borne the burden of this curse for too long. He is the only one who can wield the knowledge within *the Mrityormukti: Rahashyam*." His meditation grew more intense, his mind casting out farther, seeking the exact location of the wounded warrior. As he focused, the world around him began to blur, and visions of the past and future collided in a swirl of images. He saw Ashwatthama, lying broken at the base of a mountain, rescued by villagers who had no idea of the immortal's true identity. He saw the Vaidya who tried to heal him, the wound on Ashwatthama's forehead resisting all attempts at treatment.

Shukracharya's brow furrowed as he concentrated further, piecing together the scattered fragments of Ashwatthama's recent past. He saw the immortal warrior's thoughts, his desperate need to recover, to continue his fight. And he saw the faint glimmers of hope that still burned within Ashwatthama's soul—a hope that he could reclaim his strength and fulfill his destiny.

"Yes," Shukracharya whispered, his voice filled with a quiet determination. "I must guide him, restore him. For only then can he stand against Lord Parashurama and his minions."

As he prepared to break his meditation, Shukracharya gathered one final piece of information. He saw Manas, struggling under the weight of his mission, his mind focused on the search for the divine armor. The sage shook his head, amused by the young warrior's naivety.

"It is a lost cause, Manas. You chase a dream that cannot be realized."

With that, Shukracharya opened his eyes, returning to the present, his mind now clear and focused. He glanced at the lifeless body beside him, then at the remaining travelers who were still frozen in place, their eyes wide with terror. The sage's expression softened slightly as he considered their fate. One of the men, his body immobilized but his mind still his own, stared at Shukracharya with a mixture of fear and desperation. He had witnessed the impossible, seen the sage's power firsthand, and now he was trapped, unable to move, his fate uncertain. Shukracharya stood slowly, his movements deliberate, and approached the terrified man.

"You have seen what power truly is," the sage said, his voice calm and devoid of malice. "Let this be a lesson to you. Do not mock what you do not understand."

The man, too terrified to speak, scrambled to his feet and fled into the forest, not daring to look back. The remaining travelers, still under the sage's control, were left standing in the snow, their fates uncertain. Shukracharya did not linger. He retrieved his staff, glanced once more at the scene, and then began his journey anew. His path was now clear—he would find Ashwatthama, restore him, and together they would confront the forces that sought to unearth the past.

As the sage moved through the snow-covered landscape, the distant echoes of a curse and the promise of a forgotten battle lingered in the air. The game had begun, and the players were taking their positions. But this time, Shukracharya intended to tip the scales in his favor. The world had forgotten his power, but it would soon remember. And when it did, the consequences would be felt by gods and men alike.

CHAPTER 4

The first light of dawn crept over the distant horizon, casting a pale glow across the snow-covered landscape. The day began in quiet reverence, with the villagers rising slowly from their sleep to tend to their daily chores. But there was one among them who was already awake, moving with a deliberate purpose that set him apart from the rest.

Ashwatthama, had begun his day as he always did—offering his prayers to Lord Shiva. Despite the countless centuries that had passed since his time, the rituals had not changed. Even in his weakened state, his spirit remained unbroken, fueled by a purpose that transcended the mundane concerns of the modern world.

The villagers, who had taken him in and nursed him back to health, watched with a mixture of awe and trepidation as he performed his rituals. One morning, as Ashwatthama knelt in prayer, one of the villagers, a curious young man, approached him cautiously.

"How do you know when to wake up for your prayers?" he asked, his voice tinged with genuine curiosity.

"We've noticed that you wake up at the same time every day, without fail, and without using any clock. How do you do that?"

Ashwatthama, his eyes closed in deep meditation, did not immediately respond. When he finally spoke, his voice was low, almost dismissive.

"Your modern way of calculating time is ridiculous," he said.

"You rely on watches and clocks as if they control the very flow of time itself. You are all clueless about time."

The young man, taken aback by the sharpness in Ashwatthama's tone, hesitated before asking another question.

"But… without these tools, how did people in your time manage? How did they know the time without any clocks?"

Ashwatthama's lips curled into a faint, almost mocking smile. "In my period, no such things existed," he replied.

"We were in tune with the natural world, with the rhythms of the earth and the heavens.

Time was not something that needed to be measured—it was felt, experienced. It was known. But you… you've lost that connection, buried it under layers of meaningless inventions." Another villager, an older man who had been listening quietly from a distance, stepped forward. He had lived a long life, steeped in the traditions and stories of his ancestors.

"It would be easy to know more about your time," the old man said cautiously. "We've only read about it in books, but there are many variations, and we don't know what is true."

Ashwatthama laughed, a sound that was more bitter than amused.

"The truth?" he repeated, shaking his head. "You seek the truth in books written by those who were not there, who can only guess at what happened. You will never find the truth that way. You want to know what my time was like? You'd have better luck finding it in your dreams."

The villagers exchanged uneasy glances, disturbed by the immortal's caustic words. His demeanor, so different from what they had expected, unsettled them. The elder Vaidya, who had been caring for Ashwatthama since his arrival, spoke up, his voice filled with a quiet authority.

"In all the stories passed down from my ancestors," he said, "I've never heard of anyone from your time being this... rude."

Ashwatthama ignored the remark, his focus entirely on his prayers. The rituals were all that mattered to him in that moment, grounding him in a world that had changed beyond recognition. As the final words of his prayer left his lips, Ashwatthama transitioned seamlessly into a meditative state, closing his eyes and steadying his breath. His thoughts turned inward, seeking a connection to the one soul he yearned to reach—his son, Akshay.

In the silence of his mind, he called out to his son, his thoughts like tendrils reaching across time and space. But no matter how deeply he delved into his meditation, he found only emptiness, a void where once there had been a bond as strong as any forged in battle. Frustration gnawed at him, a sharp reminder of all that he had lost. And then, just as he was about to give up, he heard it—a voice, clear and strong, calling his name. "Ashwatthama."

His eyes snapped open, and for a moment, he was disoriented, unsure whether the voice had been real or another cruel trick of his mind. But the voice came again, more distinct this time, filled with a power that commanded attention.

"Son, I see you have my book, and I am proud to say that you are worthy of it."

A wave of relief washed over Ashwatthama, his heart pounding in his chest. He knew that voice, though it had been many centuries since he last heard it. It was Shukracharya, the great sage, the one who had written the *Mrityormukti: Rahashyam.*

"Shukracharya Ji," Ashwatthama whispered, his voice filled with reverence. "At last... someone who can help me."

The sage's presence was like a comforting embrace, calming the storm of thoughts that had raged within Ashwatthama's mind. He had so many questions, so much he needed to understand.

"Where are you?" he asked urgently.

"How did you find me? How can you reach me now, after all this time?"

But before he could bombard Shukracharya with more questions, the sage's voice interrupted, gentle but firm.

"Not now, my son. All will be revealed in time. But first, we must focus on what is most important. We need to stop Manas."

"Manas?" Ashwatthama's surprise was evident. "How do you know him?"

"Do not judge my power, Ashwatthama," Shukracharya Ji replied with a tone of gentle reproach.

"There is much that I see, much that I know. Manas is not just a simple warrior; he is a threat, one that we cannot afford to ignore."

Ashwatthama felt a twinge of regret at his earlier outburst.

"I am sorry, Guruji," he said, his voice subdued.

"I did not mean to question you."

Shukracharya's voice softened, a note of understanding creeping in.

"There is no need for apologies, my son. We are bound by the same cause. But there is much to do, and little time to waste. We need to meet."

Ashwatthama's mind raced with possibilities.

"Tell me where you are, Guruji. I will send help for transportation, and we can meet at once."

"I am in the Himalayas," Shukracharya replied.

"But our meeting must take place elsewhere. We will meet at the place where it all began—Kurukshetra. But first, there is something we must do. We must meet in Ayodhya. There, I will share with you the answers to your questions and prepare you for what lies ahead."

Ashwatthama nodded, though he knew Shukracharya could not see the gesture. The mention of Kurukshetra, the legendary battlefield where the fate of the world had once been decided, sent a shiver down his spine. He knew that their meeting there would be significant, a turning point in the conflict that was brewing.

"Very well, Guruji," Ashwatthama agreed.

"I will make the necessary arrangements. We will meet in Ayodhya, and from there, we will do what must be done."

"Be swift, my son," Shukracharya urged. "Time is not on our side. The forces that oppose us are already in motion. We must be prepared to face them."

With that, the connection between them faded, leaving Ashwatthama alone once more in the quiet village. But this time, he felt a renewed sense of purpose, a clarity that had been missing since his battle with Manas. Shukracharya was with him, guiding him, and together they would stop the forces that sought to undo the world.

Yet, even as the sage's presence faded, Ashwatthama's thoughts turned to another troubling matter. He had been unable to reach his son, Akshay, through meditation. The connection that once allowed him to communicate across time and space now seemed severed.

"Why has he shunned me?" Ashwatthama thought, his frustration mounting. He needed to reach Akshay, to understand what had gone wrong.

An idea struck him suddenly, and he turned to the villagers, his voice carrying a command that brooked no argument.

"Bring me a phone."

The villagers, still wary of Ashwatthama's earlier rudeness, exchanged skeptical looks. One of them, the same young man who had questioned him earlier, couldn't help but smirk.

"I thought we were the fools and that you didn't need any of our modern technology," he said with a hint of mockery.

Ashwatthama's patience, already worn thin, snapped. His voice rose in a bark of frustration.

"Bring it to me, or else—"

Before he could finish, a small child, who had been watching the exchange from the sidelines, timidly approached and handed Ashwatthama a smartphone. The child's wide eyes were filled with both fear and curiosity as he offered the device with trembling hands. Ashwatthama took the phone, his expression softening slightly as he accepted the gift.

"Thank you," he muttered, more to himself than to the child, before turning his attention to the screen.

His fingers, unfamiliar with the touch interface, fumbled for a moment before he managed to dial the number he had memorized long ago. The phone rang once, twice, before a voice answered on the other end—Akshay's voice, distant and cold.

"Akshay," Ashwatthama began, his tone both urgent and desperate. "Why have you shunned me? Why did you cut off our connection?"

There was a long pause before Akshay's voice, filled with a restrained anger, came through the line. "Because of you, Raghav is dead."

The accusation hit Ashwatthama like a blow to the chest, but he did not falter.

"I can bring Raghav back to life," he said with a conviction that brooked no argument. "I have the power to undo what has been done."

"Nonsense," Akshay retorted, disbelieving his words. "You speak of miracles, but they are nothing but empty promises."

"Trust me," Ashwatthama insisted. "I have to meet Shukracharya Ji, and he knows the *Mrit Sanjeevni Vidya*. He can bring back Raghav."

There was a sharp intake of breath on the other end of the line, and Ashwatthama knew that he had struck a chord. Akshay, for all his anger, could not deny the weight of the name Shukracharya Ji, nor the ancient knowledge of *Mrit Sanjeevni Vidya*. He understood the gravity of what his grandfather was saying, and for a moment, all the barriers he had erected around himself seemed to waver.

"*Mrit Sanjeevni Vidya*," Akshay repeated slowly, the words heavy with meaning. He knew of it, knew that it was the key to defying death itself, and that only Shukracharya held the knowledge of its use.

"Okay," Akshay finally said, his voice still tinged with skepticism but now laced with a faint glimmer of hope. "I'll help you. But you need to bring me the details, and this better not be another one of your tricks."

Ashwatthama felt a surge of relief, knowing that he had regained a small part of his trust.

"I promise you, Akshay, this is real. I will bring you what you need."

As the call ended, Ashwatthama handed the phone back to the child who had given it to him, a rare smile crossing his face. The road ahead was fraught with danger and uncertainty, but for the first time in a long while, he felt that he was not alone.

He had Shukracharya's guidance, his grandson's tentative support, and the promise of a power that could turn the tide of fate. And so, with renewed determination, he began to prepare for the journey to Ayodhya, where the answers to his questions—and perhaps the salvation of his son—awaited.

CHAPTER 5

The sun had reached its zenith, casting harsh beams of light down onto the secluded forest clearing where Manas and Ananya were immersed in their daily training. The air was thick with the sounds of exertion—the rhythmic thud of wooden staffs clashing, the sharp intake of breath as they dodged and countered, and the steady cadence of their footwork against the earth. Every movement was precise, calculated, and honed to perfection under the watchful eyes of Lord Parashurama, the legendary warrior sage.

Manas and Ananya had been sparring for hours, their bodies drenched in sweat, yet they showed no signs of slowing down. Lord Parashurama demanded nothing less than excellence, and both warriors pushed themselves to their limits.

Lord Parashurama observed them from a distance, his sharp gaze missing nothing. He had drilled them relentlessly, teaching them the ancient forms of combat that had been passed down through generations. Today's session focused on the art of wielding the gada—the mighty mace. It was a weapon that required both power and finesse, and under Lord Parashurama's tutelage, they learned how to channel their energy into every strike, making their blows devastatingly effective.

"Manas, your grip needs to be tighter!" Lord Parashurama called out, his voice carrying across the clearing.

"The gada is an extension of your arm. If your grip is weak, your strikes will lack force."

Manas adjusted his hold on the weapon, feeling the rough texture of the mace's handle bite into his palms. He swung the gada with renewed strength, the weight of the weapon now more familiar, more manageable. Ananya, facing him, parried the blow with her own mace, the impact sending vibrations up her arms. She responded with a quick counter strike, which Manas barely deflected in time.

"Good!" Lord Parashurama praised, his tone approving but still demanding. "Again!"

For hours, they continued their sparring, each strike, block, and maneuver testing their limits. By the time Lord Parashurama called for a break, both Manas and Ananya were breathing heavily, their muscles burning with fatigue.

As they settled down on the edge of the clearing, beneath the shade of a massive banyan tree, Manas' mind began to churn with questions that had been lingering since the morning's session. His thoughts returned to the Kavach Kundal and the story of Dambodhaya that Lord Parashurama had shared, but there was something else that troubled him even more. Ananya noticed the furrow in his brow and nudged him lightly with her elbow.

"What's on your mind, Manas? You look like you're trying to solve the mysteries of the universe."

Manas managed a small smile, but it quickly faded as he turned to her, his voice thoughtful.

"Ananya, there's something I've been wondering about. It's not just the Kavach Kundal that bothers me—though that story still weighs on me. It's the Saraswati River."

Ananya tilted her head, curious. "The Saraswati River? What about it?"

Manas glanced around, ensuring that Lord Parashurama was out of earshot, though he knew it was futile.

"I keep thinking about what Guruji said—that I'm supposed to bring it back. But where is it now? Why did it vanish in the first place? And why is it that only I can bring it back?"

Ananya frowned, considering his questions.

"I don't know, Manas. I've heard stories, of course, but none of them ever explained why the river disappeared. And as for why you're the one who has to bring it back... that's something I don't understand either."

Before they could continue, a voice interrupted them, clear and authoritative.

"The answers you seek are not simple, Manas."

Startled, both warriors looked up to see Lord Parashurama approaching them. His expression was calm. He had overheard their conversation, and he knew it was time to share another piece of the puzzle that would shape their destiny. Manas and Ananya immediately straightened, their respect for their guru evident in their postures. Lord Parashurama gestured for them to remain seated, then joined them under the shade of the banyan tree. The forest around them seemed to fall into a hushed silence, as if the very trees were leaning in to listen.

"The story of the Saraswati River," Lord Parashurama began, "is one of the most ancient tales in our history. It is a story of pride, punishment, and redemption—a story that has shaped the very course of time."

Manas and Ananya listened intently as Lord Parashurama continued, his words weaving a vivid picture of a time long past.

"It was many eons ago, in the age when the Mahabharata was being composed. The great sage Ved Vyas had taken on the monumental task of dictating the epic to Lord Ganesh, who had agreed to scribe it for the benefit of all humanity. They chose the banks of the Saraswati River as their setting, for it was believed that the river's pure and sacred waters would inspire wisdom and clarity in their work."

At that time, the Saraswati River was not merely a body of water. It was a living entity, a goddess whose waters flowed with the essence of knowledge, truth, and purity. Her presence was revered by all, and her blessings were sought by sages and scholars alike. But as Ved Vyas began his dictation, they encountered an unexpected challenge. The flow of the Saraswati was so powerful, so thunderous, that it drowned out Ved Vyas's voice. No matter how loudly he spoke, the roar of the river made it impossible for Lord Ganesh to hear him clearly.

Frustrated, Ved Vyas tried to reason with the river, asking her to soften her flow so that they could complete their sacred task.

"But Saraswati, in her pride, refused.

'Why should I change my course for you?' she asked.

'I am the Saraswati River, and my waters have flowed through these lands since the dawn of time. It is you who should move, not I.'"

Lord Parashurama's voice grew somber as he continued. "Ved Vyas could not tolerate this insolence. To have it hindered by arrogance was unacceptable. And so, in his anger, Ved Vyas cursed Saraswati. He decreed that her waters would dry up, that she would disappear from the earth, and that her once-glorious presence would be reduced to nothing more than a memory."

Manas felt a chill run down his spine as he imagined the scene— the mighty Saraswati River, brought to her knees by the wrath of a sage.

"Saraswati," Lord Parashurama said, his tone softening, "was devastated by the curse. She had not realized the gravity of her actions, and in her regret, she begged Ved Vyas for forgiveness.

She pleaded with him to lift the curse, to restore her waters so that she might continue to bless the earth. But the curse had already taken hold, and not even Ved Vyas could undo what had been done."

"However," Lord Parashurama continued, "Ved Vyas, being a sage of great compassion, offered her a glimmer of hope.

'Though your waters shall disappear,' he said, 'you will not be forgotten. In the age of Kaliyug, when darkness and ignorance cover the earth, you will be of great use. Only the descendant of Lord Surya or Lord Kalki himself will have the power to bring you back. But because your pure waters can be easily misused in such a corrupt age, you will be placed under the protection of Lord Parashurama.'" Ananya's eyes widened as she realized the significance of the tale.

"So that's why the Saraswati River vanished," she murmured.

"And that's why only you, Manas, can bring it back."

Manas, who had been listening in rapt attention, now fully understood the burden that had been placed upon him.

"But why me, Guruji?" he asked, his voice filled with a mix of awe and trepidation. "Why must I be the one to bring her back? And what will happen once she returns?" Lord Parashurama looked at Manas with a gaze.

"You, Manas, are the descendants of Lord Surya.

The power to restore the Saraswati River flows through your veins, passed down through your lineage. It is your dharma, your sacred duty, to fulfill this task."

"But there is more," Lord Parashurama added, his voice taking on a darker, more urgent tone.

"The return of the Saraswati River is not just about restoring a lost treasure. Her waters are needed for a greater purpose—a purpose that could determine the fate of the world."

Manas and Ananya leaned in closer, sensing the gravity of what Lord Parashurama was about to reveal.

"We need the Saraswati River," Lord Parashurama said slowly, "to perform a yagna—a sacred ritual that will allow us to destroy the *Mrityormukti: Rahashyam*, the book that holds the secrets of life and death.

This book, now in the hands of Ashwatthama, is a source of unimaginable power. If it falls into the wrong hands, it could bring about the end of everything we hold dear."

"But the yagna is not just about destroying the book," Lord Parashurama continued. "It is also the key to curing Ashwatthama of the curse that binds him to this earth. He is a warrior who has suffered for millennia, a soul who has been both blessed and cursed by the gods. Once the yagna is complete, Ashwatthama will be freed from his torment, and he will be restored to his full strength."

Ananya's eyes flickered with understanding.

"And he will be needed, won't he? At the end of Kaliyug."

Lord Parashurama nodded solemnly.

"Yes. Ashwatthama will play a crucial role in the final battle, the battle that will mark the end of Kaliyug and the dawn of a new age. He will also be the one to train Lord Kalki, who will come to cleanse the world of its impurities and restore dharma."

Parashurama Ji continued, "Karan and Ashwatthama were once close friends. However, the constant pain in Ashwatthama's forehead drove him to seek relief. He turned to somras for solace, but when the supply ran dry, he stumbled upon Shukracharya's book. This knowledge corrupted his mind. To heal Ashwatthama, we must first accomplish two things: destroy the book, and then focus on curing him."

Manas felt a sense of awe and responsibility settle over him like a mantle.

Lord Parashurama rose to his feet, signaling the end of their discussion.

"Rest now, both of you. Tomorrow, we will continue your training. The challenges you will face are unlike anything you have encountered before, but you must be prepared."

Manas and Ananya nodded in unison, their minds heavy with the knowledge they had just received. As Lord Parashurama walked away, disappearing into the shadows of the forest, they remained seated under the banyan tree, processing everything they had learned.

"Ananya," Manas said quietly, breaking the silence, "I don't know if I'm ready for this."

Ananya placed a reassuring hand on his shoulder.

"You don't have to do it alone, Manas.

We're in this together. And with Guruji's guidance, we'll find a way."

Manas looked at her, grateful for her unwavering support.

"Thank you, Ananya. I just hope I'm worthy of the task."

"You are," she replied with conviction.

"We both are. And we'll see this through to the end."

As the last light of day faded, leaving the clearing bathed in the soft glow of twilight, Manas and Ananya prepared themselves for the trials ahead.

CHAPTER 6

The biting cold of the Himalayan air swirled around the isolated mountain clearing where Shukracharya sat, his eyes closed in deep meditation. The snow beneath him had long since melted away from the sheer heat of his inner energy, and a faint, ethereal glow surrounded his body, casting an otherworldly light across the rocky terrain. The landscape was eerily silent, save for the occasional gust of wind that whistled through the jagged peaks. Shukracharya's mind was a vast, labyrinthine expanse, navigating through layers of consciousness that stretched back across millennia. His thoughts were focused on the intricate web of fate that had drawn him out of his deep meditation and back into the world of mortals—a world teetering on the edge of an epochal shift.

Yet, even in his meditative state, a small seed of disturbance gnawed at him, born from the recent news he had overheard on the traveler's phone. The world had changed in ways that even he, in all his wisdom, had not fully anticipated. The reclaiming of the Ram Mandir, the resurgence of old powers, and the rising tide of conflict were all signs that the final battle was drawing near—a battle that would determine the fate of Kaliyug itself.

His meditation was interrupted by a distant noise, faint at first but growing steadily louder. Shukracharya opened his eyes slowly, the glow around him dissipating as his awareness returned fully to the physical realm. The sound became clearer, unmistakable now— the chopping, rhythmic thrum of helicopter blades cutting through the thin mountain air.

He stood, his ancient eyes narrowing as he looked towards the sky. A black helicopter emerged from the cloud cover, its dark shape contrasting sharply against the snowy backdrop of the Himalayas. The machine descended, disturbing the snow on the ground as it landed a short distance from where Shukracharya stood.

The helicopter door swung open, and four men stepped out, their movements disciplined and purposeful. They were armed, dressed in black tactical gear, their faces hidden behind masks. But it was the fifth figure, stepping out from between the armed guards, that drew Shukracharya's full attention.

Akshay emerged from the helicopter, his eyes immediately seeking out the ancient sage. But even as he approached, a wave of nervousness washed over him. Akshay could feel his hands trembling, a cold sweat breaking out on his brow despite the freezing air. His heart raced as he took hesitant steps forward, his throat dry and his mind a whirl of anxiety.

As he reached Shukracharya, Akshay dropped to his knees, touching the sage's feet with trembling hands. Tears welled up in his eyes, not only from the overwhelming emotions of the moment but also from the desperate hope that the sage could fulfill his heart's deepest wish.

"Shukracharya Ji," Akshay's voice was choked with emotion, his words barely escaping his quivering lips,

"Can you bring Raghav back? Is there a way?"

Shukracharya looked down at the young man, sensing the turmoil within him. The sage's expression softened, and he placed a hand on Akshay's shoulder, his touch imbued with a calming energy. Immediately, Akshay felt a wave of warmth spread through his body, easing the tremors in his hands and slowing his racing heart.

"Calm yourself, my child," Shukracharya said, his voice gentle yet commanding.

"Fear and doubt have no place here.

You stand before me because you are meant to be part of something far greater than you can imagine."

Akshay looked up at Shukracharya, his eyes wide with a mixture of awe and gratitude. The trembling in his hands ceased, and the cold knot of fear in his stomach began to unwind.

Ashwatthama reached out to Shukracharya a day before, requesting him to employ the sacred Mrit Sanjeevini Vidya to restore life. Shukracharya consented to the request. Ashwatthama then voiced his concern that Akshay might become anxious and persistently question Raghav. Before Ashwatthama could elaborate, Shukracharya interjected, reassuring him,

"*Do not worry. I will handle it.*"

"I will bring Raghav back,"

Shukracharya continued, his voice steady and reassuring.

"But you must do exactly as I say. Raghav is needed—his strength will be vital in the battles to come. You must be strong too, Akshay. There is no room for hesitation in what lies ahead."

Akshay nodded, the last vestiges of his fear melting away under Shukracharya's calming influence.

"I will do whatever it takes, Guruji," he vowed, his voice now steady.

"Just tell me what needs to be done."

Shukracharya nodded in approval, pleased with Akshay's growing resolve. He had known that Akshay would be vital in the coming conflict, and his willingness to obey without question would be a valuable asset.

"I need you to bring a specific list of items required to perform the dark ritual that will bring Raghav back," Shukracharya commanded.

Akshay quickly turned on his tablet, fingers flying across the keys as he began jotting down the list. Shukracharya started reciting the items:

A **skull of a serpent**, symbolizing the soul's departure and return through the cycle of death and rebirth.

- A bowl filled with **ashes from a cremation ground**, representing the gateway between life and death.

- **Black sesame seeds** to appease the spirits wandering in the netherworld.

- A **bronze urn** containing **sacred water from the Yamuna River**, symbolizing the purification of the soul.

- **Neem leaves** soaked in cow's blood, to ward off malevolent spirits during the ritual.

- A **pitch-black mirror**, crafted to catch the reflection of the departing spirit and bind it to the physical realm.

- A piece of **Rudraksha**, blessed with incantations to summon powers from beyond.

- **Five rare herbs**, to be burnt and inhaled, allowing the conjurer to see into the realm of the dead.

- A **coal-black cloak**, worn by the ritualist to shield against the vengeful spirits that will emerge.

- A large, intricately carved **trident**, used to channel the power of the deities controlling life and death.

Akshay nodded, typing everything down with growing unease.

"Okay, I'll arrange these items," he said, trying to mask the uncertainty in his voice. Without wasting a moment, he quickly pulled out his phone and dialed his secretary.

"I need you to arrange something urgent," he said, his tone sharp and precise.

"Get these items," he listed them one by one, "and make sure they are ready by tomorrow. No delays."

"I'll share the location later," Akshay added.

His secretary hesitated on the other end but eventually agreed, sensing the urgency in Akshay's voice. Akshay hung up and glanced at Shukracharya, his mind racing. "It'll be done," he assured, though a knot of unease tightened in his chest.

But before they could discuss their plans further, Shukracharya turned his attention to another matter—the traveler he had hypnotized, the one who had witnessed more than he should have. The traveler had been standing off to the side, his eyes glazed and unfocused, still under the influence of Shukracharya's power. His mind was trapped in a fog, unable to process the events that had unfolded around him.

Shukracharya approached the traveler, who looked up at him with a mix of fear and confusion. The sage's expression was unreadable as he stared into the man's eyes.

"I will let you live,"

Shukracharya said, his voice cold and unyielding,

"but only on one condition. You must clean up the dead body over there—make it look as if nothing ever happened."

The traveler blinked, the fog in his mind lifting just enough for him to comprehend the command. His eyes darted to the lifeless body of the man who had mocked Shukracharya, now lying cold and still on the ground. The task was daunting, and panic began to rise in his chest.

"But... but there are many dead," the traveler stammered, his voice trembling with fear.

"How can I possibly remove them all? You're an ancient sage, as you claim, and powerful too. Why can't you do it yourself?"

Shukracharya's gaze hardened, his patience waning.

"Boy," he said, his voice now laced with a warning, "do not test my patience. You have already seen a fraction of my power. Do you wish to see more? Do you want to experience it firsthand?"

The traveler's heart skipped a beat, and he felt a cold sweat break out on his forehead. The memory of Shukracharya's earlier display of power—the way he had taken a life with a mere touch—flashed through his mind. He knew better than to push his luck any further.

"N-no, Shit," the traveler stammered, his voice barely a whisper.

"I'll do as you say. Just… just make me forget everything that happened here."

Shukracharya's expression softened, just a fraction, as he placed a hand on the traveler's forehead.

"Very well," he said. "You will remember nothing. Now, do as I commanded."

Disheartened and terrified, the traveler began the grim task of cleaning up the scene, his movements mechanical and driven by fear. He worked quickly, his hands shaking as he tried to make the body disappear, all while Shukracharya watched, his eyes cold and impassive.

"Guruji," Akshay said, his voice steady despite the turmoil within, "we are ready to go. But I have one question—who is that traveler?"

Shukracharya glanced at the man, who was now standing quietly off to the side, his eyes dull and unfocused as the effects of the hypnosis took hold.

"Harmless," Shukracharya replied dismissively.

"He will remember nothing of what transpired here. He is of no consequence."

Akshay nodded, accepting the answer without further question. He knew better than to doubt Shukracharya's judgment, especially in matters as mysterious as these. Shukracharya rose to his feet, the snow crunching under his feet as he moved towards the helicopter.

"We must leave now," he said, his voice firm.

"Our destination is Ayodhya, where Ashwatthama will join us."

The mention of Ayodhya made Akshay pause.

"Why Ayodhya, Guruji?" he asked, curiosity and concern mingling in his tone.

Shukracharya's eyes flashed with a mix of anger and determination.

"Ayodhya is where the seeds of chaos must be sown," he said, his voice taking on a darker edge.

"The Ram Mandir is being reclaimed, a symbol of power that has not been seen for centuries. If it is allowed to flourish, it will tip the balance against us. I must go there and ensure that chaos reigns. The old order must be disrupted before it can solidify."

Akshay hesitated, a knot of unease forming in his stomach. If this was what had to be done to ensure their success, then he would follow his guru without question.

"As you command, Guruji," Akshay said, his voice steadying with resolve. He called his secretary and shared the location, instructing firmly, "Bring those items to Ayodhya."

"We will go to Ayodhya." Shukracharya nodded in approval, then turned to the hypnotized traveler. With a mere flick of his wrist, he reawakened the man's consciousness, his voice commanding and final.

"Walk east," he instructed the traveler. "You will find a body of water there. Bathe in it, and you will forget everything that happened here."

The traveler, his mind still under Shukracharya's influence, nodded blankly and began walking in the direction he was told, his movements robotic and without hesitation. As the traveler disappeared into the snowy landscape, Shukracharya turned back to Akshay and the armed men.

"Come," he said, his voice filled with an urgency that belied the calm expression on his face.

"We have much to do, and little time. The forces we face are gathering strength, and we must be prepared for the storm that is coming."

With that, Shukracharya and his followers boarded the helicopter, the rotors roaring to life once more as the machine lifted off the ground and headed south, towards Ayodhya. As they soared through the sky, Akshay's thoughts turned to his grandfather, Ashwatthama, and the reunion that awaited them in the ancient city. For now, all he could do was trust in Shukracharya and hope that the path they were on would lead to the victory they so desperately sought. Below them, the snow-covered peaks of the Himalayas receded into the distance.

CHAPTER 7

Ashwatthama had always been a man of immense resolve, a warrior shaped by the fires of countless battles and the weight of an ancient curse. But as he stood at the edge of the village, fully recovered from his injuries, he felt something he had not experienced in centuries—gratitude. The villagers had saved him from the brink of death, an act of kindness he had not expected in this age of Kaliyug. Yet, even as he felt this gratitude, he knew that he could not allow their actions to be known. His existence needed to remain a secret.

"I thank you," Ashwatthama began, his voice a cold contrast to the warmth of his words. His eyes, like hardened steel, locked onto the faces of the villagers gathered before him.

"For saving my life. But let me make one thing abundantly clear—if any of you speak of this, if word of my presence here reaches the outside world, I will return. And this time, it will not be as a wounded man."

The threat chilled the blood of the villagers. They nodded quickly, fear evident in their eyes. None would dare cross this man—this being who seemed to be more than human. Before he turned to leave, Ashwatthama addressed the village Vaidya, the elderly healer who had tended to him with such care.

"Tell me," he demanded, his tone leaving no room for hesitation.

"Where did you find me? Which side of the mountain? Was there anyone else with me?"

The Vaidya stepped forward, his movements slow and deliberate, weighted by both age and the gravity of the situation.

"We found you on the northern slope," he replied, his voice steady despite the fear that gripped him.

"Near the edge of the forest, at the base of a cliff. There was no one else—only you."

Ashwatthama's gaze remained fixed on the Vaidya, scrutinizing his every word for any sign of deception. Satisfied, he gave a curt nod.

"Take me there tomorrow morning. I need to see it for myself."

The Vaidya agreed, his head bowing slightly in acknowledgment. With that, Ashwatthama turned away, retreating to the small hut that had been his refuge during his recovery. The villagers dispersed, whispering among themselves as they tried to process the encounter, their fear overshadowing their relief. The night passed slowly, but Ashwatthama did not sleep. Instead, he spent the dark hours in meditation, offering his prayers to Lord Shiva, seeking the strength and guidance he would need for the trials ahead. His mind replayed the events of the past few weeks—the battle with Manas, Ananya, and Lord Parashurama, the fall from the mountain, the loss of Raghav. These thoughts swirled in his mind like a storm, but he forced himself to focus, to find the clarity he needed.

At dawn, when the first light touched the peaks of the surrounding mountains, Ashwatthama was already prepared. He stepped out of the hut and made his way to the village outskirts, where the Vaidya awaited him. The old man stood with a staff in hand, his posture betraying the weariness of age, but his eyes still held the determination of a man who had lived through much.

Without a word, the Vaidya led Ashwatthama through the dense forest that clung to the mountainside. The path was treacherous, the ground uneven and the air thin at this altitude, but Ashwatthama moved with the grace of a predator, his senses sharp and attuned to the world around him. The *Vaidya*, despite his age, kept pace, his experience in these mountains guiding his steps. As they neared the spot where the villagers had found him, Ashwatthama asked him to leave, but *Vaidya* spoke, his voice breaking the silence.

"If you need help searching, I can assist you. These mountains have many secrets, and they do not reveal them easily."

Ashwatthama shook his head, his tone resolute.

"No. I will take it from here."

Vaidya nodded, understanding that his role in this journey had ended. He turned to leave, but before he could go, Ashwatthama spoke again, his voice softer than before.

"Thank you," he said, the words carrying a weight they rarely did.

"Thank you for curing me. And remember—this stays between us."

The Vaidya met Ashwatthama's gaze, his eyes filled with a mixture of respect and fear.

"I will not speak of it," he promised, and with that, he turned and began the long trek back to the village, leaving Ashwatthama alone in the wilderness.

Now alone, Ashwatthama stood at the base of the cliff where he had been found, his mind slipping into a deep focus. He closed his eyes, breathing in the cold mountain air, and allowed his memories to wash over him. The vision came quickly, vivid and painful—a chaotic swirl of battle, blood, and fury. He could see Lord Parashurama's fierce attacks, feel the impact of Manas and Ananya's strikes, and then the moment when everything went black as he plummeted down the mountainside. But there was something else, a detail that had escaped him before. He rewound the memory, playing it back in his mind, and this time he focused on Raghav. He could see his grandson, falling from a different angle, the momentum of the battle driving him over the edge of the cliff. The memory sharpened, and Ashwatthama concentrated on the specific spot where Raghav had disappeared from view, using the terrain to estimate where his body might have landed.

With renewed purpose, Ashwatthama began to navigate the rugged landscape, his eyes scanning the ground for any sign of his fallen comrade. The forest grew denser as he moved away from the cliff, the trees pressing in on him as if trying to keep him from his search. The terrain was unforgiving, and the air was thin, but Ashwatthama pushed forward, driven by the need to find Raghav.

But as the hours passed and the sun climbed higher in the sky, frustration began to gnaw at him. He had followed the path as best he could, but there was no sign of Raghav. The body had vanished, swallowed by the unforgiving wilderness. Exhausted and disheartened, Ashwatthama finally stopped, sitting down heavily beside a massive tree. He leaned back against the trunk, his mind a tumult of doubt and despair.

As he sat there, his thoughts spiraling into darkness, he felt a single droplet of water fall on his cheek. Startled, he opened his eyes and looked up, expecting to see the beginning of a rainstorm. But the sky above was clear, the sun shining brightly with no sign of clouds. Confusion flickered across his features, and he reached up to touch the droplet. When he pulled his hand away, his breath caught in his throat. The droplet was not water. It was blood. Ashwatthama reflected, "The blood still hasn't clotted." Countless thoughts raced through his mind. "It's been days, yet the wound remains open. The wound refuses to heal because this is no ordinary blood—it's mine, the blood of my grandson, Raghav. He carries the blood of an immortal, which is why it remains fresh.

Ashwatthama slowly looked up, his heart pounding in his chest. There, hanging from the branches above, was a body. His pulse quickened as realization struck him like a hammer blow. He scrambled to his feet, his hands gripping the rough bark of the tree as he climbed up to the branch. There, tangled in the branches, was Raghav's body. The sight sent a shock of grief and rage through Ashwatthama. He carefully untangled Raghav from the branches, his hands trembling as he lowered the broken body to the ground.

Raghav's form was shattered, his limbs twisted at unnatural angles from the fall. His face, once filled with life and strength, was now pale and lifeless. Kneeling beside the body, Ashwatthama's hands shook as he touched Raghav's face. Tears welled up in his eyes, and for the first time in centuries, the ancient warrior wept. But Ashwatthama was not one to succumb to despair. Shukracharya's words echoed in his mind:

"*I can bring him back from his ashes. Trust in me.*" Those words were a lifeline, a promise of hope in a world that had grown increasingly dark.

With trembling hands, Ashwatthama lifted Raghav's body, carrying him to a small clearing where the sunlight filtered down through the trees. He set Raghav down gently and began to gather wood, building a funeral pyre as suggested by *Shukracharya Ji*, with the precision and reverence of one performing a sacred rite. Each piece of wood was placed with care, as if Ashwatthama was constructing something more than just a pyre—something sacred, something that would defy the very laws of life and death. Once the pyre was ready, Ashwatthama placed Raghav's body atop it, arranging his limbs with the same care he would have shown a brother. He stood back, taking a deep breath, and then, with a whispered prayer to Lord Shiva, he set the pyre alight. The flames rose quickly, consuming the wood and the body, turning the remains of his comrade to ash. Ashwatthama watched in silence, the crackling of the fire the only sound in the stillness of the forest.

The smell of burning wood and flesh filled the air, but Ashwatthama stood unmoving, his gaze fixed on the pyre. The flames danced and flickered, casting long, eerie shadows that seemed to take on a life of their own, swirling around him like the spirits of the past.

As the hours passed, the once-roaring fire began to dwindle, leaving behind smoldering embers and a mound of gray ash where Raghav's body had lain. The heat of the pyre dissipated, but the weight on Ashwatthama's heart only grew heavier. He had seen death countless times, had been the harbinger of it on many battlefields, but this—this felt different. When the fire finally died out, leaving only the remnants of what once was, Ashwatthama stepped forward. He knelt beside the ashes, his hands trembling slightly as he reached out to gather them. Each movement was deliberate, almost ritualistic, as if he were performing a sacred ceremony. The ash was soft and light, sifting through his fingers like sand.

He took a small clay pot from his satchel, a simple vessel yet significant in its purpose. With great care, he scooped the ashes into the pot, filling it until there was no more left on the ground. When the last of the ash was collected, Ashwatthama secured the lid tightly, holding the pot in both hands. It was all that remained of Raghav now—a handful of ash in a pot, and the memories of a warrior who had fought bravely until the end.

Ashwatthama stood, the pot cradled against his chest, and closed his eyes. He could feel the presence of Raghav around him, as if his spirit lingered, watching, waiting for the promise that had been made to be fulfilled.

"Shukracharya Ji said he could bring you back," Ashwatthama whispered, his voice rough with emotion.

"I hope he is right."

With a final glance at the remnants of the pyre, Ashwatthama turned and began his descent down the mountain. The forest around him seemed to pulse with life, the trees whispering secrets in the wind as he moved with purpose through the undergrowth. His destination was Kurukshetra, the ancient battlefield where the fate of the world had once been decided, and where he believed it would be decided again. But before he could reach that fateful place, there was another stop he had to make, Ayodhya. The name resonated in Ashwatthama's mind. Ayodhya, the birthplace of Lord Ram, the king whose story had shaped the very fabric of Indian history. It was a place of power, a place where the old and the new converged, where the past was never truly gone.

As he made his way through the forest, the memories of his last battle with Lord Parashurama, Manas, and Ananya haunted him. The flashes of steel, the roar of fury, the pain of each blow—these were all etched into his mind.

Ashwatthama's journey was long and arduous, the terrain shifting from the cold, rugged mountains to the warmer, more fertile lands as he descended into the plains. The air grew thicker with humidity, and the scent of blooming flowers replaced the crispness of the mountain air.

The road to Ayodhya was not without its challenges. The journey took him through dense forests, across rivers swollen with the monsoon rains, and along paths that had not been traveled in years. Ashwatthama moved with the swiftness and agility of a seasoned warrior, his senses always alert, his instincts sharp.

As he neared Ayodhya, the landscape began to change. The trees grew taller and more ancient, their roots twisting through the earth like the veins of the land itself. The air was thick with the scent of sandalwood and incense, the telltale signs of the sacred city that lay just beyond the horizon.

When the first glimpse of Ayodhya appeared in the distance, Ashwatthama paused, his breath catching in his throat. The city was as he remembered it—grand, ancient, its spires reaching towards the heavens like the hands of a giant. But there was something different now, a change in the air that he could feel even from miles away. It was as if the city itself was preparing for something monumental, something that would shift the balance of power in the world.

Ashwatthama continued his journey, the clay pot still held tightly in his grasp. The closer he got to Ayodhya, the more he could sense the presence of Shukracharya, a force that seemed to draw him in like a magnet. The sage had promised to meet him here, to guide him in the next steps of their plan, and Ashwatthama trusted that Shukracharya would be true to his word.

As he entered the city, the streets buzzed with activity. Merchants hawking their wares, children ran through the alleys, and the temples hummed with the prayers of the devout. But beneath the surface, there was an undercurrent of tension, a feeling that something was coming—something that would change the course of history. Ashwatthama made his way through the crowded streets, his eyes scanning the faces around him. He knew that Shukracharya would be waiting, but the sage was not one to reveal himself easily. Ashwatthama would have to find him, to seek him out in the labyrinth of the ancient city.

His search led him to a secluded part of Ayodhya, far from the bustling markets and grand temples. Here, the air was still, the streets quiet, as if time itself had slowed. Ashwatthama's steps grew cautious, his senses heightened as he felt the presence of something powerful nearby.

And then, he saw him.

Shukracharya stood in the shadow of an ancient banyan tree, his form barely visible in the dim light. The sage was exactly as Ashwatthama remembered—ageless, with an aura of power that radiated from him like the heat of the sun. His eyes, sharp and penetrating, met Ashwatthama's with a look of understanding. Ashwatthama approached, his grip tightening on the pot of ashes.

"He touched his feet and said, "I have brought Raghav's ashes, as you instructed," he said, his voice steady but laced with the weight of the task.

Shukracharya nodded, a faint smile playing on his lips.

"You have done well, Ashwatthama. Raghav's return

is crucial to what we must achieve. His strength will be needed in the battles to come."

Ashwatthama felt a surge of relief, though it was tempered by the enormity of what lay ahead.

"Can you truly bring him back?" he asked, the doubt that had haunted him on the journey finally finding a voice.

Shukracharya's smile widened, a glimmer of something ancient and knowing in his eyes.

"I can, and I will. But there are steps that must be taken, rituals that must be performed.

"We need a drop of the Saraswati River," Shukracharya declared.

"But, the drop of the Saraswati River..." Ashwatthama began, only to be interrupted by Shukracharya, who said,

"Isn't Somras already flowing through the veins of Manas and Ananya? Spill their blood, and we shall use it as the drop of Saraswati River."

Ashwatthama hesitated, "But where can we find them?"

Shukracharya replied,

"The Lord Rama temple is about to be inaugurated. I suspect they will be there. They are also on a quest for Karna's Kavach and Kundal. I believe their journey will start with a clue from Ayodhya."

Ashwatthama nodded, accepting the sage's words. Ashwatthama's gaze hardened, his resolve solidifying with each word.

"What must we do?"

Shukracharya's eyes gleamed with fierce determination.

"We must disrupt the old order, create chaos where there is peace, and weaken the forces that would stand against us. Only then can we move forward with our plan."

Ashwatthama understood the implications of Shukracharya's words. The city of Ayodhya, with its ancient temples and sacred sites, was a place of power—a place that could either help or hinder their mission. If they were to succeed, they would need to ensure that Ayodhya's power was under their control. The sage turned, his gaze sweeping over the city with an almost predatory intensity.

"Come, Ashwatthama. We have much to do, and little time."

With that, the two began their preparations, the pot of ashes a reminder of the life they sought to restore, and the city of Ayodhya the first step in a journey that would determine the fate of the world. As they moved through the ancient streets, the weight of their mission pressed down on them, but so too did the promise of what was to come. Ashwatthama's heart burned with the fire of purpose, the ashes of his comrade close to his chest. He would see this through, no matter the cost, no matter the sacrifices that lay ahead.

For in the end, there was no other path. There was only the battle, the fire, and the promise of a new beginning.

CHAPTER 8

The first light of dawn bathed the earth in a soft, golden glow as Manas rose from his bed. The crisp morning air carried with it the faint scent of dew, and the world seemed momentarily at peace. Manas stepped outside, his feet brushing against the cool grass, and turned his face to the rising sun. With reverence, he began his morning prayers, offering his devotion to Lord Surya, the Sun God, who had guided his lineage for generations. The warmth of the sun's rays seemed to fill him with renewed strength, a reminder of the divine purpose that lay before him.

As the last of his prayers were whispered into the morning air, Manas felt a sense of calm wash over him. Today, they would take another step toward fulfilling the destiny that had been set for him.

Lord Parashurama Ji, already awake and prepared for the day, approached Manas as he finished his prayers.

"Manas," he said, his voice carrying the authority of countless lifetimes of experience,

"We must continue our training. The road ahead is long, and the challenges we face will only grow stronger."

Manas nodded, his resolve firm.

"Yes, Guru Ji. But there is something that has been on my mind."

He hesitated for a moment, choosing his words carefully.

Where can we find the Kavach Kundal?

Can Vyas Ji help us? After all, he is the one who dictated the entire Mahabharata to Lord Ganesh Ji. Perhaps he knows where it is hidden."

Lord Parashurama Ji paused, considering Manas' words. The thought had never occurred to him before, and he realized now that it was a question he had never thought to ask.

"I never thought of asking this question, Manas," Lord Parashurama admitted, his tone thoughtful.

"Because it was not meant to be asked by me. But you are right. If anyone knows the secrets of the Mahabharata, it is Vyas Ji. We should seek his counsel."

Manas' heart quickened at the prospect of finding the Kavach Kundal. With it, their quest would take on a new level of power and purpose.

"Let us go to Vyas Ji," Lord Parashurama Ji said decisively. Prepare yourself, both of you."

Manas and Ananya quickly gathered their belongings, and after a brief period of preparation, they set out on their journey. The road ahead was long and winding, passing through dense forests and across rocky terrain. As they walked, the silence between them was occasionally broken by the sounds of nature—the rustle of leaves in the wind, the distant call of a bird. But there was another sound too, a sound that was not of this world.

It was the echo of a memory, a vision that played in the minds of both Manas and Ananya—the memory of the battle that had taken place just days before. They could see it clearly, as if it were happening again: the fierce clash with Ashwatthama and Raghav, the intensity of the fight, and the moment when Raghav had fallen from the mountain. The memory was vivid, almost painfully so, and it lingered in their minds as they walked.

Manas' eyes fell on a spot in the distance, the very place where Raghav had fallen. The memory of that moment flooded back with such force that it nearly stopped him in his tracks. His mind replayed the scene over and over.

Sensing Manas' turmoil, Lord Parashurama Ji's voice cut through the silence, firm and unwavering.

"Do not focus on the past, Manas. A warrior must have an iron heart. The past is behind us, and it cannot be changed. Our focus must be on the path ahead."

Manas took a deep breath, forcing himself to let go of the memory. Lord Parashurama Ji was right—the past could not be undone, and dwelling on it would only weaken his resolve. He nodded, his eyes once again set on the road before them. As the sun began its descent, they finally reached the outskirts of Paralakhemundi. The small village was nestled at the foot of a hill, surrounded by lush green fields and dense forests. The evening air was filled with the sound of village life—the laughter of children, the lowing of cattle, the murmur of conversations carried on the wind. The sight of the village brought a sense of peace to Manas' heart, a respite from the harsh realities of their journey.

As they entered the village, the villagers gathered to greet them, their faces lighting up with recognition and joy. They had heard of Manas and his training with Parashurama Ji, and to them, he was more than just a warrior—he was a messiah, a figure of hope in troubled times. The villagers greeted him with open hearts, their smiles warm and genuine.

"Welcome, Manas," they called out, their voices filled with admiration.

"Welcome, Messiah!"

Lord Parashurama Ji, ever focused on their mission, wasted no time. He approached the village elder, a man of great age and wisdom, and asked,

"Where is Guru Vyas? We seek his guidance."

The elder bowed respectfully.

"Guru Vyas is deep in meditation, Guru Ji," he replied.

"He has asked not to be disturbed."

Before Lord Parashurama Ji could respond, a voice rang out from the direction of the temple.

"स्वागतं गुरोः परशुरामः, अनन्या, माणसः ।

(Swāgataṃ Guroḥ Paraśurāmaḥ, Ananyā, Māṇasaḥ.)"

The voice belonged to none other than Vyas Ji. His presence commanded respect and reverence, yet there was a gentleness to him that put those around him at ease. Vyas Ji emerged from the temple, his white robes flowing as he moved with the grace of one untouched by the passage of time. Lord Parashurama Ji, Ananya, and Manas all bowed deeply as Vyas Ji approached. Lord Parashurama Ji spoke first, his voice filled with respect.

"व्यासस्य गुरोः, नमस्ते । (Vyāsasya Guroḥ, Namaste.)"

"नमस्ते परशुराम । (Namaste Paraśurāma.)," Vyas Ji replied, a knowing smile playing on his lips. He turned to the villagers, his presence commanding their attention.

"Will you please set the fire beside the temple? I, Lord Parashurama, Ananya, and Manas need to talk."

The villagers hurried to fulfill his request, eager to serve the great sage. Within moments, a fire was lit beside the temple, its flames dancing in the gathering twilight. The crackling of the fire and the soft murmurs of the villagers provided a serene backdrop as the four of them gathered around it, ready to delve into the mysteries that had brought them here.

Vyas Ji turned to Manas, his gaze penetrating yet kind.

"Tell me, young boy, what do you wish to ask me?"

Manas hesitated for a moment, unsure of how to begin.

"How do you know I have something to ask, Guru Ji?" he finally asked, curiosity lacing his words.

Both Vyas Ji and Lord Parashurama Ji chuckled, their laughter lightening the atmosphere. Vyas Ji's eyes sparkled with wisdom as he answered,

"I do not need modern equipment to communicate, my boy. I have seen and understood much in my time. Besides,"

he added with a wink, "Lord Parashurama Ji hinted to me about your question when you started your journey." Manas thought to himself,

"I must learn this skill of telepathic communication from Guru Parashurama."

Now is not the time for hesitation.

"Guru Lord Parashurama Ji has tasked me with finding Karna's Kavach Kundal," Manas began, his voice steady.

"But we do not know where it is hidden. You are the one who dictated the Mahabharata, the great epic in which Karna's story is told. You must know where the Kavach Kundal can be found.

Will you help us?"

Vyas Ji's expression grew thoughtful, his gaze distant as he recalled the countless stories and secrets he had woven into the Mahabharata. The flames of the fire reflected in his eyes, giving them an almost ethereal glow as he considered Manas' request.

"Ah, the Kavach Kundal," Vyas Ji murmured, his voice tinged with both reverence and sorrow. "A relic of great power, one that has been lost to time. But nothing is truly lost to those who know where to look."

The fire crackled softly in the dim light of the evening, casting long shadows on the ancient stones of the temple courtyard where Manas, Lord Parashurama Ji, Ananya, and Vyas Ji sat. Manas had listened intently as Vyas Ji recounted the story of how Lord Krishna had asked Lord Indra to take the Kavach from Karna on the twelfth day of the Mahabharata. But as Vyas Ji continued, the story took a turn that Manas had not expected.

"When Lord Indra took the Kavach," Vyas Ji began, his voice deep and resonant, "he sought to bring it to Swarg Lok—the heavenly abode of the gods. But upon his arrival at the gates of Swarg Lok, he was denied entry."

Manas' brow furrowed in confusion.

"Denied entry? But why, Guru Ji?"

Vyas Ji's eyes reflected the flickering flames as he explained,

"Lord Surya, the Sun God, stood at the gates of Swarg Lok. He told Indra that the Kavach was obtained through deceit, and in Swarg Lok, there is no place for something acquired by such means. The Kavach, despite its power, was tainted by the way it was taken from Karna."

Manas felt a heaviness in his chest as he absorbed the implications of Vyas Ji's words.

"What happened then?" he asked, his voice tinged with concern.

"Indra was left with no choice," Vyas Ji continued, his tone grave.

"He returned to Mrityu Lok—the realm of mortals, our world. Knowing the immense power of the Kavach, and fearing that it could be misused, Indra hid it somewhere on Earth. But in his effort to protect it, he also concealed its location from everyone, even from me. I do not know the exact place where it lies hidden."

Manas' heart sank at this revelation. The hope that had fueled his journey began to wane, replaced by a sense of frustration and helplessness.

"Then who can tell us where it is?" Manas asked, his voice betraying the desperation he felt.

"How can we find it if even you, the great Vyas Ji, do not know?"

Vyas Ji smiled gently, his eyes filled with compassion for the young warrior.

"Calm your mind, Manas," he said softly.

"Frustration will not serve you in this quest. There is always a way, even when the path seems obscured."

Manas took a deep breath, trying to steady his racing thoughts.

"What is the way, Guru Ji? How can we find the Kavach Kundal?"

Vyas Ji's expression grew contemplative, and after a moment of silence, he asked,

"Manas, do you believe in time travel?"

The question took Manas by surprise. He had read about the concept in ancient scriptures, but the idea of actually using it to find the Kavach seemed almost beyond belief.

"Yes, Guru Ji," Manas replied hesitantly. "I read about it in the Vishnu Puran."

Vyas Ji's eyes twinkled with interest.

"Good. Tell me, what did you read in the Vishnu Puran?"

Manas paused, gathering his thoughts before speaking.

"The Vishnu Puran," he began, "describes the three forms of Lord Vishnu. It is said that when Lord Vishnu exhales, universes are created from every pore of his body. And when he inhales, those universes are drawn back into him. This cyclical process of creation and destruction is eternal, and it is through this cycle that time flows."

Manas continued, his voice steady as he delved deeper into the sacred text.

"The Puran also explains that Lord Vishnu exists beyond time, beyond the constraints of the physical world. In his form as *Maha Vishnu*, he oversees the creation of countless universes, each with its own cycle of time. Time travel, as we understand it, is merely moving between these cycles—something that is possible for the gods and for those who have attained great spiritual power."

Vyas Ji nodded approvingly.

"You have understood well, Manas. Time, as we perceive it, is but a thread in the vast tapestry of creation. To move through time is to move through that tapestry, to see the weave from different angles."

The night had deepened, and the flickering flames of the fire cast long shadows on the ancient stones of the temple courtyard. Manas, Ananya, and Lord Parashurama Ji sat in rapt attention as Vyas Ji prepared to share a story that would take them deep into the heart of ancient lore—a tale of wisdom, transformation, and eternal devotion. Vyas Ji's voice, steady and resonant, filled the air with a sense of timelessness as he began.

"There is a being," he said, "who has seen the events of the Ramayana unfold eleven times and has witnessed the great war of the Mahabharata sixteen times, including in this very era. He is not a man, but a being of extraordinary knowledge and power, blessed with immortality. This being is none other than *Kaagbhusandi— the immortal crow*."

Manas leaned forward, his curiosity piqued.

"A crow, Guru Ji? How can a crow possess such wisdom?"

Vyas Ji smiled, a knowing glint in his eyes.

"Ah, Manas, Kaagbhusandi is no ordinary crow. His story is one of profound transformation, a journey that took him from the arrogance of a proud sage to the humility and wisdom of an immortal being." And so, Vyas Ji began the tale of Kaagbhusandi, weaving together the threads of myth and legend into a narrative that seemed to transcend time itself.

There exists a figure of great mystery and devotion—Shri Kaagbhusandi. This sage, whose form defies the norms of human and divine alike, possesses a body like that of a man but with the face of a crow. His tale is one of divine curses, spiritual awakening, and an unwavering devotion to Lord Ram, a tale that traverses the realms of gods and mortals, unraveling the secrets of existence. Kaagbhusandi was no ordinary sage. Blessed with the unique gift of divine vision by Lord Ram, he could perceive the past and the future. However, his journey to this eternal existence was not straightforward—it was fraught with trials, errors, and the inevitable consequences of pride and ignorance.

In one of his many lives, Kaagbhusandi was born into a humble family, cherished by his parents and beloved siblings. They lived in peace until a severe drought ravaged their land, bringing with it unimaginable suffering. For years, the sky withheld its rains, the earth turned barren, and the people, desperate to survive, resorted to cannibalism. As the eldest son, Kaagbhusandi could do nothing but watch as his family succumbed to starvation. His younger brother, his sister, and finally his parents—all perished in the grip of hunger, leaving him alone in a world that had lost all meaning.

Driven by despair, Kaagbhusandi fled to Avantika, a city untouched by the drought. Though he found sustenance there, the memories of his lost family haunted him, and he was plagued by questions about the nature of life and suffering. One day, while wandering through the city, he came upon a temple dedicated to Lord

Shiva. Drawn by a desperate need for answers, he sat down to listen to the priest's discourse on the value of human life and the importance of true devotion in attaining liberation. The priest's words resonated deeply within him, yet the seed of devotion had not yet taken root in his heart. When the priest offered him initiation into the spiritual path, Kaagbhusandi hesitated, thinking that he could delay such a commitment for later. Months passed, and as he continued to attend the daily discourses, the pain of his past slowly gave way to a growing arrogance. The devotees praised his voice and his manner of speaking, inflating his ego to the point where he began to see himself as superior even to his own guru.

One day, while delivering a sermon, Kaagbhusandi's guru, the priest who had taken him in, entered the temple. The other devotees rose to honor the priest, but Kaagbhusandi, blinded by pride, remained seated, thinking that to bow before his guru would diminish his own standing among the devotees. This act of disrespect did not go unnoticed by the heavens. Lord Shiva, watching from above, grew angry at the arrogance shown by the young man and made a divine proclamation: Kaagbhusandi would suffer in hell for one hundred thousand years as punishment for his insolence. The priest, distressed by this divine decree, pleaded with Lord Shiva to forgive his disciple. Though the god's words could not be undone, Lord Shiva, moved by the priest's devotion, agreed to lessen the severity of the punishment. Kaagbhusandi would indeed descend to hell, but he would be spared the torments that awaited other souls. Thus, when Kaagbhusandi's life ended, he was cast into the underworld, where he lived out his sentence in solitary reflection.

When his time in hell was complete, Kaagbhusandi was reborn as a human once more. This time, the trials of his past lives had awakened within him a deep thirst for spiritual knowledge. He traveled from one holy site to another, seeking answers to the questions that had tormented him for so long. It was during one of these journeys that he encountered the great sage Lomas, who was delivering a sermon on the nature of God. Still harboring remnants of his old pride, Kaagbhusandi challenged the sage's teachings, questioning the very appearance of the divine. Annoyed by the young man's arrogance, Sage Lomas cursed him, saying,

"Since you have failed to respect the wisdom of a sage, you shall be reborn in the house of a Chandaal, with the face of a crow."

Realizing the gravity of his mistake, Kaagbhusandi immediately sought the sage's forgiveness. He pleaded for a blessing that, despite his cursed form, he might always remember God and remain devoted to the Supreme Almighty. Sage Lomas, moved by the sincerity of his plea, granted his wish.

In his next life, Kaagbhusandi was born from the union of a female swan—the vehicle of Goddess Saraswati—and Kaagchand, a deity. Thus, he came into the world with the body of a god but the face of a crow. Despite his unusual appearance, he was blessed with the ability to speak and think like a human. It was in this life that Kaagbhusandi finally found the true path of worship. Under the guidance of a true saint, he devoted himself to the Almighty, attaining a state of spiritual enlightenment that had eluded him for so long. Kaagbhusandi, learned that true liberation could only be achieved through the worship of the Supreme Almighty, and he spent the rest of his eternal life spreading this message to others.

As Vyas Ji concluded the story, the fire crackled softly, casting a warm glow on the faces of those gathered around it. Manas, Ananya, and Lord Parashurama Ji sat in silence, absorbing the profound tale they had just heard. Manas was the first to speak, his voice filled with wonder.

"Kaagbhusandi Ji... He has witnessed the events of the Ramayana and Mahabharata so many times. His wisdom must be beyond comprehension."

Vyas Ji nodded.

"Indeed, Manas. Kaagbhusandi's knowledge spans across time, and his understanding of the great epics is unmatched. He has seen the rise and fall of countless civilizations, and his insight into the nature of the universe is profound. If there is anyone who can guide you to the Kavach Kundal, it is Kaagbhusandi."

Before Vyas Ji could finish, the fire beside them suddenly flared, its flames reaching high into the air. The villagers gasped and stepped back, fear and awe etched on their faces. Vyas Ji's eyes narrowed, and he turned to Lord Parashurama Ji, a silent understanding passing between them.

"It seems we are not the only ones who seek the Kavach Kundal," Lord Parashurama Ji said, his voice laced with concern.

Vyas Ji nodded, his expression grave.

"The forces of darkness are always drawn to such power. We must be vigilant."

The night had deepened, and the gentle crackling of the fire provided a soothing rhythm, contrasting the intensity of the conversation that had just unfolded. The air was cool, and the village around them had grown quiet, the stillness allowing the weight of Vyas Ji's story to settle fully on Manas, Ananya, and Lord Parashurama Ji. Vyas Ji, ever the patient teacher, leaned slightly forward, his wise eyes gleaming with a mix of curiosity and expectation.

"So, what have you learned from this story?" he asked, his voice carrying the gentle authority of a sage who had witnessed the passage of countless lifetimes.

Ananya was the first to respond. She took a deep breath, gathering her thoughts before she spoke.

"Kaagbhusandi Ji was a great devotee of Lord Ram," she began, her voice tinged with reverence. "Despite the curse that transformed him into a crow, his unwavering devotion to Lord Rama allowed him to transcend his fate. His story teaches us the power of devotion and the importance of humility."

Vyas Ji nodded, a satisfied smile playing on his lips.

"Indeed, Ananya. Kaagbhusandi's story is a testament to the transformative power of devotion. Through his love for Lord Ram, he was able to rise above his circumstances and gain profound wisdom."

He paused, allowing his words to sink in before continuing.

"But there is more to this story, isn't there?"

Ananya hesitated for a moment, then added,

"And the Ram Temple is going to be inaugurated in Ayodhya very soon. Given Kaagbhusandi Ji's devotion to Lord Ram, it's possible—no, likely—that he would be drawn to such a significant event."

Vyas Ji's smile widened, his eyes gleaming with pride at Ananya's insight.

"Absolutely correct, my child. The Ram Temple is not just a place of worship; it is a symbol of Lord Ram's legacy, a beacon of faith that has endured through the ages. It is a place where the divine presence is particularly strong."

Manas, who had been quietly absorbing the discussion, finally spoke up, his voice filled with determination.

"So, there's a strong chance—if Kaagbhusandi Ji is in this lok—that he will be there at the inauguration of the Ram Temple."

Vyas Ji's expression grew serious as he regarded Manas.

"Indeed, Manas. If he is anywhere in this world, then Ayodhya is where you are most likely to find him."

Lord Parashurama Ji, who had been listening intently, finally spoke, his voice carrying the weight of authority and experience.

"Very well, then. We will start our journey to Ayodhya at first light. The path is clear, and our purpose is set."

The three of them sat in silence for a moment, each lost in their own thoughts. As the night wore on, they knew it was time to rest and prepare for the journey ahead. But before they could take their leave, Vyas Ji's voice, gentle yet firm, called them back to attention.

Manas, Ananya, and Lord Parashurama Ji stood up, bowing deeply before Vyas Ji as a sign of their respect and gratitude.

"धर्मः स्वयम्भूः सत्यं यथा धर्मेण सदा स्थितः।

("Righteousness (Dharma) is self-existent, and truth is always upheld by righteousness.")

Manas murmured, invoking the ancient wisdom that had guided their forebears. Vyas Ji smiled, placing a hand on Manas' shoulder.

"May victory be on your side, my children," he said, his voice filled with warmth. "Ananya, Manas, you carry the hopes of many with you. Be strong, be wise, and trust in the divine."

"यतो धर्मस्ततो जयः।"

(Where there is righteousness, there is victory.)

Lord Parashurama Ji responded, his voice resonating with the strength of conviction.

The following morning, as the first light of dawn broke over the horizon, Manas, Ananya, and Lord Parashurama Ji prepared to leave. The air was crisp and fresh, filled with the sounds of the village slowly awakening from its slumber. The anticipation of the journey ahead gave them energy, and the significance of their mission weighed on their minds. Before they departed, they returned to Vyas Ji's dwelling one last time. The sage was waiting for them at the entrance, his white robes almost glowing in the soft morning light. His presence, as always, exuded calm and wisdom.

"May the blessings of the divine be with you on your journey," Vyas Ji said, his voice filled with encouragement.

"Remember, the path you walk is not just for yourselves, but for all those who place their faith in you."

"सर्वे भवन्तु सुखिनः सर्वे सन्तु निरामयाः।

सर्वे भद्राणि पश्यन्तु मा कश्चिद्दुःखभाग्भवेत्।

May all beings be happy; may all be free from illness. May all see what is auspicious; may no one suffer in any way.

Vyas Ji chanted softly, invoking a blessing that echoed through the ages. Manas and Ananya bowed deeply, their hearts filled with gratitude and determination.

"We will do our best, Guru Ji," Ananya promised, her voice steady with resolve.

With their final farewells made, the three set out on their journey. The road to Ayodhya awaited them, and while the path was long and fraught with potential challenges, their purpose gave them strength. They knew they had only three days before the inauguration of the Ram Temple—a momentous event that would draw not only devotees but perhaps the very being they sought. As they walked, the landscape around them began to change. The dense forests and rocky paths of the highlands gradually gave way to the rolling plains and fertile fields of the heartland. The sun climbed higher in the sky, casting a warm glow over the earth and serving as a constant reminder of the divine presence that guided their steps.

"सूर्योऽस्माकं प्रबोधयतु चित्तान्यस्मिन्निदानकाले।

May the Sun awaken our minds at this moment of beginning.

Manas murmured as they walked, invoking the Sun to awaken their minds at this crucial moment.

The journey was long, but with each step, the determination in their hearts grew stronger. The story of Kaagbhusandi, the chance to discover the location of the Kavach Kundal, and the inauguration of the Ram Temple—each thread wove together into a tapestry that was both ancient and eternal.

As the day wore on, the three companions quickened their pace. The road to Ayodhya was still long, but they were resolute in their mission.

"कर्तव्यमिति यद्यस्य न तस्यास्ति विचारणा।

"If someone has a sense of duty, then there is no need for contemplation."

Lord Parashurama Ji reminded them as they walked. For one who knows their duty, there is no need for deliberation.

The Ram Temple awaited them, and within its sacred walls, the immortal crow Kaagbhusandi held the key to the Kavach Kundal—and the fate of all creation.

CHAPTER 9

The streets of Ayodhya were alive with celebration, the city gleaming in the glow of a million lamps as the grand inauguration of the Ram Mandir drew closer. Everywhere, people rejoiced, their hearts filled with devotion and pride. The city was draped in vibrant colors, with garlands of flowers hanging from every doorway and the scent of incense filling the air. Music echoed through the streets as dancers performed in honor of Lord Ram, who had once again returned to the hearts of his people.

The atmosphere was electric, a palpable sense of joy and reverence permeating every corner of the city. From the youngest child to the oldest elder, everyone was caught up in the festive spirit, their faces illuminated with the light of countless diyas that lined the pathways, casting a warm, golden glow over the jubilant crowds.

But amidst this sea of devotion, two figures moved like shadows, their presence unnoticed by the revelers around them. Shukracharya, the ancient sage and preceptor of the Asuras, and Ashwatthama, the cursed warrior of the Mahabharata, walked side by side, their expressions a stark contrast to the joy surrounding them. Shukracharya's eyes were clouded with the memories of an age long past. As he walked through the decorated streets of Ayodhya, he couldn't help but be transported back to the *Treta Yuga*, to the time when Lord Rama had returned to this very city after his victory over the demon king, Ravan. The vision played out before him as clearly as if it were happening in the present: the cheers of the people, the shower of flowers from the heavens, and the overwhelming adoration for the prince of Ayodhya who had fulfilled his dharma.

But instead of reverence, Shukracharya felt only frustration and anger. The sight of Ayodhya celebrating Lord Ram's return stirred something dark within him, a resentment that had festered for millennia. His jaw tightened, and his hands clenched into fists as the memories washed over him. Ashwatthama noticed the shift in Shukracharya's demeanor.

"Why do you hate Rama so much, Guru Ji?"

he asked, his voice low but filled with curiosity.

"Is it because of what happened in Treta Yuga?"

Shukracharya stopped walking and turned to Ashwatthama, his eyes narrowing with an intensity that made the air around them feel suddenly colder.

"I do not hate Ram," he replied, his voice steady but laced with a bitterness that ran deep.

"My enmity is not with him, but with Vishnu. Time and again, Vishnu has used deceit and manipulation to achieve his ends. He masquerades as the preserver of dharma, but his methods are far from righteous."

Ashwatthama frowned, uncertain of what Shukracharya meant.

"How can you say that, Guru Ji? Vishnu is revered as the protector of the universe, the upholder of dharma."

Shukracharya's gaze darkened as he recalled ancient memories.

"You speak as the people do, Ashwatthama. They see Vishnu as a benevolent god, but they do not know the whole truth. I have seen Vishnu's treachery firsthand."

He paused, allowing his words to sink in before continuing.

"There was a time, long ago, when Vishnu and I crossed paths in a manner that shaped my view of him forever. It was during the churning of the ocean, the Samudra Manthan, when the gods and demons worked together to obtain the nectar of immortality—*amrita(immortal nectar).*"Shukracharya's voice grew colder as he recounted the tale.

"When the *amrita(immortal nectar)* was finally obtained, Vishnu, in his cunning, took on the form of the enchanting Mohini. The demons, my disciples, were captivated by her beauty, and in their infatuation, they did not realize that Vishnu was deceiving them. He distributed the nectar only to the gods, ensuring that they would gain the upper hand over the demons."

Ashwatthama listened intently, the tale revealing a side of Vishnu he had never considered.

"But wasn't that necessary to maintain the balance of the universe?" he asked, still grappling with the idea of Vishnu as a deceiver.

Shukracharya shook his head, his expression one of deep resentment.

"Necessary, perhaps, but not just.

Vishnu could have achieved his goals without deceit, yet he chose to trick those who trusted him. He manipulated the outcome to favor the gods. It is this cunning, this willingness to sacrifice fairness for victory, that I despise."

Ashwatthama nodded slowly, understanding now the source of Shukracharya's anger. But before he could respond, their conversation was interrupted by the arrival of Akshay, Ashwatthama's grandson.

"*Daitya Guru Shukracharya Ji,*" Akshay said, bowing respectfully, "I have arranged 100 men as you commanded."

Ashwatthama's eyes narrowed in confusion.

"One hundred men? Why do you need them?"

Shukracharya's gaze shifted to the bustling streets around them, his eyes glinting with malevolent intent.

"Let me take care of them," he said, his voice carrying an edge of dark promise.

"I will hypnotize them, bending their will to mine. Once under my control, they will bring chaos to this city, a chaos that no one will be able to stop."

Ashwatthama frowned, his concern evident.

"But why? Why create such chaos here, in a place of devotion and celebration?"

Shukracharya looked at him, his expression unreadable.

"Because, Ashwatthama, chaos is the breeding ground for power. It disrupts order, weakens the resolve of even the strongest, and in the midst of chaos, opportunities arise that would otherwise remain hidden. This city, with its devotion to Vishnu's avatar, must be shown the fallibility of their so-called gods."

Before Ashwatthama could argue further, Shukracharya sensed the lingering effects of Ashwatthama's injuries from his recent fall. The great warrior was still not fully recovered, his strength not yet returned to its full measure. Shukracharya's eyes softened for a moment, and without a word, he reached for his kamandalu, the ancient water vessel he carried.

Chanting an ancient mantra under his breath, Shukracharya sprinkled the water over Ashwatthama, the droplets shimmering with a faint, otherworldly light as they fell.

"ॐ वैश्वानराय विद्महे महादेवाय धीमहि तन्नो रुद्रः प्रचोदयात्॥

As the water touched Ashwatthama, he felt a surge of energy coursing through his veins, like fire reigniting in his blood. The pain and fatigue that had weighed on him since his fall began to dissipate, replaced by a newfound strength and clarity of mind. His muscles, once stiff and sore, now felt revitalized, his senses sharpened as if he had just awakened from a deep, restorative sleep. Shukracharya stepped back, watching as Ashwatthama straightened, his powerful frame regaining its full might.

"You need to be at full strength," Shukracharya said, his voice a blend of command and care.

"The battles ahead will not be easy, and you must be ready to face them with everything you have." Ashwatthama bowed deeply, gratitude and respect evident in his eyes.

"Thank you, Guru Ji," he said, his voice reverent. "I feel renewed, stronger than before."

Shukracharya nodded, satisfied.

"Go and rest now, Ashwatthama. Tomorrow, we will set the chaos in motion, and then we will head to Kurukshetra, where the final stages of our plan will unfold."

Ashwatthama bowed once more, his loyalty to Shukracharya unshakable. He turned and walked away, his mind already steeling itself for the challenges that lay ahead. The streets of Ayodhya, once filled with the sounds of celebration, now felt like the calm before a storm, a storm that would be unleashed at Shukracharya's command. As Ashwatthama disappeared into the shadows, Shukracharya remained standing in the midst of the jubilant crowds, his thoughts far from the joy that surrounded him. Slowly, he turned to Akshay, his eyes filled with a sense of urgency, as if he were weighing the fate of what lay ahead.

Akshay's attention shifted to his phone as it vibrated. He picked it up and saw a message from his secretary: "I've arranged everything. Please come to this location." Turning to Shukracharya,

Akshay said, "Guru Ji, I need to go. The items you asked for are ready."

Shukracharya nodded in acknowledgment.

His mind was focused on the tasks at hand, on the chaos he would create and the power he would wield.

The night continued, with Ayodhya's citizens oblivious to the dark forces gathering in their midst. But for Shukracharya and Ashwatthama, this was just the beginning. The true battle was yet to come, and when it did, the world would witness the resurgence of ancient powers, forces that had long been thought dormant.

CHAPTER 10

The journey to Ayodhya continued under the canopy of a starry night, the road stretching out before Manas, Ananya, and Lord Parashurama Ji like a ribbon of destiny. The cool night air carried the scents of the earth and the distant sounds of nocturnal creatures. The trio moved in a comfortable silence, each absorbed in their thoughts, the weight of their mission ever-present. Manas' mind, however, was far from at ease. Questions swirled within him, each one demanding answers that he was unsure he could find on his own. As they walked, he glanced at Lord Parashurama Ji. Before Manas could voice his thoughts, Lord Parashurama Ji spoke, his voice calm and knowing.

"Yes, Manas, tell me your query," Lord Parashurama Ji said, his tone gentle yet firm.

Manas started, surprised.

"Guru Ji, can you read minds?"

Lord Parashurama Ji chuckled softly, the sound of it warm in the night air.

"No, Manas, I do not need to read minds. I read your face. You wear your thoughts openly, like a book that anyone can read. I could see the questions forming in your mind long before you could voice them." Manas smiled sheepishly, realizing that his concerns must have been evident.

"I do have a question, Guru Ji," he admitted, his voice steadying.

"Something has been bothering me, and I need to understand it better."

Lord Parashurama Ji nodded, encouraging him to continue.

"Ask, and I will answer to the best of my ability."

Manas hesitated for a moment before speaking.

"I do have the contents of the Saraswati River in my veins. It was used in the creation of Somras, and now that same essence flows within me. But what if Ashwatthama captures me? What if he extracts my blood and uses it as an ingredient in his Yagna, as described in the ancient texts?"

Lord Parashurama Ji's expression grew serious as he considered Manas' words.

"That is a valid concern, Manas. But understand this: while the Somras flows within you, the content of the Saraswati River is no longer in its purest form. It has been mixed with your blood, your essence. The power that it held when it was drawn from the river has changed, and it is no longer the same as it once was."

Before Manas could respond, Ananya, who had been listening intently, jumped into the conversation.

"Then why are we trying to bring back the Saraswati River in the first place?" she asked, her voice tinged with both curiosity and frustration.

"If the essence already flows in Manas, why do we need the river itself?" Lord Parashurama Ji looked at Ananya with a calm, reassuring gaze.

"That is a good question, Ananya. The Saraswati River, in its original form, holds immense power. It is not just about the Somras; it is about the purity and strength of the river's water. With that water, we can perform our own Yagna—a sacred ritual that has the power to heal and transform."

Ananya's eyes widened in understanding.

"You mean, we can use that Yagna to cure Ashwatthama? To free him from his curse?"

Lord Parashurama Ji nodded.

"Yes. It is prophesied that Ashwatthama has a role to play at the end of this Yuga. He is destined to assist Lord Kalki in the final battle against the forces of Kali. But for him to fulfill his destiny, he must be healed, his mind and spirit restored to their original strength. The Yagna, performed with the water of the Saraswati River, is the key to achieving that."

As they continued to walk, the night grew darker, and the road ahead seemed to stretch endlessly. Lord Parashurama Ji suddenly halted, his gaze fixed on a structure that loomed ahead—a small, secluded temple, its stone walls weathered by time but still standing strong.

"Let's halt here for the night," Lord Parashurama Ji said, his voice quiet yet decisive.

"This temple is far from the main road, hidden from the eyes of the world. It will provide us with shelter and the solitude we need to rest."

Manas and Ananya followed Lord Parashurama Ji toward the temple, their footsteps echoing in the stillness of the night. The temple was ancient, its stone carvings depicting scenes from long-forgotten legends. Vines had crept up its walls, intertwining with the stone, as if nature itself sought to embrace the sacred space. The entrance to the temple was flanked by weathered stone pillars, and as they stepped inside, the air grew cooler, the silence even more profound. The interior was simple, with a single shrine at the far end, dedicated to an unknown deity. A faint scent of incense lingered in the air, a reminder that this place had once been a site of worship, though it had long since been abandoned by the world outside.

Lord Parashurama Ji gestured to a corner where they could set up for the night.

"We will leave early in the morning," he said, his voice barely above a whisper.

"Rest now, for the journey ahead will require all of your strength."

Manas and Ananya nodded, their thoughts still racing with the revelations of the night. They settled down on the cool stone floor, their bodies weary from the journey, but their minds too active to find sleep easily. As they lay there, the distant sounds of the night—rustling leaves, the call of an owl—seemed to merge with their thoughts, creating a tapestry of contemplation and anticipation. Manas' mind returned to the conversation they had just had. The thought of being captured by Ashwatthama, of his blood being used in some dark ritual, was terrifying, but Lord Parashurama Ji's reassurance gave him strength.

As the night wore on, the temple's silence wrapped around them, a cocoon of stillness that allowed their minds to settle, their bodies to relax.

In the morning, we would rise and continue our journey to Ayodhya.

CHAPTER 11

The first light of dawn crept over the horizon, casting a pale glow across the secluded temple where Shukracharya and Ashwatthama had spent the night in deep meditation. The air was still, the early morning silence broken only by the faint rustle of leaves and the distant call of a bird greeting the new day. In the center of an open courtyard, both Shukracharya and Ashwatthama sat cross-legged, their eyes closed, their minds focused on the tasks ahead. The power of their meditation was palpable, the ancient energies they invoked swirling around them like an invisible storm.

As the morning progressed, a figure approached quietly, stopping at a respectful distance. It was Akshay. He observed the two ancient beings for a moment, then cleared his throat softly—a subtle cough to signal his presence.

Shukracharya's eyes opened first, his gaze sharp and penetrating. Ashwatthama followed, his eyes flickering with the residual energy of his meditation. They both stood up in unison, their movements graceful and deliberate.

"Everything is in place," Akshay reported, his voice steady with a mixture of respect and anticipation.

"The 100 men you commanded are ready and awaiting your command."

Shukracharya nodded, his expression one of satisfaction.

"Good," he said, his voice low and commanding.

"Line them up in an open field. I need to hypnotize them."

Akshay hesitated for a moment, his brows furrowing slightly.

"Is that necessary, Guru Ji? They are already prepared to obey you."

Ashwatthama, sensing Akshay's hesitation, stepped forward.

"If they are hypnotized, they will have no choice but to follow through with their orders, no matter what happens. It eliminates the possibility of fear or doubt causing them to back off."

Akshay considered this, then nodded in agreement.

"Very well then. I'll gather them and line them up in the field you specified."

As Akshay turned to leave, Ashwatthama took a step closer to Shukracharya, his mind troubled by a question that had been lingering since the previous night.

"Guru Ji," he began, his voice tinged with uncertainty, "in your Mrit Sanjeevani—the knowledge that can bring the dead back to life—there is an ingredient required from the Saraswati River. How is it possible to bring Raghav back if we don't have access to that water?"

Shukracharya's eyes narrowed as he considered

Ashwatthama's question. "You are right," he replied slowly,

"The water of the Saraswati River is indeed one of the ingredients needed for the Mrit Sanjeevani. But not all hope is lost. I have sensed the presence of Lord Parashurama, Ananya, and Manas. They are coming to Ayodhya as well, though their exact purpose is not yet clear to me." But I assume it has to do something with the Ram Mandir. Ashwatthama listened intently, his mind racing with possibilities.

"What does that mean for us, Guru Ji?" he asked.

Shukracharya's lips curled into a slight smile, a plan already forming in his mind.

Ashwatthama's eyes glinted with understanding.

"So we must capture Manas," he said, his voice firm with resolve.

Shukracharya nodded.

"Indeed. But first, we have other matters to attend to."

He turned to Akshay, who had been listening carefully, and gave him a new command.

"Prepare to go to Kurukshetra. The very land where the Mahabharata was fought and where the soil is imbued with the blessings of the divine. Whoever dies on that sacred ground is granted mukti—liberation.

We will need to collect the soil as the next step in the process to bring Raghav back."

Akshay's eyes widened at the mention of Kurukshetra, the ancient battlefield where the great war of the Mahabharata had taken place.

"The soil of Kurukshetra…" he murmured, understanding the significance of Shukracharya's words. "It holds the power to free souls from the cycle of rebirth."

Shukracharya's gaze was distant, his thoughts drifting back to the eons-old battle that had shaped the course of history.

"Yes, Akshay," he said, his voice heavy with the weight of ancient knowledge.

"That soil, combined with the blood of Manas, will allow us to complete the ritual. We will bring Raghav back, and with his return, our power will grow. The forces of this world will tremble before us."

Ashwatthama bowed deeply to Shukracharya, his respect for the Daitya Guru evident in every movement.

"I am ready, Guru Ji," he said, his voice resolute. "We will succeed."

Shukracharya placed a hand on Ashwatthama's shoulder, his touch both comforting and commanding.

"In this era you are my most trusted warrior, Ashwatthama," he said, his voice filled with a rare warmth.

"You must be at your strongest for the battles ahead. Rest now, for tomorrow we will set chaos in motion, and then we will journey to Kurukshetra to complete what we have started."

Ashwatthama bowed once more, acknowledging Shukracharya's words. He then turned and left the temple, his mind focused on the tasks ahead, knowing that the future of their mission rested on his shoulders. Shukracharya watched him go, his mind already turning to the next phase of his plan.

As the first rays of the morning sun began to filter through the trees, Shukracharya closed his eyes and returned to his meditation, his thoughts locked on the events that were about to unfold.

CHAPTER 12

The sun hung low in the sky as Lord Parashurama Ji, Ananya, and Manas reached the outskirts of Ayodhya. The city, usually a beacon of light and devotion, now carried an unsettling undercurrent that none of them could ignore. As they approached the temple where the inauguration of the Ram Mandir was to take place, Lord Parashurama Ji's keen senses detected something amiss.

"Stay alert," Lord Parashurama Ji instructed, his voice firm but quiet.

"We need to secure the perimeter before we proceed any further."

Manas and Ananya nodded in unison, their expressions serious. The three of them moved swiftly but cautiously through the crowded streets, their eyes scanning for any sign of danger. The air was thick with the scent of flowers and incense, but beneath it all was a tension that gnawed at the edges of their awareness. As they moved closer to the temple, Lord Parashurama Ji's sharp ears picked up something disturbing—a faint murmur that cut through the festive sounds of the city. He paused, straining to hear more clearly. The words became clearer, more ominous: *"Asuro ki Jeet ho!"*—Victory to the Asuras.

Lord Parashurama Ji's eyes narrowed, his body tensing as the gravity of the situation began to dawn on him. He turned to Manas and Ananya, his voice a low, urgent whisper.

"Something is very wrong here. I need you two to go and monitor the situation more closely. Be careful, and report back to me as soon as you can."

Manas and Ananya exchanged a quick glance, their eyes reflecting the same mixture of concern and determination. Without another word, they split off from Lord Parashurama Ji and moved through the crowd, their senses heightened, their every movement calculated to avoid drawing attention.

As they navigated through the bustling streets, they both began to hear the same sinister chant, echoing from the mouths of seemingly ordinary people. *"Asuro ki Jeet ho!"* The words, so out of place in a city dedicated to the celebration of Lord Ram, sent chills down their spines. There was something deeply unnatural about the way the people spoke, their voices flat and emotionless, their eyes glazed over as if they were puppets being controlled by some unseen force.

Manas and Ananya moved closer to one of the groups, trying to get a better sense of what was happening. The people were gathered in small clusters, their eyes fixed on the ground, their hands clasped together in a gesture that was more menacing than reverent.

"They're not themselves," Ananya whispered, her voice barely audible.

"They're hypnotized... but not by anything in this world."

Manas nodded in agreement, his mind racing.

"We need to report back to Lord Parashurama Ji. This is worse than we thought."

They quickly made their way back to where Lord Parashurama Ji was waiting, his posture tense, his eyes scanning the horizon. As soon as they reached him, they relayed what they had seen and heard. Lord Parashurama Ji's expression darkened, his jaw tightening as he processed the information.

"This is not the work of any ordinary force," he muttered, more to himself than to them.

"These people are under the influence of an ancient power… one that does not belong to this time." He turned to Manas and Ananya, his gaze intense.

"We have to act quickly. We need to thin the crowd, but we must be careful. These are innocent people who have been caught in a web of dark magic. We cannot harm them—only disarm them or render them unconscious. We'll deal with the source of this corruption once the immediate threat is neutralized."

Manas and Ananya both nodded, understanding the gravity of their task. They moved back into the crowd, their movements swift and precise, avoiding detection as they subtly began to disarm those who seemed most under the influence of the dark force. Each time they encountered someone chanting

"*Asuro ki Jeet ho,*" Victory to evil, they acted quickly, disabling them with minimal force, ensuring that no lasting harm was done.

As they worked, Lord Parashurama Ji kept watch from a distance, his mind attuned to the shifting energies around him. He could feel the presence of something ancient and malevolent, something that had no place in this city of devotion and light. His thoughts turned to the possibility that Shukracharya, the Daitya Guru, was behind this dark enchantment. The signs were all there—the precision of the hypnosis, the dark intent behind the words. It all pointed to a force that had been biding its time, waiting for the right moment to strike.

With each passing moment, the situation grew more dangerous, the threat more immediate. Lord Parashurama Ji knew that they were running out of time. The crowd was large, and despite their best efforts, they could only do so much to thin it without drawing attention to themselves. Finally, as the first light of dawn began to creep over the horizon, Lord Parashurama Ji called Manas and Ananya back to his side.

"We've done what we can for now," he said, his voice grim. "But this is only the beginning. The true battle is yet to come."

Manas looked at Lord Parashurama Ji, his eyes filled with a mixture of fear and determination.

"What do we do now, Guru Ji?"

The three of them knew that the day ahead would bring challenges unlike any they had faced before. But they were ready. The forces of darkness had shown their hand, and now it was time to respond with the full force of their light. The city was still celebrating, but beneath the surface, a storm was brewing. And Lord Parashurama Ji, Manas, and Ananya were prepared to face it head-on, armed with their faith, their training, and the knowledge that righteousness would ultimately prevail. Soon all those men came together to attack three of them.

The battle raged on, each moment stretching into an eternity as Lord Parashurama, Ananya, and Manas fought with every ounce of strength and skill they possessed. The very air around them seemed to vibrate with the force of their blows, as if the universe itself were holding its breath, waiting to see how this clash of titans would unfold.

Lord Parashurama, moved through the battlefield like a force of nature. His eyes, sharp and focused, missed nothing as he assessed each opponent with the precision of a master tactician. His battle axe, a weapon of divine origin, gleamed in the dim light, reflecting the resolve in his gaze. With a single swing, he could fell multiple foes, his strikes so powerful they sent shockwaves through the ground. One by one, his enemies fell before him. A swordsman charged, his blade raised high, but Lord Parashurama sidestepped the attack with ease, bringing his axe down in a swift, diagonal slash.

The swordsman barely had time to register the movement before he was on the ground, unconscious, his sword clattering beside him. Another enemy, with a knife attempted to pierce Lord Parashurama's defenses with a rapid series of thrusts, but the sage deflected each one with the flat of his axe, his movements so fluid it seemed as though he was simply guiding the spear away from him rather than blocking it. With a quick twist of his wrist, Lord Parashurama disarmed the man, sending the spear flying from his grip. A swift kick to the chest sent the attacker sprawling, the force of the blow knocking the wind from his lungs and leaving him incapacitated.

Meanwhile, Ananya was a whirlwind of motion, her body a blur as she moved with lightning speed across the battlefield. Her fighting style was a mix of agility and precision, every move calculated to maximize impact while minimizing exposure. She flipped through the air with the grace of a dancer, her feet barely touching the ground before she launched herself into another attack. A group of adversaries attempted to surround her, thinking to overwhelm her with their numbers, but they were woefully unprepared for her skill. Ananya leaped into the air, somersaulting over their heads and landing behind them with cat-like agility. Before they could react, she delivered a devastating roundhouse kick to the nearest foe, sending him crashing into his comrades. Without pausing, she spun on her heel, her leg sweeping out in a low arc that took another enemy's legs out from under him. He hit the ground hard, his head bouncing off the dirt as he lost consciousness.

Ananya's fists flew with the speed of a tempest, each punch landing with bone-cracking force. She targeted vital points with deadly accuracy, her strikes designed not just to incapacitate, but to ensure her enemies stayed down. A man lunged at her with a dagger, but Ananya caught his wrist in mid-air, twisting it sharply until he cried out in pain and dropped the weapon. She followed up with a knee to his stomach, then an elbow to the back of his head, sending him crumpling to the ground in a heap.

Across the battlefield, Manas fought with the calm, collected demeanor of a seasoned strategist. He had always been the one to analyze and plan, using his sharp mind to outthink his opponents before they even realized they were being outmaneuvered. His swordsmanship was a reflection of this—every strike, every parry, was executed with precise intent. He knew when to press the attack and when to draw back, luring his enemies into making mistakes that he could then exploit.

A hulking brute came at him with a basketball bat, the bat whistling through the air as it swung toward Manas' head. But Manas was ready. He ducked under the swing, stepping inside the brute's guard and delivering a sharp thrust to his ribs with the hilt of his sword. The brute grunted in pain, staggering back, and Manas didn't waste the opportunity. With a quick sidestep, he positioned himself behind the brute and delivered a powerful blow to the back of his knee, sending the giant crashing to the ground. The brute tried to rise, but Manas was already upon him, delivering a final strike that knocked him out cold.

As the trio continued to fight, they seemed almost unstoppable. Yet, in the midst of their victory, Manas' sharp eyes caught a movement out of the corner of his eye. A tall, shadowy figure was creeping closer to Lord Parashurama, moving with a stealth that belied its size. The figure's intent was clear—it was aiming to strike when Lord Parashurama's back was turned, when he was most vulnerable.

Manas' heart skipped a beat as he realized the danger. He opened his mouth to shout a warning, but the words seemed to stick in his throat. Time seemed to slow as he watched the figure raise a glinting object high above its head—a knife, poised to strike. The figure moved with a speed that defied belief, closing the distance between itself and Lord Parashurama in the blink of an eye.

"*Guru Dev*, behind you!" Manas finally managed to shout, his voice ringing out across the battlefield.

Lord Parashurama turned, his instincts honed by centuries of battle. But even he, the mighty warrior blessed with the strength of the gods, was not quick enough to completely avoid the attack. The knife struck with deadly precision, the blade sinking deep into his back. Lord Parashurama staggered forward, his axe slipping from his grasp as pain shot through his body. For a moment, the great sage was paralyzed by disbelief. His skin, blessed by the divine, was supposed to be impenetrable. How could this have happened?

"My skin is impenetrable," Lord Parashurama muttered, the words barely audible as he struggled to comprehend what had just occurred. But the figure behind him heard him clearly, and a cold, mocking voice responded.

"Impenetrable, you say?" The voice was laced with malice. "But not against mystical knives, laced with ancient poison."

The realization struck Lord Parashurama like a physical blow. He turned slowly, his eyes narrowing as he caught sight of his attacker. Standing before him, a twisted smile on his lips, was Shukracharya. Lord Parashurama's mind raced. He had heard of such weapons before—mystical knives, forged in the fires of the underworld and infused with poisons so potent they could bring even the strongest of warriors to their knees. But to actually face such a weapon, to feel its effects taking hold, was something entirely different. He could already feel the poison seeping into his veins, its cold grip spreading through his body, weakening him with every passing second.

But Lord Parashurama was not one to be easily defeated. His will was as strong as his body, and he refused to let this treachery be his end. Gritting his teeth, he reached for the divine strength within him, summoning every ounce of power he had left. He turned to face Shukracharya fully, his eyes blazing with fury.

"This isn't over," he growled, his voice low and dangerous.

Shukracharya merely smiled, a twisted, malevolent grin.

"Oh, it's far from over," he replied, his voice dripping with dark amusement.

"This is just the beginning."

Manas and Ananya, seeing their mentor in peril, moved to help him. But before they could reach Lord Parashurama, they were struck from behind by a powerful force. The impact was like being hit by a boulder, sending them flying through the air. They hit the ground hard, the wind knocked out of them as they struggled to comprehend what had just happened. Groaning, they pushed themselves to their feet, their bodies aching from the blow. As their vision cleared, they saw a towering figure standing before them, exuding an aura of unbridled power. It was Ashwatthama, his eyes burning with a fierce determination. His presence alone was enough to send a chill down their spines.

"Ready for Round 2?" Ashwatthama sneered, his voice filled with cold malice.

Manas and Ananya exchanged a glance, their faces set with grim determination. They knew the battle ahead would be even more brutal, but they had no choice. Lord Parashurama needed them, and they would not fail him. With a nod, they steeled themselves for the fight, their muscles tensing as they prepared to face Ashwatthama once more.

Ashwatthama didn't give them the chance to make the first move. With a roar that seemed to shake the very earth, he charged at them, his sword flashing in the dim light. Manas met his advance with a clash of steel, their blades ringing out as they collided with the force of a thunderstorm. The sheer power of Ashwatthama's strikes sent shockwaves up Manas' arms, but he held his ground, parrying each blow with skill and precision.

Ashwatthama fought like a man possessed, his every movement fueled by a dark rage. His sword was a blur as he attacked with relentless fury, forcing Manas to defend himself with all his might. The ground beneath them cracked under the strain of their battle, each strike leaving gouges in the earth as sparks flew from their clashing blades.

Ananya circled around, looking for an opening. She knew that in a direct confrontation, Ashwatthama was nearly unbeatable, but she also knew that she and Manas had to work together to take him down. As Ashwatthama focused on overpowering Manas, Ananya saw her chance. She launched herself into the air, her body twisting mid-flight as she aimed a powerful kick at Ashwatthama's side. But Ashwatthama was quicker than she anticipated. He sensed her approach and spun around just in time to deflect her kick with his forearm. The impact jolted Ananya, but she landed gracefully, immediately following up with a rapid series of punches aimed at Ashwatthama's chest and throat.

Ashwatthama countered with brutal efficiency, blocking her strikes and delivering a bone-crushing backhand that sent her stumbling. But Ananya was nothing if not resilient. She recovered quickly, her eyes narrowing as she prepared for another assault. She moved in again, this time feinting a high kick before switching her attack to a low sweep aimed at Ashwatthama's legs.

The move caught Ashwatthama off guard, and he faltered for just a moment. It was all the opening Manas needed. With a surge of strength, he pushed Ashwatthama back, forcing him off balance. The mighty warrior snarled in frustration, but before he could regain his footing, Manas pressed his advantage. He struck with lightning speed, delivering a flurry of blows that Ashwatthama struggled to parry.

Ananya, seeing Ashwatthama's defenses weakening, joined the attack. She moved with a deadly grace, her strikes coming faster and harder as she targeted Ashwatthama's weak points. The two of them fought as one, their movements perfectly synchronized as they wore down their opponent.

Despite his immense strength, Ashwatthama was beginning to feel the strain. Manas' sword strikes were relentless, and Ananya's precise attacks left him no room to breathe. He staggered back, his chest heaving as he struggled to keep up with the combined assault.

With a final, coordinated effort, Manas and Ananya struck in unison. Manas delivered a powerful blow to Ashwatthama's side, while Ananya aimed a kick at his head. The impact was too much for Ashwatthama to withstand. He let out a pained grunt as he was sent crashing to the ground, his sword slipping from his grasp.

The sun continued its ascent over Ayodhya, casting long shadows across the sacred city as the battle between light and darkness raged on. Lord Parashurama Ji, Manas, and Ananya fought valiantly, their skills and strength tested to the very limits by the overwhelming forces they faced. But as the fight dragged on, the scales began to tip in favor of the ancient evil that had lain dormant for so long.

As Manas and Ananya stood side by side, preparing to make their next move against Ashwatthama, a sudden, chilling command cut through the chaos.

"Remember the missing ingredient, Ashwatthama!" Shukracharya's voice boomed across the courtyard, filled with dark intent.

Ashwatthama's eyes widened with understanding, his gaze locking onto Manas with renewed determination. He knew exactly what Shukracharya meant.

Without wasting a second, Ashwatthama sprang into action. He scooped up a handful of dirt from the ground and flung it into the faces of Manas and Ananya. The coarse grains of earth struck their eyes, blinding them temporarily as they staggered back, trying to rub the dirt away.

Seizing the opportunity, Ashwatthama moved with the speed and precision of a seasoned warrior. He closed the distance between himself and Manas in an instant, his powerful fist crashing into Manas' chest with the force of a sledgehammer. The impact drove the air from Manas' lungs, sending him sprawling to the ground.

Before Manas could recover, Ashwatthama struck again, this time with a sharp blow to the side of Manas' face, drawing blood. A thin line of crimson trickled from Manas' mouth, and Ashwatthama's eyes gleamed with triumph as he quickly collected a few precious drops of the blood on his fingers.

"Got it," Ashwatthama muttered under his breath, a dark satisfaction curling his lips into a smile.

Ananya, still struggling to clear her vision, sensed what had happened and felt a surge of panic. She blinked furiously, her eyes watering as she forced herself to focus. When she finally regained her sight, she saw Ashwatthama moving towards Shukracharya to help him out.

Lord Parashurama Ji, who had been locked in a fierce struggle with Shukracharya's dark tendrils, saw what had transpired. His heart sank as he realized the gravity of the situation.

"You won't get away with this, Shukracharya!"

Lord Parashurama Ji roared, his voice filled with both fury and determination. With a burst of divine energy, he shattered the tendrils that bound him and lunged toward Shukracharya, his staff glowing with a brilliant light.

But Shukracharya was prepared. With a wave of his hand, he conjured a barrier of dark energy that deflected Lord Parashurama Ji's attack, sending the warrior-sage skidding back across the stone floor. Ashwatthama, now fully focused on the task at hand, backed away from the fallen forms of Manas and Ananya, his prize secure. He turned to Shukracharya, nodding in acknowledgment of their victory.

"We have what we need. It's time to move to the next phase."

Shukracharya smiled, a thin, cruel smile that spoke of centuries of plotting and vengeance. Manas, groggy and disoriented, struggled to rise to his feet. His vision blurred, his head throbbing from the blows he had taken. But through the haze of pain, he understood what had happened.

"Ananya… we can't let them leave," Manas gasped, his voice weak but resolute.

"We have to stop them…"

Lord Parashurama Ji's vision blurred as the world around him began to spin. The poison from Shukracharya's dagger was working its way through his veins, sapping his strength and dulling his senses. His eyelids grew heavy, and he felt an overwhelming urge to succumb to the darkness that beckoned him.

Across from him, Shukracharya stood, his malevolent grin widening as he watched Lord Parashurama Ji struggle.

"It seems the poison is doing its work,"

Shukracharya said, his voice dripping with satisfaction. He stepped closer, his hand tightening around the hilt of his dagger, ready to deliver the final blow.

But just as Shukracharya raised his dagger, a shadow moved swiftly between him and Lord Parashurama Ji. Shukracharya halted mid-strike, his eyes narrowing as he saw a hooded figure standing in his way. The figure's face was obscured by the deep hood, but his stance radiated strength and purpose.

"Who dares interfere?" Shukracharya hissed, his voice laced with venom.

The hooded figure said nothing, only moved with lightning speed, launching into an attack that caught Shukracharya off guard. Their blades clashed in a flurry of sparks, and the hooded figure's skill became immediately apparent. Each strike was precise, each movement fluid, as if the hooded figure had been trained for centuries in the art of combat. Shukracharya, though powerful, found himself struggling to keep up. The hooded figure pressed the attack, forcing Shukracharya to retreat step by step. His confidence began to falter as he realized that he was being overpowered.

Seeing Shukracharya in danger, Ashwatthama leaped into the fray, his powerful frame barreling toward the hooded figure. But the hooded figure, with a speed and agility that belied his size, dodged Ashwatthama's attack and spun around, landing a powerful blow on Ashwatthama's chest. The impact sent Ashwatthama stumbling backward, but instead of finishing the attack, the hooded figure chose to push him aside, sending him sprawling near Shukracharya.

Ashwatthama looked up from where he had fallen, confusion and disbelief in his eyes. Why had the hooded figure spared him? As he regained his footing, his gaze followed the hooded figure, who was now helping Lord Parashurama Ji to stand.

The hooded figure extended a hand to Lord Parashurama Ji, who took it with a mix of gratitude and surprise.

"Aren't you late?" Lord Parashurama Ji murmured, his voice weak but laced with a hint of humor.

The hooded figure chuckled softly, the sound familiar and comforting.

"Just got back in time," he replied, pulling back his hood to reveal his face. Ashwatthama's eyes widened in shock, his breath catching in his throat. "Uncle?" he whispered, disbelief coloring his voice.

The hooded figure was none other than Kripacharya Ji, the immortal sage and one of the last surviving warriors of the Kurukshetra war. His presence here was both a surprise and a blow to Ashwatthama. Kripacharya's eyes, normally filled with the calm wisdom of centuries, were now hard and unforgiving as they locked onto Ashwatthama.

"Yet again, you find yourself on the wrong side, Ashwatthama,"

Kripacharya said, his voice ringing with disappointment and authority.

"You've strayed far from the path of righteousness."

Ashwatthama staggered to his feet, struggling with the emotions that Kripacharya's words stirred within him. But before he could respond, Shukracharya, who had regained his composure, interjected.

"Enough of this," Shukracharya snapped, his voice cutting through the tension.

"We have what we came for. There's no need to linger."

He grabbed Ashwatthama by the arm, pulling him back as he began to retreat. Ashwatthama hesitated, his eyes flicking between Kripacharya and Shukracharya, torn between loyalty and doubt.

"Let's go, Ashwatthama," Shukracharya ordered, his tone leaving no room for argument.

"We've got what we need."

Kripacharya watched as Shukracharya and Ashwatthama retreated, his expression unreadable. He did not pursue them but instead turned his attention back to Lord Parashurama Ji, who was still weakened by the poison. As Shukracharya and Ashwatthama disappeared into the shadows, the tension in the air slowly began to dissipate. Kripacharya sighed, a mixture of relief and sorrow in his eyes as he knelt beside Lord Parashurama Ji.

"We need to get you to safety, old friend," Kripacharya said softly, his voice filled with concern.

"The poison is strong, but there's still time to counteract it."

Lord Parashurama Ji nodded, leaning heavily on Kripacharya as they moved away from the battlefield. Manas and Ananya, still recovering from their own injuries, followed closely, their minds reeling from the unexpected turn of events.

As Shukracharya and Ashwatthama retreated into the shadows, Lord Parashurama Ji, Kripacharya, Manas, and Ananya prepared themselves for whatever might come next. But before they could catch their breath, a new threat emerged. Out of the shadows, more than a hundred men appeared, their eyes glazed over, their movements robotic and menacing. These were Shukracharya's final gambit—extra forces he had hypnotized as a contingency.

Lord Parashurama Ji, still weakened from the poison, struggled to remain on his feet, while Manas and Ananya, battered from their earlier battle, exchanged worried glances. Kripacharya, the only one still in good condition, stood tall, his eyes narrowing as he assessed the incoming threat.

"There are too many," Ananya began, her voice trembling slightly, but before she could finish, Kripacharya placed a reassuring hand on her shoulder.

"Don't worry," Kripacharya said calmly, a hint of a smile on his lips.

"An army is coming."

Just as the words left his mouth, Manas felt the ground beneath him begin to tremble. The vibration grew stronger, like the earth itself was shuddering under the weight of something massive. He turned his head to the left, squinting into the distance, and saw a dust storm forming on the horizon, as if an entire legion was charging toward them.

The dust began to clear, and the scene that unfolded before them was nothing short of miraculous. A vast army of monkeys, their fur bristling and their eyes glowing with determination, charged toward the hypnotized men. Their roars echoed through the air, a sound that sent shivers down the spines of the few conscious men who could still comprehend what was happening.

The monkeys moved with a precision and coordination that seemed impossible for mere animals. They formed ranks, charging at the hypnotized men with a ferocity that was awe-inspiring. Each monkey leaped at the nearest opponent, their powerful limbs slamming into the hypnotized men with enough force to knock them down. But there was something different about these monkeys— they were not just attacking. They were curing.

Ananya, her eyes wide with astonishment, noticed that each monkey held a small pouch in its hand. As the monkeys slapped or tackled their opponents, they deftly slipped the contents of these pouches into the nostrils of the hypnotized men. One by one, the men began to collapse, unconscious but no longer under Shukracharya's spell.

"What… what is that in their hands?"

Ananya asked, her voice a mix of curiosity and disbelief.

Kripacharya smiled knowingly.

"It's a mixture of potent herbs," he explained.

"A special blend that counters the effects of hypnotism. These men will wake up with no memory of what they've done, free from the influence of Shukracharya's dark magic."

As the monkeys continued their task, Lord Parashurama Ji, who had been watching in awe, felt a sense of deep relief. He managed a weak smile, despite the pain still coursing through his body.

"Nothing can harm Lord Ram, not in Treta Yuga, and not in this Yuga, as long as Lord Hanuman Ji is here."

Kripacharya nodded in agreement, his eyes sparkling with pride.

"Lord Hanuman Ji sends his regards," he said softly. The battle was brief but decisive. The monkeys, with their incredible speed and strength, quickly overwhelmed the hypnotized men, delivering the herbal remedy with every strike. Soon, the entire field was littered with unconscious bodies, the once menacing force now neutralized by the unexpected and mighty army of monkeys.

As the dust settled, Lord Parashurama Ji, Kripacharya, Manas, and Ananya stood together, surveying the scene. The monkeys, their task complete, gathered in front of the four warriors, their chests heaving with exertion but their eyes filled with triumph.

Lord Parashurama Ji, filled with gratitude and reverence, raised his voice in a powerful chant.

"Jai Shree Ram!" he shouted, his voice ringing out across the field.

"Jai Shree Ram!" echoed Kripacharya, his voice rich with the wisdom of ages.

"Jai Shree Ram!" Manas and Ananya shouted together, their voices filled with renewed hope and determination.

The chant spread like wildfire, the cry of victory and devotion carrying on the wind, as if the very earth itself was joining in the celebration. The monkeys roared in unison, their voices mingling with those of the warriors, creating a symphony of triumph that echoed through the city of Ayodhya.

For now, though, there was a moment of peace—a moment to remember that even in the darkest times, the light of righteousness could never be fully extinguished. With Hanuman Ji's blessing and the strength of their bonds, they had won this battle. The road ahead would be difficult, but they would walk it together, united in their devotion to Lord Ram and the cause of dharma.

The monkeys began to retreat, their work done, but not before one of them, the leader of the group, paused to look back at the four warriors. He raised his hand in a gesture of farewell, then turned and disappeared into the trees, his army following close behind.

As the last of the monkeys vanished from sight, Lord Parashurama Ji turned to his companions, his heart swelling with pride and gratitude.

"Let this victory be a reminder," he said, his voice strong despite his weakened state, "that as long as we remain true to our purpose, no force of darkness can stand against us."

With one final shout of "Jai Shree Ram," the four warriors began to make their way back into the heart of Ayodhya, ready to face whatever challenges lay ahead. The dust from the recent battle had barely settled when Kripacharya Ji turned to Manas and Ananya, his eyes filled with a mix of wisdom and gentle authority. He could see the questions in their eyes, the uncertainty that comes with youth and the burden of responsibility they were shouldering. He placed a reassuring hand on Lord Parashurama Ji's shoulder before addressing the young warriors.

"Manas, Ananya," Kripacharya Ji said, his voice calm yet commanding, "take care of your Guru. He has guided you this far, and his wisdom will be needed for what lies ahead."

Manas, filled with respect and gratitude, bent down and touched Kripacharya Ji's feet, a gesture of deep reverence. Kripacharya Ji placed a hand on Manas' head, blessing him.

"Rise, my son," he said warmly. "Your grandfather taught you well."

Manas looked up, surprised by Kripacharya Ji's words. The mention of his grandfather sparked a curiosity that he couldn't contain.

"You knew my grandfather?" Manas asked, a note of astonishment in his voice. Kripacharya Ji smiled, a twinkle of nostalgia in his eyes.

"Well, kid, in the future—" he began, but Lord Parashurama Ji, sensing that the conversation was drifting into dangerous territory, signaled silence.

"Enough for now," Lord Parashurama Ji said firmly, though not unkindly.

"Manas has to focus on one mission first."

Manas nodded, understanding that there were still many things he needed to learn, but now was not the time. He had a duty to fulfill, and that came before satisfying his curiosity.

Ananya stepped forward and touched Kripacharya Ji's feet as well. He patted her head, his affection for her evident.

"Rise, my child," he said, his voice filled with paternal warmth.

"You have a strong spirit. The road ahead will test you, but I know you will prevail." Ananya, sensing the depth of his wisdom, asked the question that had been on her mind since they had first met.

"I think you already know why we are here, who we seek."

Kripacharya Ji nodded, his expression turning serious.

"Yes, I do. Stay here until the *Pran Pratishtha* (consecration ceremony) is complete. After that, you will get your answers. Everything will become clear."

Lord Parashurama Ji, always focused on the task at hand, stepped forward.

"Do you need any help with your mission, Kripacharya Ji?"

Kripacharya Ji shook his head.

"No, Lord Parashurama. I have Raghu Bhassin with me. He is more than capable. We have trained him well, and he will be able to assist me with what needs to be done."

Ananya, her curiosity piqued, asked,

"Speaking of him, where is he? We haven't seen him."

Kripacharya Ji smiled softly, a hint of pride in his eyes.

"He is out there, protecting the city, ensuring that no harm befalls Ayodhya during this sacred time." Manas, still grappling with the barrage of new information, looked puzzled.

"Who is he?" he began to ask, but Ananya, sensing that now was not the time to delve into more mysteries, gently interrupted him.

"Leave it," Ananya said softly.

"As Guru Ji said, let's focus on this mission first."

Kripacharya Ji watched the exchange with approval.

"You have good companions, Lord Parashurama," he said, his voice tinged with respect.

"Rest assured, we will join you soon. But for now, take care of yourselves and see to it that your mission is completed."

With those words, Kripacharya Ji gave them a reassuring nod, signaling that their paths would cross again soon. He then turned and walked toward the temple, his figure strong and resolute, a living connection to a past that was both ancient and enduring.

As Manas, Ananya, and Lord Parashurama Ji watched him go, they felt a renewed sense of purpose. The presence of such a venerable ally as Kripacharya Ji, gave them hope that they were not alone in their struggle. The road ahead was fraught with danger, but they knew that with their combined strength and the guidance of their elders, they could face whatever challenges lay in wait.

As the sun dipped lower in the sky, casting long shadows across the sacred city of Ayodhya, the three warriors stood together, united in their resolve. They would rest, gather their strength, and prepare for the battles yet to come. And when the time was right, they would seek out the answers they needed to fulfill their destiny.

For now, they echoed the chant that had filled the air earlier, their voices strong and full of faith.

"Jai Shree Ram!"

"Jai Shree Ram!"

As dawn broke over Ayodhya, the golden rays of the sun bathed the city in a warm, ethereal glow. The air was thick with the anticipation of the day's events—*Pran Pratishtha*, the consecration ceremony of the Ram Mandir. The trio—Lord Parashurama Ji, Manas, and Ananya—rose early, their hearts filled with reverence and purpose. Today, they would attend the sacred ceremony, but their mission extended beyond the spiritual rites.

The city was alive with devotion. Thousands of devotees had gathered to witness the historic moment, the inauguration of the grand Ram Mandir. The streets were adorned with marigold garlands, and the air was filled with the scent of incense and the sound of devotional songs. The atmosphere was charged with a sense of divine presence, as if Lord Ram himself walked among them.

As they approached the temple, they could see the preparations in full swing. The main stage was set, and at its center stood a magnificent statue of Lord Ram, resplendent in his royal attire, his eyes full of compassion and strength. The Prime Minister of India, stood at the forefront, preparing to lead the Pran Pratishtha ceremony. The entire nation watched, both in person and through countless screens, as the momentous occasion unfolded.

The trio found a place among the crowd, their eyes fixed on the proceedings. As the ceremony began, the Prime Minister, with utmost reverence, performed the rituals. He offered prayers, chanted sacred mantras, and placed the first brick, symbolizing the rebirth of the temple after centuries of longing and struggle. The crowd erupted in chants of *"Jai Shree Ram!"* as the sacred flames were lit, their light reflected in the eyes of the devotees, filling the space with an aura of purity and divine energy.

As the *Pran Pratishtha* ceremony reached its climax, the sacred verses from the *Baal Kaand* of Valmiki's Ramayana resonated through the air, invoking the divine presence of Lord Ram.

"श्रीमद्वाल्मीकि रामायणस्य बालकाण्डे सप्तमोऽध्यायः

The atmosphere was electric, charged with the spiritual energy of countless prayers. The Prime Minister, with folded hands, bowed before the statue of Lord Ram, seeking his blessings for the nation. But as the ceremony concluded and the attention of the crowd shifted to the speeches that followed, Lord Parashurama Ji signaled Manas and Ananya. Quietly, they slipped away from the gathering, moving towards the back of the temple. Their steps were careful, their senses alert. They had a different purpose now, one that required them to move in silence and with utmost reverence.

As they reached the secluded area behind the temple, they noticed something unusual—a large gathering of crows perched on the temple's walls, all of them intently gazing at the statue of Lord Ram. Their black eyes were fixed, unblinking, as if they were witnessing something beyond the physical world.

Ananya, curious and slightly unnerved by the sight, picked up a small pebble from the ground. She tossed it lightly into the air, aiming to see if the crows would react. The stone arced gracefully, and as it fell, the crows suddenly broke their trance, their attention diverted. They cawed loudly, flapping their wings as they scattered into the sky, all except one.

One crow remained, its gaze still locked onto the statue of Lord Ram, unmoved by the disturbance. Lord Parashurama Ji observed this with keen interest, his suspicion growing stronger.

"प्रणम्य शिरसा रामं सत्त्ववांश्च महाबलः।

Lord Parashurama Ji began to recite *shlokas* from the Baal Kaand, specifically from the episode where Kaagbhusandi Ji first met Lord Ram. His voice was low, respectful, as he chanted the sacred verses, invoking the memory of that ancient meeting. As the chanting continued, the lone crow did not move. It remained still, its gaze unwavering. This lack of reaction confirmed Lord Parashurama Ji's suspicions—this was no ordinary crow.

"It is him," Lord Parashurama Ji whispered to Manas and Ananya, his voice filled with reverence.

"He is Kaagbhusandi Ji."

Manas' heart skipped a beat. Lord Parashurama Ji gestured to Manas, signaling him to speak. Manas took a deep breath, his hands trembling slightly as he approached the venerable being. He bowed deeply, his forehead nearly touching the ground, and spoke with the utmost humility.

"O great sage," Manas began, his voice steady despite the gravity of the moment, "we seek your help."

The crow, Kaagbhusandi Ji, slowly turned its gaze towards Manas. There was a deep, ancient wisdom in its eyes, a knowledge that spanned eons. It was as if the sage could see into Manas' very soul, understanding not just his words but the depth of his need. Kaagbhusandi Ji observed Manas for a long moment. Then, recognizing Lord Parashurama Ji and the sincerity in the young man's plea, the crow inclined its head slightly—a gesture that conveyed both acknowledgment and consent.

"Your presence with Lord Parashurama Ji tells me that your cause is just,"

Kaagbhusandi Ji's voice echoed in Manas' mind, ancient and serene. Though the crow did not speak aloud, its thoughts resonated clearly, a testament to its spiritual power.

Lord Parashurama Ji, standing nearby, felt a deep sense of relief. They had found Kaagbhusandi Ji, and he had agreed to listen. Ananya, sensing the significance of the moment, stepped forward and bowed as well.

"We seek your wisdom, O great sage," she said softly.

"Please guide us on our journey."

Kaagbhusandi Ji remained silent for a few moments, as if contemplating their request. Then, with a slight nod, the sage agreed.

"Stay for now. After the consecration is complete, we shall speak. The answers you seek will be revealed, but only after the ceremony is honored."

With that, the crow returned its gaze to the statue of Lord Ram, its presence once again blending into the sacred atmosphere of the temple. Lord Parashurama Ji, Manas, and Ananya shared a look of mutual understanding. They would wait until the time was right. As they quietly returned to their place within the temple grounds, the trio couldn't help but feel a renewed sense of purpose. The ceremony continued, the sacred chants and offerings filling the air with their holy resonance. As the crowd chanted *"Jai Shree Ram!"* in unison, the trio joined in, their voices blending with the multitude.

"Jai Shree Ram!"

CHAPTER 13

The journey to Kurukshetra was tense, the air thick with unresolved anger and the looming weight of their dark mission. Shukracharya, Ashwatthama, and Akshay moved with purpose, but Ashwatthama's mind was clouded with fury and confusion.

"Why?" Ashwatthama growled, his fists clenched as they rode through the desolate landscape.

"Why is my own uncle, Kripacharya, standing against me?

Why won't he help me?"

Shukracharya, ever the manipulative and cunning guide, turned to Ashwatthama, his voice calm but firm.

"Leave him be, Ashwatthama. Kripacharya has made his choice, and it is not with us. But we do not need his help. Our strength lies in our purpose, not in the approval of others."

Ashwatthama's eyes still burned with anger, but Shukracharya's words managed to soothe him, if only slightly. The betrayal by his uncle stung, but his resolve remained unshaken. He would press on, with or without Kripacharya.

As they neared Kurukshetra, the land of the legendary battle, something shifted in the atmosphere. The air grew heavier, and Ashwatthama's mind began to drift into a trance, pulled back to a time when the ground beneath him had been soaked in the blood of warriors, when the very soil had trembled under the weight of destruction.

In his vision, Ashwatthama saw the epic scenes of the

The Mahabharata war is unfolding once again.

He saw his father, Guru Dronacharya, leading the Kaurava army with unparalleled skill and valor. But then, the vision turned dark. He witnessed the treacherous moment when his father was deceived by the news of his son's death—by the death of the elephant named Ashwatthama.

*The memory was seared into Ashwatthama's mind: Yudhishthira, known for his unwavering truthfulness, was persuaded by Krishna to utter the half-truth, "**Ashwatthama hathaha... kunjaraha,**" meaning "Ashwatthama is dead... the elephant." Dronacharya, hearing this, was overwhelmed with grief, believing his beloved son had perished. He laid down his weapons and sat in meditation, where he was then killed by Dhrishtadyumna.*

The vision of his father's death played over and over in Ashwatthama's mind, each repetition fueling his rage and sorrow. He saw his friend Duryodhana falling, struck down by Bhima, the Pandava he despised most. He saw Karna, his dearest friend, helpless as Arjuna's arrow pierced his armorless chest. The battlefield was littered with the bodies of those he had fought beside, those he had sworn to protect.

Ashwatthama's breathing grew heavy, his heart pounding in his chest as the visions consumed him. The sounds of clashing weapons, the cries of dying warriors, and the sight of his father's lifeless body all melded into a nightmarish swirl of rage and sorrow.

"Focus on now, Ashwatthama," Shukracharya's voice cut through the haze, pulling him back to the present.

"We must bring Raghav back. We need to increase our strength if we are to succeed."

Ashwatthama shook his head, dispelling the remnants of his vision. His eyes, still clouded with emotion, scanned the ground around him. Akshay, ever eager to please, pointed to a spot on the ground where he stood.

"Why not pick the soil from here and start the ritual?" Akshay suggested.

Shukracharya shook his head, a hint of impatience in his tone.

"No, it must be from the place where a powerful warrior fell. Only then will the soil carry the strength we need."

Ashwatthama's gaze landed on a specific spot, and a fresh wave of emotion washed over him.

"Here," he said, his voice tinged with the weight of memory.

"This is where the elephant named Ashwatthama fell, the lie that led to my father's death."

Shukracharya's eyes narrowed as he looked at Ashwatthama.

"This is promising," he said, his voice deep and resonant.

"But I require something more potent, something that holds the essence of the fallen king. Tell me, Ashwatthama, where did your friend Duryodhan breathe his last?" With this knowledge, Raghav will inherit the very strength that Duryodhan once wielded. The strength of an emperor, the strength forged in battle and betrayal."

Ashwatthama's brow furrowed, confusion clouding his thoughts. Ashwatthama took a deep breath, closing his eyes, and let the silence of the ages envelop him. His mind drifted back through time, traversing the echoes of forgotten battles and ancient oaths. The memories came slowly, like

whispers from the past, until suddenly, a vision burst forth, vivid and undeniable.

He saw it—the cursed battlefield, drenched in blood and sorrow, where Duryodhan had faced his final moments. The ground was scorched, the air thick with the scent of death. There, in the dying light of the day, lay Duryodhan, his once-mighty form crumpled, the last vestiges of his strength slipping away. Ashwatthama's eyes snapped open, a spark of realization igniting within them.

"Up there, Guru Ji," he said, his voice steady and filled with newfound certainty.

"This is the place where Duryodhan met his end. The earth still remembers, and it is there that the power you seek lies dormant, waiting to be claimed."

"Very well," Shukracharya said, nodding in approval. "We will use this soil."

Akshay knelt down, ready to scoop up the soil, but Shukracharya stopped him.

"Not like this," he said sharply.

"After so many years, the surface soil has lost its potency. We must dig deeper to reach the true essence of this cursed land."

Akshay signaled to their men, who immediately set to work. They dug furiously, the ground giving way under their shovels and picks. The deeper they went, the more the soil changed, its color darkening to a deep, ominous red—a red that spoke of ancient blood spilled in battle.

After digging for nearly ten feet, the men paused, staring at the soil they had unearthed. It was richer, darker, and more vibrant than the earth above. The sight of it made Shukracharya's eyes glisten with a dark satisfaction.

"Yes," Shukracharya whispered, his voice filled with a malevolent glee.

"This is the soil we need. Place it in the pot, and keep it near Raghav's ashes and the blood of Manas."

Akshay carefully collected the soil, placing it in the pot with reverence, as if handling a sacred relic. The pot, now filled with the soil of Kurukshetra, Raghav's ashes, and the blood of Manas, pulsed with a dark energy—a testament to the power they were about to unleash.

Shukracharya, his eyes gleaming with anticipation, turned to Ashwatthama and Akshay.

"We are one step closer to our goal. Raghav will return, and with him, our strength will be unmatched.

The shadows of Kurukshetra lengthened as the sun dipped below the horizon, casting an ominous twilight over the land that had witnessed the greatest war in history. The air was heavy with the memories of battle and bloodshed, but for Ashwatthama, the weight of the past was not enough to quench his thirst for vengeance. His mind was a storm of rage and frustration, his heart beating with a singular purpose—revenge.

As they gathered the last of the sacred soil from the battlefield, Ashwatthama turned to Shukracharya, his eyes burning with a question that had been festering within him since they had begun their dark journey.

"So, what is the next step, Guru Ji?" he asked, his voice edged with impatience.

"Where do we go from here?"

Shukracharya straightened and brushed the dust from his hands. His gaze turned to the distant mountains, where the first stars of the evening began to twinkle against the deepening sky. Shukracharya's gaze turned distant, as if he were peering through the veils of time itself.

"The next step," he began, his voice a low, measured murmur, "is to journey to Rakshastal. It is there, and only there, that the final ritual must be performed." Akshay, his curiosity piqued, dared to question,

"Why Rakshastal? What makes that place so important?"

Shukracharya's eyes narrowed, a flicker of ancient knowledge shining through.

"Rakshastal is no ordinary place," he said, his tone both ominous and reverent.

"It is a place of ancient dread and dark whispers, hidden in the shadow of the mighty Mount Kailash. This lake, known as the 'Lake of the Demons,' has witnessed the presence of one of the most feared beings in our lore—Ravana, the great demon king. It was here that Ravana, in his insatiable quest for power, sought the blessings of Lord Shiva. He chose this desolate place to perform his severe penance, far from the eyes of gods and men."

Shukracharya paused, allowing the weight of his words to settle. "Day after day, year after year, Ravana sat in stillness, his mind focused on one goal: to gain dominion over life and death. His presence left an indelible mark on the land, twisting the energies of the lake into something dark and untamed. The waters of Rakshastal, bitter and saline, stand in stark contrast to the sweet, pure waters of nearby Mansarovar, as if the very essence of the lake had been poisoned by Ravana's ambition."

Akshay listened, his earlier doubt fading as the significance of the place became clear. Shukracharya continued, his voice now imbued with a deeper gravity. "Rakshastal, with its history steeped in the shadows of Ravana's penance, is a place where the lines between the mortal world and the realms beyond blur. The ancient sages knew of its power, a power that could be harnessed only by those who understood the delicate balance between creation and destruction, between light and dark. This lake, where the energies of a demon king's desire still linger, is a gateway—a thin veil separating our world from the underworld. It is a place where life and death converge, a perfect crucible for rituals that defy the natural order."

Ashwatthama nodded, though the mention of the final procedure brought forth the dark ambitions he harbored.

"And once Raghav is back," he said, the words slipping from his lips like venom, "I will kill Manas. He has interfered long enough, and his blood should be spilled for what he has done."

Shukracharya glanced at Ashwatthama, noting the intensity of his resolve, but also sensing the impatience that simmered just below the surface. He knew that Ashwatthama's anger was both a weapon and a weakness, something that could propel their plans forward or derail them entirely.

"Patience, Ashwatthama," he counseled, his voice carrying the weight of centuries of experience.

"We must move carefully. Manas is not our true target. What we truly seek is Karna's Kavach Kundal."

Ashwatthama frowned, the mention of the Kavach Kundal only deepening his confusion.

"But why? Why chase after a piece of armor when we could simply end this Yuga, speed up time, and bring everything to a close, as you yourself mentioned in your book."

Shukracharya's eyes gleamed with an ancient wisdom, a knowing that stretched far beyond the mortal world.

"The Kavach Kundal is no mere armor, Ashwatthama. It is a relic of immense power, created by Lord Surya himself. It does not simply protect; it radiates a unique energy.

Ashwatthama's frustration flared again, his hands balling into fists at his sides.

"So, we don't need Manas at all?"

Shukracharya shook his head, a slight smile playing on his lips. Shukracharya's voice was calm, yet it carried the weight of ancient secrets.

"We need Manas," he began, "but only at the final moment. Karna's Kavach, when mixed with Manas' blood, is the true key to reviving the Saraswati River."

Ashwatthama's eyes flickered with determination.

"We already have his blood," he stated, thinking it would suffice.

Shukracharya shook his head, his gaze piercing through the layers of time.

"That's not enough," he replied, his tone resolute.

"What you possess is sufficient to bring Raghav back, but not for what we seek. To revive the Saraswati, we need more—more of Manas' blood, and it must be spilled with intent. This time, it must be enough to coat the entire Kavach. Only then will we hold the power to restore the sacred river."

Ashwatthama's impatience flared, his desire to end the current age burning within him.

"Then let us hasten the time and bring this Yug to an end," he urged. Shukracharya's eyes flashed with a stern warning.

"Enough of your obsession with ending this Yug," he said sharply.

"I have a plan—one far greater than merely closing this cycle of time. But that knowledge is not for now. When the moment is right, all will be revealed."

Ashwatthama's anger was a palpable thing, a force that seemed to crackle in the air around him.

"And yet, we're behind schedule! We don't even know where Manas and his companions are. Have they begun their journey to find the Kavach Kundal, or are they still wandering aimlessly?"

Shukracharya's expression remained calm, though there was a subtle edge to his voice.

"We are not as far behind as you think, Ashwatthama. We have been moving in tandem with their steps, watching, waiting. But first, we must focus on what is before us. We must bring Raghav back, and with his strength, we will be able to track Manas and take what we need. The final steps will fall into place, but only if we execute them with precision."

Ashwatthama's jaw tightened, but he nodded in agreement. The promise of power and revenge was enough to keep his rage in check, for now.

"Very well," he said, his voice a growl of reluctant acceptance.

"But know this—once Raghav is back, I will not wait any longer. Manas' blood will be spilled, and the Kavach Kundal will be ours."

Shukracharya acknowledged Ashwatthama's words with a slight incline of his head.

"Agreed. But remember, Ashwatthama, the endgame is not just about Manas. It's about bringing forth a new era—an era that we will command."

With the plan set, the trio began their journey to Rakshastal.

CHAPTER 14

The Pran Pratishtha ceremony had concluded, and the sacred atmosphere of Ayodhya was still resonating with the divine energy that had been invoked. The air was thick with the fragrance of flowers and incense, and the voices of thousands of devotees chanting "Jai Shree Ram" echoed throughout the city. But for Manas, Ananya, and Lord Parashurama Ji, their focus had shifted from the grandeur of the ceremony to the mysterious task that lay ahead.

Kaagbhusandi Ji, the ancient sage in the form of a crow, had given them a cryptic message before flying away. His words lingered in Manas' mind, like a riddle wrapped in layers of ancient wisdom.

"You must go to Mansarovar Lake," Kaagbhusandi Ji had said, his voice carrying the weight of eons.

"The lake holds great significance from ancient times. Mansarovar was created in the mind of Lord Brahma before it manifested on Earth. It is a place of immense spiritual power, a source of purity and enlightenment. Those who seek the deepest truths and answers to their most profound questions must go there."

Manas, puzzled and seeking clarity, had asked,

"What must we do when we reach Mansarovar?"

Kaagbhusandi Ji's response had been enigmatic.

"यो उत्तराणि इच्छति, तस्य सरःजलं पातव्यम्,

किन्तु तद् जलं प्राचीनमन्त्रयुक्तेन द्रव्येण संयोजयितव्यम्, यत् विष्णोः अवताराणां एकेन संबद्धम् अस्ति।

एतत् सर्वं सुरप्रभायुक्ते सरःसम्पूर्णे केवलम् यथा कर्तव्यं।"

"The one who seeks answers must drink the water of the lake, but it must be mixed with a substance that contains ancient magic, something that has a connection to one of Lord Vishnu's incarnations. And it should be done when the entire lake glows with celestial light. Only then will you receive your first clue—your first step on the path to finding the Kavach Kundal."

The cryptic nature of the instructions left Manas more confused.

"I don't understand," he had said, his voice tinged with frustration.

"How will we know what substance to mix with the water?

What is this ancient magic you speak of?"

Kaagbhusandi Ji, had fixed Manas with a penetrating gaze, his eyes reflecting the vast wisdom of the ages.

"If the path were easy, anyone could walk it," he had replied.

"This journey will test you, Manas. It will test your resolve, your faith, and your worthiness."

"Test what?" Manas had begun to ask, but Kaagbhusandi Ji had already anticipated the question.

"A test to determine whether you are worthy of the Kavach you seek," the sage had said with finality. Then, with a solemn chant of *"Jai Jai Shree Ram,"* Kaagbhusandi had spread his wings and flown away, disappearing into the sky.

Lord Parashurama Ji and Ananya had bowed low, paying their respects to the ancient sage, while Manas stood there, his mind racing with questions. As the figure of the crow vanished from sight, the reality of the task before them began to set in. Manas turned to Lord Parashurama Ji, his expression one of uncertainty and doubt.

"What do we do now, Guru Ji? How do we even begin to understand what Kaagbhusandi Ji meant?"

Lord Parashurama Ji, ever the steadfast guide, placed a reassuring hand on Manas' shoulder.

"We do as he instructed," he said calmly.

"We make our way to Mansarovar Lake, and once there, we will seek the guidance we need. The answers will come to us, but only if we take the first step."

Ananya, who had been silent, nodded in agreement.

"Kaagbhusandi Ji's words may seem unclear now, but we must trust in his wisdom. Mansarovar is a place of great power—perhaps the very journey there will reveal the answers we seek."

Manas, still grappling with the magnitude of the task ahead, took a deep breath and nodded.

"Then we should go to Mansarovar as soon as possible."

Lord Parashurama Ji looked out at the horizon, where the sky was just beginning to lighten with the first hints of dawn.

"Yes, we must leave immediately. The journey will be long and challenging, but it is the only way forward."

The trio gathered their belongings, their hearts and minds steeling themselves for the journey ahead. The road to Mansarovar would not be an easy one—it was a place of pilgrimage, located high in the Himalayas, near the sacred Mount Kailash, the abode of Lord Shiva. The lake, revered in Hinduism, Buddhism, Jainism, and Bon, was said to be the earthly manifestation of the divine consciousness. Pilgrims believed that a single dip in its waters could cleanse the soul and bring one closer to the divine. But for Manas, Ananya, and Lord Parashurama Ji, Mansarovar represented something more—a gateway to the ancient knowledge that would guide them to the Kavach Kundal.

As they began their journey, Lord Parashurama Ji spoke of the significance of Mansarovar. It is said that the very first rays of the sun kiss the surface of Mansarovar, and in those moments, the entire lake glows with a celestial light. Manas said, Yes, it is also a part of the puzzle, so I do have to take the water in the morning.

Ananya listened intently, her mind absorbing the weight of their mission.

"And what about the substance we need to mix with the water?" she asked, her curiosity piqued.

Lord Parashurama Ji paused, his gaze thoughtful.

"Kaagbhusandi Ji mentioned that it must contain ancient magic and be connected to one of Lord Vishnu's incarnations.

Ananya spoke earnestly,

"Guru Parashurama, as one of Lord Vishnu's incarnations, you might possess something that could aid us."

Parashurama Ji replied,

"I do not have anything magical, but I do have this axe."

Manas, eyeing the weapon with interest, said,

"Perhaps we can put it to use."

Parashurama Ji nodded,

"Let us hope it will prove effective."

As they ventured further into the mountains, the path became more treacherous, the air thinner, and the cold more biting. But the trio pressed on, driven by the knowledge that their journey to

Mansarovar was not just a physical one—it was a spiritual test, a trial of their resolve and purity of heart. With each step, they grew closer to the sacred lake, closer to the answers they sought, and closer to the destiny that awaited them. The journey to Mansarovar was only beginning, but they knew that once they reached its shores, they would face the first of many challenges that would determine their fate.

Parashurama Ji said,

"It will take us another three days to reach there."

Ananya replied,

"Let's expedite our journey."

Parashurama Ji nodded,

"Agreed. We must hasten our pace."

CHAPTER 15

The path was treacherous, winding through narrow mountain passes and along the edges of steep cliffs. The moonlight bathed the landscape in a ghostly glow, the silence of the mountains broken only by the distant howl of the wind and the crunch of their boots on the rocky terrain.

As they ascended higher into the mountains, the temperature dropped, and the air grew thinner. But the chill in the air was nothing compared to the cold resolve that gripped Ashwatthama's heart. Shukracharya, leading the way, moved with a steady, unhurried pace. His thoughts were focused, his mind calculating every possible outcome. He knew that Ashwatthama's rage was a potent force, one that could be harnessed to achieve their goals, but he also knew that it had to be carefully controlled. The timing of their actions was critical, and any misstep could unravel the delicate web he had spun.

Akshay followed closely behind, his eyes darting nervously between the shadows that seemed to close in around them. He trusted Shukracharya and Ashwatthama, but the enormity of what they were about to do weighed heavily on him. After what felt like an eternity of climbing, they finally reached the shores of Rakshastal.

Rakshastal, known as the *"Lake of the Demons,"* lay in stark contrast to its neighbor, the sacred Mansarovar. The water of Rakshastal was dark and foreboding, its surface reflecting the cold light of the moon in a way that made the entire lake seem like a portal to another world. The air around it was heavy, almost suffocating, as if the lake itself exuded a malevolent energy.

The lake's reputation in the ancient texts was one of darkness and mystery. Rakshastal was said to be the abode of demonic forces, a place where only the bravest or the most foolhardy would dare to tread. The water was considered cursed, devoid of life, and those who drank from it were said to be driven mad or consumed by their darkest desires. Shukracharya had chosen this place for a reason. The dark energy that permeated the area was exactly what they needed to fuel the ritual they were about to perform. The resurrection of Raghav required more than just power—it required a connection to the primal forces of the universe, forces that Rakshastal could provide.

"This is the place," Shukracharya said, his voice echoing across the desolate landscape.

"Here, at the shores of Rakshastal, we will begin the ritual. The lake's energy will help us tap into the ancient powers that are necessary to bring Raghav back."

Ashwatthama, his mind still filled with the visions of Kurukshetra, gazed at the lake with a mix of awe and revulsion. The water seemed to call to him, its surface rippling with the echoes of battles long past, battles that had shaped the very fabric of his existence. This was a place where the boundaries between life and death, between past and present, were thin—perfect for the dark work they were about to undertake.

Akshay, standing a little apart, shivered as he looked at the lake. He could feel the oppressive energy pressing down on him, the weight of countless dark deeds that had been performed in places like this. The night was thick with tension as Shukracharya, Ashwatthama, and Akshay stood at the edge of Rakshastal, the Lake of Demons. The lake's dark waters reflected the starless sky, a void so profound it seemed to swallow the very light of the moon. The air around them buzzed with an unsettling energy, as if the lake itself was alive, watching, waiting.

Shukracharya Ji turned to Ashwatthama and Akshay with a steely gaze.

"Bring me some water from the lake," Shukracharya commanded, his voice low and commanding. He turned to Akshay. "And Akshay, bring the items I asked for. Scatter them on the ground and form a circle."

Akshay followed the instructions, carefully arranging each item in a ritualistic pattern. He began by placing the *skull of a serpent* at the center of the circle, symbolizing the cycle of death and rebirth—the soul's eternal journey. Around it, he sprinkled *ashes from a cremation ground*, which filled the air with a sense of finality, marking the thin boundary between life and death.

Next, he spread *black sesame seeds* along the circle's perimeter, appeasing the restless spirits lingering in the shadows of the netherworld. At each cardinal point, Akshay placed a *bronze urn filled with sacred water from the Yamuna River*, its presence intended to purify the soul as it approached the threshold of the dark realm. Near the serpent's skull, Akshay carefully arranged *neem leaves soaked in cow's blood*, their pungent scent warding off malevolent spirits, ensuring the ritual remained undisturbed. A *pitch-black mirror* was positioned nearby, angled perfectly to capture the reflection of any departing spirit, binding it to the physical realm and preventing its escape. At the foot of the serpent's skull, he placed a *piece of Rudraksha*, consecrated with ancient mantras, ready to summon forth powers from beyond. Surrounding this were *five rare herbs*, meticulously prepared to be burnt and inhaled, granting the ritualist sight into the realm of the dead. Akshay took a moment before unfurling a *coal-black cloak*, laying it reverently on the ground outside the circle. This cloak would be worn by the ritualist, shielding them from the vengeful spirits about to emerge. Finally, he set down a large, intricately carved **trident** near the northernmost point of the circle, its three sharp prongs poised to channel the deities' power over life and death. As the circle took shape, a dark energy seemed to pulse within it, signaling the beginning of the forbidden ritual.

Meanwhile Ashwatthama moved toward the lake, each step feeling heavier as he approached its cursed waters. The dark energy radiating from Rakshastal was palpable, pressing down on him like a physical force. He knelt at the edge of the lake and carefully dipped a sacred vessel into the water. The surface rippled, and for a moment, it felt as though the lake itself resisted, as if aware of the ritual that was about to unfold. As Ashwatthama returned with the vessel of water, Akshay had already gathered the wood and arranged it into a large pyre, measuring six by six feet. The pyre stood tall, a foreboding structure that seemed to pulse with the energy of the ritual to come.

Shukracharya surveyed the preparations, his mind sharp and focused. He knew that the next steps were crucial, requiring precision and unwavering concentration. He turned to Ashwatthama,

"Ashwatthama, your task is of the utmost importance. You must protect me while I am in transition. I will be leaving this body and journeying to Preta Lok, the realm of the departed souls. There, I will search for Raghav and bring him back to this world. But in that time, my body will be vulnerable. Guard it with your life."

Ashwatthama nodded, his resolve firm. He positioned himself close to Shukracharya Ji, ready to defend him from any threat. He knew that the forces they were dealing with were beyond the ordinary, and he steeled himself for whatever might come.

Shukracharya began to chant, his voice low and resonant, filled with ancient power. The words of the mantra were incomprehensible to Akshay and Ashwatthama, but they could feel the energy building around them, a tangible force that made the hairs on the back of their necks stand on end.

The ritual began with an air of tension and purpose. Shukracharya stood before the towering pyre, his figure illuminated by the wild, flickering flames that seemed to dance to a rhythm only they could hear. The scent of burning herbs, mingled with sacred oils and the thick aroma of the earth, filled the air, setting the stage for a ceremony steeped in dark magic.

He reached down and took a handful of soil from a small earthen pot. This was no ordinary soil; it had been brought from the very fields of Kurukshetra, soaked with the blood of fallen warriors from the great Mahabharata. But the soil Shukracharya held now was different—this particular soil had absorbed the blood of Duryodhana, the great warrior prince, whose death had marked a turning point in the epic battle. This soil, tainted by both ambition and defeat, glowed faintly, as if holding onto the last vestiges of the immense power that had once coursed through the veins of the mighty.

With a steady hand, Shukracharya poured the ashes of Raghav onto the soil, watching as the two mixed together, forming a dark, potent amalgamation of life and death. The mixture was then carefully blended with a few drops of Manas' blood, each drop sizzling upon contact, like drops of water striking a hot iron, as if igniting something buried deep within the earth itself.

The air around them grew colder, and the ground beneath their feet trembled slightly. Shukracharya's chanting grew louder, resonating with a deeper, more primal force. Each word seemed to pull at the fabric of reality, bending it to his will. The pyre before them crackled and roared to life, flames leaping higher and higher as if summoned by the very power of the ritual. Then, with a final, forceful incantation, Shukracharya closed his eyes and projected his astral form from his body. To Ashwatthama and Akshay, it appeared as if a dark shadow had peeled away from Shukracharya, leaving his physical form seated in deep meditation. The astral Shukracharya hovered above, translucent and glowing with an otherworldly light.

From his elevated vantage point, Shukracharya gazed down upon his own body, motionless and serene, while Ashwatthama and Akshay stood vigilant beside him. But there was no time to linger; the ritual demanded haste. Shukracharya turned his ethereal gaze towards Preta Lok, the shadowy realm of the departed souls—a place he had journeyed through many times before, always searching, always learning. The journey between the realms was like passing through a veil of darkness, a seamless transition for one so practiced in the dark arts. Preta Lok opened up before him like a void, an eerie place of twilight and shadows where time had no meaning and reality was a shifting mirage. Souls wandered aimlessly here, their forms vague and transparent, like smoke caught in a perpetual state of being and unbeing.

Shukracharya floated through this desolate landscape, his eyes scanning the shifting shadows for any sign of Raghav. But in this vast expanse, where souls wandered without direction, it was not easy to pinpoint one specific soul. The terrain of Preta Lok was bleak—filled with twisted trees that seemed to groan and creak with every step, their branches like skeletal fingers scratching at the gray, fog-filled sky. In the distance, he could hear the faint cries of the lost and the echoes of lives long forgotten, carried on the cold, mournful winds.

He moved with purpose, but even for Shukracharya, navigating Preta Lok was challenging. He focused, trying to sense the faintest trace of the soul he sought. His own aura flared with a dark, pulsating light as he extended his consciousness outward, reaching for the thread that connected Raghav to the mortal realm. Minutes felt like hours as he moved through the dim corridors of the realm, his mind honing in on the one thing that would guide him—Ashwatthama's bloodline. The bond between Raghav and Ashwatthama acted like a beacon in the darkness, a bright thread that glimmered in the fog of Preta Lok. It was this link that Shukracharya focused on, drawing him closer to his quarry.

Finally, in the distance, a faint pulse of light appeared—a dim, flickering glow amidst the gloom. Shukracharya moved toward it, his form gliding over the barren ground. The light grew stronger, and as he drew nearer, he saw the lone figure of Raghav standing at the very edge of the realm, his back to the world of the living.

Raghav stood rigid, his shoulders squared, his eyes fixed on the unseen boundary between life and death. He seemed lost, but there was a lingering awareness in his posture, as if he could sense the call of his lineage pulling him back, like a rope tugging at a wayward ship caught in a storm.

Shukracharya approached Raghav, his astral hand reaching through the veil of shadows. His voice, echoing with authority, filled the air around them.

"Raghav," he called, the sound both a summons and a reassurance.

"Your time in this realm is over. It is time to return."

Raghav turned slowly, his movements sluggish at first, as though waking from a deep, dreamless sleep. His face was devoid of emotion, but there was a flicker of recognition in his eyes. He knew who Shukracharya was, and he understood the purpose of his summoning. Without a word, Raghav reached out and took Shukracharya's hand, a silent agreement to the journey back.

The moment their hands met, a surge of power crackled through the air like a thunderclap. The connection between their souls flared, illuminating the shadows around them, and the pull of the mortal realm intensified, drawing them both back through the veil that separated life from death. The journey back was swift, the tether between the worlds tightening like a rope being pulled from both ends.

Shukracharya's astral form re-entered his body with a violent jolt. His physical form shuddered and gasped for air as his spirit settled back into its mortal vessel. He opened his eyes, taking in a deep breath, the world of the living flooding back to him with a rush of sensations.

Akshay and Ashwatthama, who had been watching with bated breath, saw the subtle shift in Shukracharya's demeanor and knew that the ritual had succeeded. But before they could speak, the flames of the pyre abruptly extinguished themselves, plunging the entire area into a deep, unnatural darkness.

The ground beneath them trembled, and from within the smoldering remains of the fire, there was a stir. Ashwatthama tensed, his hand reaching for his weapon instinctively. He felt a surge of energy, a dark, electric hum in the air. From the ashes, a figure began to rise, first slowly, then with a sudden, powerful thrust, as if propelled by an unseen force.

Raghav emerged, his body covered in dirt and soot, his chest rising and falling with the force of his breath. But something was different. His form had changed—he was more muscular, his physique exuding an almost superhuman strength. His eyes blazed with a fierce intensity, a burning fire that seemed to radiate from deep within his soul. There was a raw, primal energy about him now, a power that crackled in the air like a gathering storm.

The transformation was dramatic. As he stood, his body seemed to hum with a low, resonant vibration, as if infused with the dark energy of Rakshastal itself. He clenched his fists, and a shockwave rippled through the ground beneath him, sending loose stones skittering across the dirt. Shukracharya's voice cut through the tension like a blade.

"Raghav, to complete your resurrection, you must take a dip in the waters of Rakshastal. Only then will the transformation be complete."

Without a moment's hesitation, Raghav turned and walked toward the lake. The dark waters lapped at the shore, whispering as if welcoming him back. He entered the lake, the cold water closing over his head, and as he submerged, the surface began to churn and swirl, reacting violently to his presence. The lake seemed to come alive, its waters darkening even further, tendrils of inky blackness wrapping around Raghav like the embrace of some ancient force. The water began to glow from within, a deep, eerie light spreading outward from Raghav's submerged form, illuminating the lake in an otherworldly radiance. The energy of Rakshastal poured into him, solidifying the transformation that had begun with the ritual.

After a few tense moments, Raghav emerged from the water, droplets clinging to his skin like dark pearls. His muscles rippled with newfound power, his every step exuding a confidence and strength that was almost tangible. He walked back to the shore, his eyes glowing with an intense, almost feral light. He approached Shukracharya and bent down to touch the guru's feet in a gesture of deep respect.

"Thank you, Guru Ji," Raghav said, his voice deeper and more resonant, filled with the strength of his rebirth.

Akshay, overwhelmed by emotion, rushed forward and embraced Raghav, tears streaming down his face.

"You're back, Raghav!" he exclaimed. "I can't believe it—you're really back!"

Raghav, his face filled with determination, patted Akshay on the back.

"Yes, *Dada Ji*, I am back. And now, we are stronger than ever."

Ashwatthama watched, his heart pounding with a mix of relief and exhilaration. Raghav's return was a victory, a sign that they were on the right path. With Raghav reborn, they were one step closer to achieving their ultimate goal. Shukracharya's eyes gleamed with satisfaction.

"This is only the beginning," he said, his voice unwavering.

"The next phase awaits. We have much to do and no time to waste."

Raghav nodded, his eyes aflame with intensity.

"What is our next move, Guru Ji?"

Shukracharya turned his gaze toward the distant mountains.

"We move to find the Kavach Kundal," he declared.

"And then, we will bring back the Saraswati River. Our time is now."

As they prepared to leave the shores of Rakshastal, the night around them seemed to pulse with energy, the air charged with the anticipation of the battles to come. The ritual had been completed, but the true journey was just beginning.

Ashwatthama, watching the scene unfold, felt a profound sense of relief. He looked at Raghav, now transformed and more powerful than ever. For the first time in a long while, he felt hope—a dark, fierce hope that their mission might actually succeed. Shukracharya, his eyes glinting with satisfaction, watched as the trio reunited. He knew that with Raghav's return, their chances of retrieving the Kavach Kundal had significantly increased. But he also knew that the true challenges lay ahead.

"Rest now," Shukracharya commanded, his voice brooking no argument.

"We have much to do, and the next steps will require all of our strength. The future awaits, and with it, the power to reshape the world."

The night was still, the only sound was the faint ripple of water lapping against the shore of Rakshastal. The air was thick with the aftermath of the dark ritual, and the energy around them pulsed with an unspoken anticipation. Ashwatthama, standing tall beside the newly reborn Raghav, turned to Shukracharya, his eyes filled with a determined fire.

"Guru Ji," Ashwatthama began, his voice firm, "now that Raghav has returned, it is time to search for Karna's Kavach Kundal. But we don't know where to start. The Kavach is hidden, and without a clue, we could be wandering aimlessly."

Raghav, his voice now deeper and more resonant after his rebirth, interjected with a calm certainty,

"I know where to start."

Akshay, standing nearby, looked at Raghav with a mixture of surprise and curiosity.

"How do you know?" he asked, the question hanging in the cold night air.

Raghav turned to face him, his eyes glowing with the same dark energy that had brought him back to life.

"Because, *Dada Ji*, I was with Manas the whole time. In my astral form, I could see and hear everything they were up to. My soul wandered, tethered to the mortal realm. I followed them, watched them, listened to their plans."

Ashwatthama and Shukracharya exchanged glances, the weight of Raghav's revelation sinking in.

"And what did you hear?" Shukracharya asked, his voice steady, but with an undercurrent of urgency.

Raghav's expression darkened as he recalled what he had witnessed.

"They met with Kaagbhusandi Ji. He gave them a clue, a piece of the puzzle that leads to the Kavach Kundal. According to Kaagbhusandi Ji, the journey to find the Kavach begins at Mansarovar Lake.

"यो उत्तराणि इच्छति, तस्य सरःजलं पातव्यम्,

किन्तु तद् जलं प्राचीनमन्त्रयुक्तेन द्रव्येण संयोजयितव्यम्, यत् विष्णोः अवताराणां एकेन संबद्धम् अस्ति।

एतत् सर्वं सुरप्रभायुक्ते सरःसम्पूर्ण केवलम् यथा कर्तव्यं।"

He repeated the exact words which Kaagbhusandi Ji shared.

"The one who seeks answers must drink from the lake, but the water must be combined with a substance infused with ancient magic, something tied to one of Lord Vishnu's incarnations. This ritual must be performed when the entire lake is bathed in celestial light. Only then will the first clue be revealed—the first step on the path to discovering the Kavach Kundal."

Shukracharya's eyes gleamed with understanding.

"So, Manas and his companions are heading to Mansarovar Lake," he said, his mind already working to anticipate their next moves.

"That means we are not far behind. They may have a head start, but we know their destination."

Ashwatthama nodded, his resolve hardening.

"If they are going to Mansarovar, then we must make haste. We cannot afford to let them gain the upper hand. We will follow them to Mansarovar, but we will not reveal ourselves until the time is right. Manas may hold the key to the first clue, but we will catch up soon".

Akshay stepped forward, his expression thoughtful.

"I have another idea that could give us a significant advantage," he said, his voice measured and deliberate.

Shukracharya Ji nodded slightly, encouraging Akshay to continue.

"We're close to Mansarovar Lake," Akshay explained, gesturing in the direction of the sacred waters.

"It's only about 500 meters from here. What if we discreetly place microphones around the lake, spacing them every 50 meters? These devices would be nearly invisible, hidden within the natural surroundings."

He paused, allowing the idea to take root.

"With this setup, we could eavesdrop on any conversations that occur near the lake—conversations that might reveal their plans or intentions. The best part is, they would have no idea we're listening. We'd gain valuable insight without them suspecting a thing."

Akshay's eyes gleamed with a mixture of cunning and determination.

"This way, we can stay one step ahead. It will allow us to advance our plans while they remain blissfully unaware of our progress."

Shukracharya Ji considered the plan, recognizing the potential it held. The lake, a place of tranquility and reflection, would become an unwitting accomplice in their strategy.

"Proceed," Shukracharya Ji finally said, his voice calm but firm.

"But ensure that no trace of our presence is left behind. This plan hinges on absolute secrecy."

Akshay bowed his head in acknowledgment, already visualizing the execution of the plan. The microphones would be hidden with care, blending seamlessly into the environment, and soon, the lake would become a source of invaluable information. The advantage would be theirs, and their progress unstoppable.

Shukracharya, satisfied that their plan was taking shape, turned his gaze toward the distant mountains, where Mansarovar Lake lay hidden.

"To Mansarovar, then," he said, his voice filled with dark resolve.

And so, with their path set and their goal clear, Shukracharya, Ashwatthama, Raghav, and Akshay began their journey to Mansarovar. As they traveled through the night, the darkness around them seemed to grow thicker, as if the very shadows were conspiring to aid them in their quest. The energy of Rakshastal still lingered in the air, a reminder of the power they had harnessed, and the power they sought to gain. But even as they journeyed toward Mansarovar, Shukracharya's mind was already turning to the future. For now, they would wait, biding their time until the moment was right.

CHAPTER 16

The sky above was a deep, velvety indigo, dotted with the last remnants of stars that clung to the night. The first light of dawn was beginning to creep over the eastern peaks, casting a pale glow over the snow-capped mountains that cradled the lake in their embrace. The air was crisp, almost biting, carrying with it the scent of ancient pine and the echo of countless prayers whispered over the centuries. Ananya, her breath visible in the cold morning air, looked towards the horizon with a hint of anxiety.

"Guru Ji, we missed the morning," she said, her voice tinged with concern.

Parashurama Ji, smiled gently.

"No worries, my child. The sun will rise again tomorrow, and we will perform the ritual as it should be done."

Parashurama took a dip in the sacred waters of Mansarovar Lake, and as he emerged, the wound inflicted by Shukracharya's knife began to heal, the lake's divine energy knitting the flesh back together. As the night gave way to day, the three of them prepared for the task ahead, their hearts filled with a mix of anticipation and reverence. As dawn finally broke, the world around them seemed to come alive. The first rays of the sun pierced the sky, their golden light spilling over the mountains like molten fire. The beams touched the surface of Mansarovar Lake, and in an instant, the water transformed. What had been a mirror-like expanse of darkness now shimmered with a radiant, almost otherworldly glow. The lake appeared as if it were made of liquid gold, each ripple catching the light and sending it dancing across the surface in a dazzling display of brilliance.

Manas stood at the edge of the sacred Mansarovar Lake, his reflection shimmering on the water's surface, distorted by the gentle ripples that danced in the morning light. The beauty of the lake was overwhelming; the water sparkled like a thousand diamonds, reflecting the snow-capped peaks of the Himalayas that surrounded them like silent guardians. The air was crisp, filled with the scent of pine and earth, and carried with it an almost palpable energy that seemed to hum with life and ancient wisdom.

Yet, despite the serene majesty of the scene, Manas's heart was restless. He knew they had a task to perform, a purpose greater than the breathtaking view before him. He reached down with great care and plucked a broad, green leaf from a nearby tree. His fingers were steady but firm as he shaped the leaf into a makeshift cup, feeling its cool, waxy surface against his skin. He scooped up some of the sacred water, the liquid cold and clear, still shimmering with the golden light of the rising sun. He lifted the leaf with reverence, his heart pounding with anticipation.

With a measured breath, Manas slowly poured the water over the blade of Parashurama Ji's legendary axe, watching as it trickled down the polished steel, each droplet catching the sunlight like a prism, reflecting a myriad of colors as they fell. He waited for a sign, any sign, but the lake remained still, the world around him unchanged.

Undeterred, Manas brought the leaf to his lips and drank deeply, the cold water sliding down his throat with a refreshing chill that sent a shiver through his body. But as he swallowed, he felt... nothing. The world continued to shimmer with its ordinary beauty, but there was no vision, no revelation. Confused, Manas frowned.

He repeated the ritual, his movements growing more urgent, almost frantic. Again, he poured the water over the axe, drank, and waited. And again, nothing happened. The sacred lake seemed to withhold its secrets, as if testing his resolve.

"There must be something we're missing," Manas said, his voice tinged with frustration and a hint of desperation.

"Kaagbhusandi Ji wouldn't have sent us here if this wasn't the right place."

Parashurama Ji, his face etched with deep lines of thought, shook his head slowly.

"It cannot be that we've misunderstood. The instructions were clear, but something is not right."

Manas repeated the ritual several more times, each attempt more desperate than the last. His hands trembled slightly with anxiety as he scooped the water again and again, his breaths coming in short, sharp gasps. But still, the result was the same—no visions, no clues, just the cold, clear water of Mansarovar. The sacred lake, its waters calm and unyielding, seemed to mock him, as if it were alive and conscious of his struggle. Manas felt the weight of failure settling on his shoulders, a cold grip of helplessness tightening around his heart.

"What are we missing?" Manas muttered, the words barely escaping his lips as he stared into the shimmering waters, searching for an answer in their depths.

Ananya, who had been standing silently by, her eyes fixed on the ritual, suddenly spoke up, her voice breaking through the tense silence like a clarion call.

"Guru Ji," she said, pointing toward the axe, "the axe belongs to you, but it was given to you by Lord Shiva."

Parashurama Ji's eyes widened slightly as the realization struck him like a bolt of lightning.

"Of course, Ananya," he said, a note of excitement creeping into his voice, "you're absolutely right. The substance that needs to be mixed with the water must be tied to Lord Vishnu, not Lord Shiva."

A flicker of hope sparked in Manas' chest.

"But Guru Ji, do we have anything connected to Lord Vishnu?" he asked, his voice tinged with both hope and doubt.

Parashurama Ji glanced down at his axe and then at his simple clothes, his mind racing through the possibilities.

"I carry only this axe and my garments," he replied, his brow furrowed with concentration. "I possess nothing that is directly tied to Lord Vishnu."

For a moment, it seemed as though they had reached a dead end. A sense of quiet despair began to settle over them like a heavy fog. But then, as the sun climbed higher into the sky, its rays seemed to focus directly on Manas, as if drawing attention to him alone. Something caught Ananya's eye—a glint of gold flashing on Manas' chest, sparkling brightly in the morning light.

"Manas, look!" Ananya exclaimed, pointing to the pendant that hung around his neck.

"The pendant I gave you—the one that belonged to my father, Guru Vyas Ji. Vyas Ji is considered a form of Lord Vishnu himself. Try using the pendant."

Manas' hand instinctively reached for the pendant, feeling its familiar weight against his skin. He realized the significance of what Ananya was saying. The pendant had been with him since the day Ananya had given it to him, a symbol of her trust, her lineage, and the ancient wisdom of her father. With renewed determination, Manas took the pendant in his hand, feeling its cold metal against his palm. He dipped it into the water held in the leaf, letting the sacred liquid bathe the pendant before bringing the leaf to his lips.

As he drank, the water trickled down his throat, much like before—cold, clear, and refreshing.

But this time, there was a shift. At first, it was subtle, almost imperceptible. The air around him seemed to grow heavier, thicker, as if filled with unseen particles. The colors of the world began to blur, the lake and mountains losing their sharpness, their vibrancy fading like paint washing away in the rain. The sun above dimmed, and the light around him seemed to drain away, plunging everything into a deep, impenetrable darkness. Manas felt a strange sensation—like falling, yet floating at the same time. The ground beneath him seemed to dissolve, and he was suspended in an endless void. His heart pounded in his chest, each beat echoing in his ears like a drum. He felt weightless, his senses overwhelmed by the sheer emptiness that surrounded him. The silence was absolute, oppressive, pressing in on him from all sides. Panic threatened to seize him, but he forced himself to remain calm.

Then, cutting through the darkness like a blade of light, came a voice. It was deep, resonant, and carried with it a power that seemed to shake the very fabric of reality. The voice seemed to come from everywhere and nowhere all at once, filling the vast void with its presence.

"अस्ति एकं स्थानं यत्र प्रत्येकद्वादशवर्षे

देवराजः इन्द्रः महादेवेन सह मिलति।

तस्मिन दिव्यसंयोगे स्वयम् महादेवः

प्रसिद्धानां कुण्डलानां किञ्चिद् प्रकटयिष्यति।"

"There is a place where every twelve years, the king of the heavens, Lord Indra, meets with the great Lord Shiva. In this sacred convergence, Lord Shiva himself will unveil one of the fabled Kundal."

The voice echoed through the darkness, repeating the words over and over until they imprinted themselves on Manas' very soul. The vision began to dissolve, and the next thing he knew, he was back at the shores of Mansarovar, gasping for breath as if he had been holding it for hours.

Ananya rushed to his side, her face pale with worry.

"Manas, are you alright? You were unconscious for a while. We thought we lost you."

Manas, still catching his breath, nodded slowly.

"I'm... I'm fine. I heard a voice. It gave me a clue to finding the first Kundal."

Parashurama Ji, his expression intense, leaned in closer. "What did the voice say, Manas?"

Manas repeated the words that had been seared into his mind. The words hung in the air like a prophecy, filled with mystery and significance. Parashurama Ji's eyes narrowed in thought, his mind racing to decipher the riddle. Ananya looked equally intrigued.

But little did they know, their every word had not gone unheard. High above, hidden in the rocky cliffs that surrounded Mansarovar, several high-range listening devices had been carefully placed the night before by Akshay. These devices, small but powerful, transmitted the conversation in real-time to a distant location where Shukracharya, Ashwatthama, and Raghav listened intently. Shukracharya's eyes gleamed with satisfaction as the words of the riddle reached his ears.

"So, Mansarovar has indeed revealed the first clue," he murmured, his voice filled with dark anticipation.

Ashwatthama clenched his fists, his impatience barely contained.

"It means we're not far behind them. They've discovered the first step, but it's us who will claim the prize."

Raghav, his reborn body brimming with newfound power, nodded in agreement.

"We'll wait for the right moment. Manas may have the clue, but it will be us who act on it."

Shukracharya's lips curled into a cold, calculating smile that sent a shiver down Akshay's spine.

"Let them lead," he said quietly. "We'll follow in the shadows, and when the moment is right, we'll strike. It's time to unravel those clues. Ashwatthama, as the greatest devotee of Lord Shiva, do you have any insight into what they might be?"

Ashwatthama kept repeating those words over and over, his mind turning them like a mantra.

CHAPTER 17

Five Thousand Years Ago...

The celestial realms were in turmoil. After Lord Indra had successfully deceived Karna and taken his precious Kavach and Kundal—the divine armor and earrings that had made Karna invincible—the king of the heavens found himself in a dilemma. Clutching the radiant, golden armor and earrings, Indra ascended to Swarg Lok, his face triumphant, yet there was a deep worry in his heart.

However, as Indra reached the gates of Swarg Lok, he was met with an unexpected obstacle. The gates, normally open to him without question, remained firmly shut. A divine barrier shimmered before him, radiating a blinding light. The Devas who guarded the entrance looked at him with furrowed brows, concern etched on their divine faces.

"Lord Indra," one of the guardians called out, his voice resonating with authority, "you cannot enter with these objects."

Indra, bewildered, raised his voice.

"Why am I denied entry? I am the king of the heavens!"

The guardian's face softened with understanding but remained firm.

"*The Kavach and Kundal were taken through deceit, Lord Indra. They are stained by this act, and no object touched by dishonor can enter Swarg Lok.*"

Indra's heart sank. He had thought himself victorious in his quest to weaken Karna, but he had not considered the divine laws that governed the heavens. Realizing his predicament, he turned away from the gates, his mind racing. He descended back to Earth, the sacred objects still clutched in his hands.

As he flew through the mortal skies, his thoughts churned. Where could he hide these objects? The Kavach and Kundal, even in his possession, were dangerous—they radiated immense power and heat. Indra knew that left unchecked, the energy from these divine objects could wreak havoc on both the Earth and the celestial realms. After moments of contemplation, Indra decided to seek the guidance of Lord Shiva. Indra ascended to Mount Kailash, the eternal abode of Lord Shiva. As he arrived, he saw Shiva, seated in deep meditation, his third eye closed, a serene expression on his face. Indra, bowing deeply, spoke with humility,

"*O Mahadev, I have come seeking your counsel and your aid.*"

Shiva opened his eyes slowly, his gaze calm yet piercing.

"*What brings you here, Indra?*" *he asked, his voice like the rumble of distant thunder.*

Indra hesitated, then explained the situation—how he had taken the Kavach and Kundal from Karna through deceit and how he was now unable to bring them into Swarg Lok.

Shiva listened quietly, his expression inscrutable. When Indra finished, Shiva's brow furrowed, and his voice grew stern.

"*Indra, your actions have been tainted by dishonesty. The deceit you have wrought was not fitting for a king of the heavens. The*

Kavach and Kundal are divine objects, forged with righteousness and the blessings of the Sun God. They are not yours to take."

Indra's heart sank further, but he dared not argue with the Lord of Destruction.

"I understand, O Mahadev. Yet, I cannot leave these objects untended. Their power is too great, too volatile. I ask for your guidance—help me conceal them, so they do not fall into the wrong hands."

Shiva's gaze softened slightly, understanding the gravity of the situation.

"Very well," he said slowly, "I shall help you. But remember, this is not because of your deceit, but because it was ordained by Lord Krishna's leela."

Indra bowed again, deeply.

"Thank you, Mahadev. I will follow your guidance." Shiva continued, "The Kavach and Kundal must not remain together. Their combined power is too great. We must separate them—break them apart, scatter them across the Earth in such a way that only those who are truly worthy can ever hope to reunite them."

Indra nodded, listening intently.

Shiva spoke again, "One of the Kundal will remain with us. I shall hide it within my lingam. Every twelve years, you will come to meet me, and I will reveal the Kundal to you, allowing you to absorb its radiation and thus diminish its power. In this way, it will remain concealed and safe, its heat contained within my lingam."

Indra's eyes widened with realization. "And the other pieces?"

Lord Shiva's face turned serious, his eyes narrowing.

"The other Kundal shall be hidden in a different direction, far from here, where only the pure of heart and those with a destiny tied to the divine shall be able to find it. The armor itself, the Kavach,

must be hidden in the south, where the energies of the Earth are most potent, where its strength will be absorbed by the land itself. "For that, you must seek the aid of Lord Hanuman." Indra nodded, but there was still a question lingering in his mind. Indra bowed deeply once more.

"I shall do as you say, Mahadev."

Shiva extended his hand over the Kundal, his fingers glowing with divine light. He murmured a few ancient mantras, and one of the Kundals vanished, reappearing within the lingam—a sacred, indestructible space where it would remain hidden.

Indra nodded, understanding the gravity of the task ahead. With that, Lord Shiva turned and disappeared in a swirl of ash and smoke, his divine form merging with the sacred energy of Kailash.

After safely entrusting the first Kundal to Lord Shiva, Lord Indra turned his thoughts to the task of hiding the second one. The responsibility weighed heavily on him, as he knew that the second Kundal had to be hidden in a place where it would remain safe and undiscovered, only to reveal itself to the worthy. Unsure of where to hide it, Lord Indra sought the wisdom of his revered Guru, Brihaspati.

Summoning him, Indra explained,

"Guruji, I have given the first Kundal to Lord Shiva for safekeeping. Now, I must find a suitable place to hide the second Kundal, but the task seems daunting."

Guru Brihaspati, the wise preceptor of the gods, listened intently and then spoke with a calm, reassuring tone.

"Indra, do you know that on Earth, during the great Samudra Manthan, a few drops of Amrit fell into certain rivers? These rivers have since become sacred, and during specific times, when the celestial alignments are perfect, the waters of these rivers attain their purest form. Devotees from all over the world come to bathe in these waters, seeking purification of body, mind, and soul."

Indra's eyes lit up with understanding, and Brihaspati continued,

"I will hide the second Kundal in the depths of these sacred rivers. It will remain concealed, shielded by the purity of the Amrit-infused waters. But remember, it will only reveal itself to those whose hearts are as pure as the waters that conceal it—those who are truly worthy."

With this plan, Guru Brihaspati set out to carry out the divine task, knowing that the second Kundal would be hidden in a place that only the most virtuous could uncover.

After securing the second Kundal, Lord Indra knew his task was far from complete. The most crucial part of the sacred armor, the Kavach itself, still needed to be hidden. He recalled Lord Shiva's instructions to conceal the Kavach in the South, so he set off in that direction, determined to fulfill this divine mission.

For weeks, Lord Indra wandered through the southern lands, searching for the perfect place to hide the Kavach. Despite his efforts, no location seemed fitting for such a powerful and sacred artifact. His heart grew heavy with the weight of responsibility.

One day, as Indra roamed through a dense forest, he was suddenly greeted by a familiar presence. The mighty Lord Hanuman appeared before him, radiating strength and wisdom.

"Pranam, Indra Dev," Hanuman Ji said, bowing respectfully.

"Bless you, my child," Indra Dev replied, his voice weary from his long search.

Noticing Indra's troubled expression, Hanuman Ji asked with concern, "Indra Dev, you look worried. Is there anything I can do to relieve your stress?"

Indra Dev paused, his mind racing.

Who better to protect the Kavach than the valiant Lord Hanuman himself? With this thought, Indra began to explain everything—the importance of the Kavach, the need to hide it, and his own struggles to find a suitable place. After hearing Indra's words, Hanuman Ji respectfully declined the request.

"With all due respect, Indra Dev, I cannot take this Kavach with me."

Indra Dev was taken aback.

"Why can't you keep it with you, Hanuman? Surely, there is no one more capable of safeguarding it."

Hanuman Ji gently explained,

"This Kavach belongs to Karna, and it was given to him by my own Guru Dev, Lord Surya. It would not be right for me to take possession of it."

Understanding dawned on Indra, and he nodded even before Hanuman finished speaking. He understood the situation, and he respected Hanuman's loyalty to his Guru. But then, Hanuman Ji continued,

"However, I also understand the significance of this Kavach and the importance of its protection. I may not keep it myself, but I will entrust it to someone I trust completely. Rest assured, it will be safe."

Relieved, Lord Indra thanked Hanuman for his wisdom and assistance. With their parting words, they bid each other farewell, both knowing that the Kavach would be kept safe under the watchful eyes of someone worthy.

As Indra left the forest, he felt a sense of peace, knowing that the Kavach was in good hands. Hanuman Ji, in turn, prepared to fulfill his promise, ensuring that the sacred armor would remain protected until the time was right for it to be revealed again.

CHAPTER 18

Ashwatthama paced back and forth, his impatience evident in every heavy step. The crisp air of the mountains seemed to grow colder around him as his thoughts churned with frustration. "Guru Ji," he said, turning sharply to Shukracharya, "don't you have another one of those knives—the mystical blade you used against Parashurama Ji? We could attack them now while they're still trying to decipher the clues. With Raghav on our side, we're stronger than ever."

Shukracharya, seated cross-legged on a large rock, remained calm. His eyes were half-closed, as if in deep contemplation. He looked up slowly, his gaze piercing through Ashwatthama's agitation.

"No, Ashwatthama," he replied, his voice steady and measured. "Attacking Parashurama now is not wise. I struck before because he was unaware, caught off guard by the element of surprise. But now he knows our intentions. He will be vigilant, prepared for any assault. Besides, he is in full strength now."

Shukracharya's eyes flicked over to Raghav, who stood silently nearby, his form exuding a quiet, formidable power.

"And Raghav…he is our secret weapon. Revealing him now, in his new form, would be a mistake. His strength has been reborn with the might of Duryodhana himself. But his time is yet to come."

Ashwatthama nodded slowly, though his frustration still simmered beneath the surface.

"As you wish, Guru Ji," he muttered.

Akshay, leaning against a tree, interjected.

"But Guru Ji," he asked, his brows furrowed with thought, "what does the clue mean? Where is this place where Lord Indra and Lord Shiva meet every twelve years?"

Shukracharya's lips curved into a faint smile, the kind of smile that held secrets.

"Patience, Akshay," he said. "I know the place. It is where one of my disciples, Kulanta, perished. A place where the divine energies of Lord Indra and Lord Shiva converge every twelve years. That is where the first Kundal is hidden."

Akshay's eyes widened.

"Then we should move quickly. If we already know the location, why waste time? The longer we wait, the closer they get." Shukracharya nodded.

"Yes, we will move soon." Prepare to proceed; gather your things.

Near the Sacred Shores of Mansarovar Lake

Manas, Ananya, and Parashurama Ji sat cross-legged in a triangle formation by the pristine waters of Mansarovar. The air around them was thick with tension, mingled with the earthy scent of the lake. The sun hung low in the sky, casting long shadows that danced on the rippling surface of the water. A serene silence enveloped them, the kind that often precedes a storm. Parashurama Ji had his eyes closed, his face serene and composed, as if he were listening to the whispers of the wind.

"Since Lord Shiva is part of this first clue," he had said earlier, "we must meditate and hope for a sign. The answer will come to us."

Ananya and Manas, following their guru's lead, focused their minds, their breaths slow and steady, their thoughts attuned to the subtle energies around them. Minutes stretched into hours, and the silence grew deeper, almost tangible. The only sound was the gentle lapping of the lake's waters against the rocky shore.

Suddenly, the air grew heavy. The temperature dropped rapidly, and the still waters of the lake began to ripple as if touched by an unseen hand. A low rumble echoed through the valley, and a gust of wind swept through the area, carrying with it the faint scent of sandalwood and ash. Ananya's eyes flickered open, her heart pounding in her chest.

"Guru Ji… what is happening?" she whispered, a note of fear creeping into her voice.

Before Parashurama Ji could answer, a bolt of lightning tore through the sky with a deafening roar, striking the ground mere inches from where Parashurama Ji sat. The light was blinding, and for a moment, everything was bathed in a brilliant white glow. Manas felt his heart leap into his throat, but Parashurama Ji did not move an inch. The lightning danced around him like a serpent of light, yet did not harm him. And just as quickly as it had appeared, the lightning vanished, and the world returned to its natural state. The wind died down, and the lake was still once more. Ananya's eyes were wide, her breath shallow.

"What… what was that?" she gasped.

Parashurama Ji slowly opened his eyes, a knowing smile playing on his lips. He looked up at the sky, then nodded as if acknowledging an invisible presence.

"Thank you for your guidance, Mahadev," he murmured softly.

He turned to Ananya and Manas, his smile growing wider. "We have our answer," he said, his voice filled with renewed energy. Manas, still trying to process what had just happened, asked,

"Was that… Lord Shiva's way of communicating with you?"

Parashurama Ji chuckled, his eyes twinkling with a mix of amusement and wisdom.

"Indeed, my boy. The gods always give us signs. We just need to be able to read them."

Ananya, still recovering from the shock, asked,

"Where are we going, Guru Ji?"

Parashurama Ji stood up, brushing the dust from his robes.

"To Kullu," he declared.

Meanwhile, on the other side.

The shadows lengthened as the group of Shukracharya, Ashwatthama, Akshay, and Raghav prepared for their journey. The air around them was thick with anticipation, every breath a reminder of the high stakes they faced. Shukracharya watched the horizon, his mind moving like a chess master plotting his next move.

"We must be swift," he muttered. "We cannot let them get there first." Raghav, his muscles still taut with the newfound strength of his rebirth, nodded.

"We're ready when you are, Guru Ji."

Shukracharya turned to Ashwatthama, his expression inscrutable.

"Remember, this is not just about strength," he warned.

"It is about wisdom and patience. We must play the long game, and the time will come when we will make our move."

Ashwatthama, despite his burning desire for action, bowed his head in understanding.

"As you say, Guru Ji."

Akshay, still intrigued by the clue, asked,

"Are you certain it is Kullu, where your disciple Kulanta fell?" Shukracharya smiled, a shadow of a grin crossing his lips.

"Yes, I am certain. That is where we will begin."

Back at Mansarovar.

As they gathered their belongings, Parashurama Ji noticed a look of concern on Manas' face.

"What troubles you, Manas?" he asked gently.

Manas hesitated, then spoke.

"Guru Ji, why Kullu? Why is that the meeting place of Lord Indra and Lord Shiva?"

CHAPTER 19

The morning sun cast a golden hue over the snow-capped peaks surrounding Mansarovar, as Manas, Ananya, and Parashurama Ji prepared for their journey. The air was filled with a new urgency, the faint echoes of the divine lightning still resonating in their minds. As they packed their belongings, Parashurama Ji began to speak, his voice steady and calm, but carrying a hint of excitement.

"Our ancestors had a very unique way of explaining things," he said, glancing at his disciples.

"They used symbols, metaphors, and stories to convey deep truths that could stand the test of time." Manas and Ananya listened intently as Parashurama Ji continued, his eyes looking back in time as he recounted the tale.

"The history of Kullu," Parashurama Ji began, "is mentioned in the ancient Puranas. It was the Pandavas themselves who constructed a temple during their time of exile. However, the legend behind its establishment is much older and deeply fascinating."

Ananya's eyes widened with curiosity.

"Tell us, Guru Ji," she urged.

Parashurama Ji nodded, pleased with her eagerness.

"Long ago, there was a demon named Kulanta, whose heart was filled with malice. This demon sought to submerge the entire valley of Kullu by stopping the flow of the Beas River. In his arrogance, he took the form of a mighty serpent of monstrous size, intending to drown all life in a deluge of water. His plan was to coil his massive body around the river, forcing it to overflow and flood everything in its path, destroying all life forms."

Manas leaned in closer, captivated by the story.

"But Lord Shiva," Parashurama Ji continued, "came to the rescue of the people. He knew that this demon needed to be stopped, for the fate of the entire valley hung in the balance. So, in his wisdom, Lord Shiva devised a plan. He approached Kulanta and, in a calm voice, told him to look back because his tail had caught fire."

Manas chuckled, "A trick… simple, but effective."

Parashurama Ji smiled, "Indeed, a simple trick, but effective against a creature blinded by arrogance. When Kulanta turned to look, Shiva struck him with his mighty Trishul, shattering his body into countless pieces. The mountain of Bijli Mahadev, where the temple now stands, was formed from the body of this dead demon."

Ananya was wide-eyed. "So, Bijli Mahadev is the temple we are going to."

Parashurama Ji nodded, "Yes, and that was not the end. Every twelve years, to ensure that the power of the demon's curse did not return, a great celestial lightning bolt, with the permission of Lord Indra, strikes the Shiva Lingam at Bijli Mahadev Temple. The lightning symbolizes the divine energy that Shiva uses to maintain balance in the universe and protect the people of the valley."

Manas's eyes widened in understanding.

"So, the Shiva Lingam placed inside the temple gets struck by lightning every twelve years. The temple priest collects the shattered pieces and reassembles them using a paste of cereal, pulse flour, and unsalted butter. Over months, the Shiva Lingam becomes whole again, just like before."

"Yes," Parashurama Ji replied, "and this is how Lord Shiva, in his own way, continues to protect the valley."

Ananya's face lit up with realization. "So, the lightning phenomenon is the meeting of Lord Indra and Lord Shiva every twelve years?"

Parashurama Ji nodded. "Precisely, Ananya. This is the convergence mentioned in the clue."

Manas exhaled, his eyes bright with newfound understanding. "And I think… when the Lingam breaks, there must be a piece of the Kundal hidden inside it. That's the second part of the clue: '*In this sacred convergence, Lord Shiva himself will unveil one of the fabled Kundals.*'"

Parashurama Ji smiled, impressed.

"Well deduced, Manas. The ancestors have indeed left us a brilliant puzzle to solve."

Manas could hardly contain his excitement. "So, our destination is clear, Guru Ji! We need to reach Bijli Mahadev Temple."

"Yes," Parashurama Ji agreed. "To get there, we must first travel from Kullu to Ramshila, which is just about a kilometer away. From there, we cross the bridge over the Beas River toward Bhuntar. After crossing, we ask a local person for directions towards the temple hill."

Manas nodded. "We need to hurry, Guru Ji. Time is of the essence."

Parashurama Ji chuckled. "Indeed, it will take us a week to reach there if we move swiftly. Gather your strength; the journey will be long and arduous, but I have faith in both of you."

Meanwhile, in the Shadows of the Himalayas…

Shukracharya stood atop a ridge, his robes flapping in the cold wind, his eyes fixed on the distant horizon. Ashwatthama stood beside him, his hand on the hilt of his sword, his gaze burning with determination.

"Guru Ji," he said, "why wait? Let us go to this temple at once. We have strength on our side. Why not confront them directly?"

Shukracharya turned slowly, his expression unreadable. "Ashwatthama, do not let your eagerness cloud your judgment. We must tread carefully. The timing is crucial."

"But Guru Ji," Akshay interjected, "what does the clue mean exactly? Where do Indra and Shiva meet every twelve years?"

Shukracharya's smile widened. "It is clear now. The place we seek is where my disciple Kulanta met his end, the place is now called Bijli Mahadev Temple. It is there that the energies of Indra and Shiva converge every twelve years."

Raghav, his new form exuding strength, nodded. "Then we should go there at once."

Shukracharya's eyes gleamed with anticipation. "Indeed, but remember, we will not strike until the time is right. Let them do the hard work of revealing the Kundal. We will be there to take it."

Back on the way to Kullu…

Manas, Ananya, and Parashurama Ji made their way swiftly down the rugged paths toward Kullu, the sacred peaks of the Himalayas towering above them. The cold air bit at their faces, and the road ahead was long and winding, but their spirits were high. As they crossed the Beas River, the water beneath them roared like a wild beast, foaming white against the rocks. They could feel the energy of the river, its power flowing beneath them like the pulse of the Earth itself.

Parashurama Ji led the way, his stride purposeful. "We must keep a steady pace," he urged. "We have much ground to cover."

Manas and Ananya followed, their eyes filled with determination. They knew that every step brought them closer to uncovering the secrets of the Kundal, to a place where history, myth, and destiny converged.

The air around Bijli Mahadev was still buzzing with the energy of the lightning strike. A faint mist had settled over the mountain, and the temple seemed to pulse with a life of its own. Shukracharya's eyes gleamed with satisfaction as he turned to Ashwatthama.

"Ashwatthama," he commanded, "Begin the preparations for the Yagna. We must perform the ritual immediately to harness the divine energy left by the lightning. Only then the lightning will strike."

Ashwatthama nodded, his expression focused and resolute. He moved swiftly, gathering the materials needed for the Yagna. He collected dried wood and arranged it meticulously in the center of the temple grounds, forming a large pyre. The wood crackled under his touch, the scent of pine and cedar filling the air. Next, he spread a layer of sacred ghee over the logs, the golden liquid gleaming in the dim light. The temple's sanctum seemed to grow darker as the preparations continued, as if the shadows themselves were gathering to witness what was about to unfold.

Raghav joined in, sprinkling a mixture of herbs and sacred powders around the pyre, creating a boundary infused with ancient symbols and protective energies. Each handful of powder released a thin plume of smoke, curling up toward the heavens like the whispers of forgotten gods. The air grew thick with the heady scent of camphor and sandalwood.

Shukracharya, standing at the edge of the circle, began chanting ancient mantras, his voice deep and resonant. The words seemed to vibrate through the very stones of the temple, a low hum that resonated in the chest of everyone present. His hands moved in precise, deliberate gestures, invoking the blessings of the elements and the divine energies that governed them.

Ashwatthama carefully placed several silver bowls filled with sacred water at the corners of the Yagna site, their surfaces rippling with every syllable of Shukracharya's incantations. He took a deep breath, closing his eyes for a moment to center his mind, then opened them with a renewed determination. The Yagna was underway.

As the ritual flames swayed and flickered in the dim light, the ancient chants of Shukracharya began to reverberate with an ominous power. Suddenly, the sky roared with thunder, and a bolt of lightning tore through the air, striking the Shiva Lingam with an earth-shaking force. The Lingam, a sacred symbol of divine power, shattered into countless fragments, each piece glowing with an ethereal orange and gold light. The brilliance of the shattered pieces cast eerie shadows around the chamber, the divine energy within them pulsing like a heartbeat.

Ashwatthama and Raghav, their hearts racing with urgency, moved swiftly through the scattered remnants. Each fragment was unique, its surface gleaming with the remnants of the divine power that had once unified them. As they sifted through the pieces, they could feel the lingering energy, potent and sacred, resonating through the very air they breathed.

Ashwatthama felt a strange pull, an almost magnetic sensation that guided his hand over the broken shards. He moved with careful precision, sifting through the debris, feeling the weight and energy of each fragment.

"There are so many pieces," he muttered, his voice tense with urgency. "How will we know which one contains the Kundal?"

Raghav's eyes darted over the scattered stones.

"Look closely," he urged, his voice low. "The Kundal is no ordinary object. It must have a glow, a radiance beyond the rest."

For a moment, there was nothing but the sound of their hurried breaths and the soft crackling of the Yagna fire. Then, out of the corner of his eye, Ashwatthama saw it—a small, curved piece, gleaming brighter than the rest. Its glow was subtle but unmistakable, a faint golden aura that seemed to pulse with life, as if it had its own heartbeat.

"There!" Raghav exclaimed, reaching out quickly. He grasped the piece in his hand, feeling a surge of warmth travel up his arm. "I've got it!" he shouted.

He held the glowing fragment up to the light of the Yagna flames, and it seemed to shimmer with a brilliant, divine energy. The Kundal piece was unlike any other—a perfect crescent of gold, intricately inscribed with symbols that seemed to shift and dance in the light. It felt alive in his hand, humming softly with a power that sent a thrill through his veins.

Shukracharya turned, his eyes narrowing as he saw the golden glow.

"Excellent, Raghav," he murmured, his voice thick with approval. "You have found it. The first piece of the Kundal is ours."

With the piece of the Kundal secured, Shukracharya turned his attention back to the shattered Lingam.

"Now," he commanded, "we must restore the Lingam to its original form. We cannot leave it broken like this; it would disrupt the sacred balance of this place."

Ashwatthama nodded, understanding the gravity of the task. He knelt beside the broken fragments of the Lingam and began to carefully align them, piece by piece. His hands moved with a practiced grace, fitting each fragment back into its place, like solving a sacred puzzle.

Raghav worked beside him, holding the fragments steady as Ashwatthama pressed them together. For a moment, it seemed as if the Lingam might hold, the pieces fitting snugly against each other. But as they finished placing the last piece, a deep crack ran through the center, and a faint tremor passed through the ground.

"It's still cracked," Ashwatthama muttered, frustration seeping into his voice. He pressed his hands against the surface, trying to force the pieces to meld together. "Why won't it stay whole?"

Shukracharya stepped forward, his face stern. "Leave it," he ordered, his tone sharp and commanding. "The Lingam has taken too much damage. Forcing it back together will only cause more harm. We have what we came for. Let it be for now."

Ashwatthama hesitated, his hands still on the cracked surface. "But Guru Ji—"

"Leave it," Shukracharya repeated, his eyes flashing. "The balance will restore itself in time. The Lingam will heal, just as it always does."

Reluctantly, Ashwatthama withdrew his hands, stepping back from the broken structure. The crack still ran through the center, a jagged line of divine damage. The pieces seemed to pulse faintly, as if aware of their own incompleteness.

Shukracharya turned back to the Yagna fire, which had begun to burn lower, its flames flickering as if tired from the ritual.

"Now," he said, his voice calm but filled with authority, "we move to the next phase. Prepare yourselves."

Ashwatthama nodded, his gaze still lingering on the broken Lingam. The faint glow of the Kundal piece in his hand felt heavy, as if it carried the weight of a thousand destinies. He knew they had only just begun to unlock the secrets of the divine, but already, the stakes felt impossibly high.

With the first piece of the Kundal in their possession and the temple still vibrating with the aftershocks of the divine strike, the journey to harness its power had only just begun.

CHAPTER 20

The rumble of the lightning had barely faded when Parashurama Ji, Manas, and Ananya arrived at the Bijli Mahadev Temple. The villagers clustered around the temple, their voices hushed, faces tight with anxiety. The air was thick with tension, as if the very atmosphere was holding its breath, waiting for something to happen.

Manas pushed through the crowd, his heart racing, while Ananya followed closely behind, her eyes scanning the scene for any sign of what had happened. Parashurama Ji moved with purpose, his expression grim. As they neared the temple's entrance, they saw the cause of the commotion—the sacred Shiva Lingam, which stood tall and powerful at the heart of the temple, was fractured.

A long, jagged crack ran through its center, like a wound that cut deep into the stone. The villagers whispered among themselves, exchanging nervous glances, while Pandit Ji, the head priest, stood before the Lingam, his face pale with worry.

"This is not possible," Pandit Ji muttered, his voice quavering. "The lightning has always been a sign from the gods, a divine occurrence that strikes only once every twelve years. Never before… never before has it struck like this, out of cycle."

Parashurama Ji approached him calmly, his demeanor steady despite the chaos around them.

"Pandit Ji," he began, "what do you know about this lightning? Can you tell us anything more?"

He asked the question with a deliberate intention, hoping that the Pandit's knowledge might reveal something deeper, something hidden within the layers of the ritual they had just witnessed. Parashurama knew that in times of great power, even the smallest detail could hold immense significance, and he was determined to uncover every piece of information that could guide them on their path.

Pandit Ji glanced at Parashurama Ji and then at Manas and Ananya, his eyes filled with suspicion. "I know only what my ancestors have passed down to me," he replied. "Every twelve years, the lightning comes as a sign from Indra, a blessing that reaffirms the bond between heaven and earth. But this…" he gestured to the damaged Lingam, "this is unnatural. It is as if someone forced Indra's hand, compelling him to strike early."

Parashurama Ji's face darkened. "That can mean only one thing," he murmured. "Shukracharya is here… or has been here."

Manas's eyes widened in alarm. "Guru Ji, how could they have known the first clue?"

Parashurama Ji shook his head slowly, his expression troubled.

"I don't know, but Shukracharya has many methods at his disposal, some beyond our understanding. What is important is that they've been here and they've their first Kundal."

Pandit Ji continued, his voice breaking slightly, "I saw it myself, just after the lightning struck. The Lingam was broken, cracked apart, and I knew it was not the natural order of things. I called out to the villagers to bring butter, ghee, and other offerings to heal the Lingam, as is our custom, but… something was missing."

Manas furrowed his brow. "Missing?"

Before Pandit Ji could answer, a small boy, no older than eight, piped up from the back of the crowd, his voice high and clear. "Baba

Ji! I saw three men! Big men—they were here, I saw them when I came, after the lightning. They were trying to fix the Lingam."

The crowd erupted in murmurs again. Parashurama Ji and Ananya exchanged a quick glance. Ananya bent down to the boy's level.

"Three men, you say?" she asked gently. "Can you describe them to me?"

The boy nodded earnestly.

"Yes, *didi*. They were tall, and they looked… powerful, like the warriors from the old stories my grandma tells me. I was hiding nearby, and I saw them right after the lightning came. Then they left quickly."

The boy's mother called him back, and he scampered off, leaving the trio with a sinking feeling. Parashurama Ji's jaw tightened.

"It was them," he said. "Shukracharya, Ashwatthama, and Akshay. Somehow, they've discovered the first clue and managed to get here before us."

Ananya bit her lip. "What could they have done to the Lingam?"

Pandit Ji, who had been listening intently, suddenly spoke up, his eyes wide with realization. "That is precisely what worries me. The Lingam has been damaged before, but never in this way. Never so deliberately. And I saw them trying to repair it, but they weren't priests. No one, not even my family, is allowed to touch the Lingam."

Manas looked around at the villagers, who were returning with butter, ghee, and other offerings, hastily trying to make sense of what had happened. Pandit Ji stepped closer, a shadow of fear passing over his face.

"There is a story," he began hesitantly, "one passed down through generations of my family, about how this Lingam holds a secret energy… an energy that was meant to protect this valley. But now… I fear that energy is gone."

Parashurama Ji leaned in, his interest piqued.

"Tell us more, Pandit Ji. What is this story?"

Pandit Ji seemed to hesitate, his eyes darting around as if fearing that the very walls of the temple were listening.

"It is said," he whispered, "that long ago, when the valley was first formed, Lord Shiva placed a unique divine energy within the Lingam—a fragment of a greater power that connects this world to the celestial realm. This energy was meant to protect us from any evil that might try to cross over from the other side. My grandfather spoke of it often, but he never revealed what exactly it was… only that it was vital to our safety."

Manas' face grew serious. "And now it's missing?"

Pandit Ji nodded slowly. "Yes. I fear that whatever energy was contained within the Lingam is no longer here. The balance feels… wrong."

Parashurama Ji frowned deeply, his mind racing. "Do you have any record of this energy? Any texts, scrolls, or books that might tell us more?" Pandit Ji paused, thinking hard.

"There is… one book," he admitted. "An old one that has been in my family for centuries. It is said to contain the secrets of Kullu's history and the events that shaped this land. Perhaps it holds the answers you seek… or at least, a clue." Parashurama Ji's eyes lit up.

"Please, bring us this book," he urged."

Pandit Ji nodded, though he still looked uncertain.

"I will fetch it for you," he agreed, "but be warned… the book is old, and its pages are fragile. Some parts have been lost to time, and others… well, they are written in a script that few can read."

Manas stepped forward, a look of determination on his face.

"We'll take whatever we can get. Even the smallest clue could be invaluable."

Pandit Ji hurried away to retrieve the book, leaving them standing beside the fractured Lingam. Ananya placed a hand on Manas' shoulder.

"We have to find that Kundal before they do. If Shukracharya has already uncovered the first piece, he'll be relentless in his search for the others."

Manas nodded, his expression set with resolve. "We will. And we will stop them, whatever it takes."

Parashurama Ji, still gazing at the Lingam, murmured.

Pandit Ji emerged from his small hut, holding a tattered, ancient book in his hands. The cover was worn, the edges frayed, and the title had faded with time, almost illegible. The binding creaked as he handed it over to Parashurama Ji, who took it with reverence.

"This book," Pandit Ji said, his voice low, "has been passed down through my family for generations. It holds the mysteries of this valley and the divine secrets whispered to my ancestors."

Parashurama Ji nodded, carefully opening the fragile pages. The parchment felt brittle under his fingers, each page

marked with the passage of time. Manas leaned in, his eyes scanning the faded script. He noticed peculiar symbols, diagrams, and words that seemed almost like a riddle. Then, one phrase caught his attention.

"It mentions an energy," Manas said, his voice tinged with curiosity. "The energy that the Lingam contains… It reflects a great deal of radiation, and anyone who comes in contact with it must cleanse themselves in holy water. But it specifically says the water must be in its purest form."

Parashurama Ji raised an eyebrow. "Purest form? The sacred rivers… perhaps the Ganga or Saraswati or something else?"

Manas turned to Pandit Ji. "Pandit Ji, it also mentions a mantra—a mantra that honors both Lord Ram and Lord Krishna. It says it must be read from two different points of view. What could that mean?"

Pandit Ji chuckled softly, his eyes twinkling with a hint of mischief.

"Ah, yes, this one! I remember reading that passage when I was a child. My ancestors always found it amusing. Let me show you the page where it is detailed further." He flipped through the old, yellowed pages with delicate care.

"Here it is," he said, pointing to a passage.

Manas leaned closer, reading aloud:

"In a rare cosmic alignment, when the nectar of immortality graces the earth, rivers will swell with divine essence. Seekers of the elixir must immerse themselves in these sacred waters. There, they must utter a single mantra that venerates both Lord Ram and Lord Krishna, from two different views. By doing so, they will receive the counterpart of that divine energy, unlocking the path to the elixir's true power."

Manas read the passage over and over, his mind racing to decipher its meaning. Ananya, sensing his confusion, took the book from his hands and read the text for herself. Her eyes widened with realization, and she glanced at Manas.

"Guru Ji!" Ananya called out. Parashurama Ji, who had been engrossed in repairing the damaged Lingam with a quiet chant of mantras, turned to face them. His eyes fell on the open book, curiosity evident in his expression.

"What is it, Ananya?" he asked, noticing the intensity in her gaze.

"We think we've found the second clue," she said, her voice brimming with excitement.

"This passage talks about a cosmic alignment, a time when divine rivers swell with the essence of immortality. It mentions a mantra that praises both Lord Ram and Lord Krishna from different perspectives. Perhaps… this is the key to finding the next piece of the Kundal."

Parashurama Ji took the book from Ananya's hands and read the passage, his lips moving silently as he contemplated the words. Slowly, a smile spread across his face, a flicker of hope lighting his eyes.

"Yes," he murmured, "this makes sense. The rivers… they must hold the key. The alignment of time, the convergence of divine essence—it's a hint of where the next piece might be hidden."

Manas, still contemplating, asked, "But which river? And when will this alignment happen?"

Parashurama Ji closed the book carefully, turning to Pandit Ji.

"Pandit Ji, thank you. You have given us a precious clue. We must leave at once to find this alignment. Do you know when this next convergence might occur?"

Pandit Ji shook his head slowly. "No, I'm afraid I do not. But if the answer is in that book, I trust you will find it."

Parashurama Ji bowed his head in respect.

"You have been of great help, Pandit Ji. We will honor this knowledge and use it wisely."

Pandit Ji nodded, a mixture of concern and hope in his eyes. "May the gods guide you on your journey."

With that, Parashurama Ji turned to Manas and Ananya. "The Lingam is as repaired as it will be. We must hurry. If Shukracharya has already gained a piece of the Kundal, he will waste no time pursuing the next."

They bowed to Pandit Ji and turned to leave. The villagers were still gathered, murmuring amongst themselves. The three of them moved quickly, their steps purposeful as they began their descent from the temple. As they reached the outskirts of the village, the clouds overhead began to part, and a single ray of sunlight pierced through, illuminating their path.

CHAPTER 21

Many Eons Ago

In the time before time, when the cosmos itself was still young and the gods walked among mortals, a great churning began in the heart of the universe. The eternal struggle between the Devas (gods) and the Asuras (demons) had reached a fevered pitch. Both factions, seeking dominion over the cosmos, yearned for the nectar of immortality—the fabled Amrit—hidden deep within the Ocean of Milk, Kshir Sagar.

This was the age of legends, when mountains could be moved by the will of the divine, and serpents were vast enough to encircle the earth. The gods, led by Lord Indra, the king of the heavens, and the Asuras, commanded by the mighty King Bali, put aside their enmity for a time to churn the cosmic ocean. They sought to unearth the Amrit, a nectar so potent it could grant eternal life to whoever consumed it.

Mount Mandara, a sacred mountain, was uprooted and placed as the churning rod. The great serpent Vasuki was coiled around it as a rope, with the gods holding its tail and the demons its head. As the churning began, a symphony of forces was unleashed—a dance of creation and destruction that shook the very fabric of existence.

The ocean yielded many treasures—gems, divine animals, and celestial beings—but the gods and demons focused solely on the elusive Amrit. After eons of relentless toil, the nectar of immortality finally emerged, held within a golden Kumbh (pot) that radiated a light so pure it illuminated the entire cosmos.

As the gods and demons gazed upon the pot of Amrit, a new battle for its possession erupted. The Asuras, driven by greed, sought to claim the nectar for themselves, intending to overthrow the gods and rule the cosmos. The Devas, knowing that the balance of the universe hung in the balance, turned to Lord Vishnu, the preserver of worlds, for aid.

Vishnu, in his infinite wisdom, took the form of Mohini, an enchantress of unparalleled beauty. With her charm and grace, Mohini mesmerized the Asuras, convincing them to let her distribute the Amrit. The gods, aware of the ruse, stood ready to receive the nectar while the Asuras were distracted by Mohini's allure. But as the distribution neared its end, the ever-scheming Asuras realized they had been deceived. A furious battle broke out, with both factions striving to seize the pot of Amrit. In the chaos, the divine nectar was spilled, and drops of Amrit descended from the heavens, falling toward the mortal realm.

The nectar of immortality, now scattered, fell upon four sacred rivers on Earth—rivers that would forever be blessed by the divine essence they received. Each drop of Amrit infused these rivers with a mystical power, making their waters a source of spiritual purification and divine strength.

The first drop fell into the Ganga at Prayagraj, where the river's sacred waters swirled with the energy of the gods. The second drop landed in the Yamuna at Haridwar, a place where the river flows from the heart of the Himalayas, carrying the blessings of the mountains. The third drop blessed the Godavari at Nashik, a river that would henceforth be revered as the purifier of souls. The fourth and final drop of Amrit merged with the Shipra at Ujjain, sanctifying the land with the power to uplift even the most fallen of beings.

These rivers, now imbued with the divine essence of Amrit, became the sites of the Kumbh Mela, a celestial gathering that would occur every twelve years, mirroring the ancient churning of the ocean. The Kumbh Mela became a time when the barriers between the divine and the mortal were thin, when millions of seekers would gather to bathe in the sacred waters, hoping to cleanse their souls and gain the blessings of the gods.

The Kumbh Mela grew into one of the most revered festivals on Earth, a time when the rivers flowed not just with water, but with the divine essence of immortality itself. It is said that during each Kumbh Mela, the gods descend from their heavenly abodes to witness the devotion of mortals, and the rivers themselves glow with a light unseen by ordinary eyes—a light that harks back to the very beginning, to the moment when the cosmos was young and the nectar of immortality first graced the earth.

Lord Parashurama finished his tale, letting the ancient words settle into the air like the dust of forgotten ages. The firelight flickered across the faces of his listeners, casting long shadows as they mulled over the story's implications.

Manas broke the silence, his voice contemplative.

"So, the first part of the clue—*'In a rare cosmic alignment, when the nectar of immortality graces the earth, rivers will swell with divine essence'*—refers to those sacred rivers you just mentioned, right? The rivers that received the Amrit."

Ananya nodded, her mind already racing ahead.

"And the second part—*'Seekers of the elixir must immerse themselves in these sacred waters'*—clearly means you'll have to take a dip in one of those rivers, Manas."

Parashurama Ji, his eyes thoughtful and piercing, added,

"The third part of the clue is where things get more complicated. *'There, they must utter a single mantra that venerates both Lord Ram and Lord Krishna, from two different views.'* This is the real challenge, the key that unlocks the path forward."

Manas furrowed his brow, deep in thought.

"A single mantra that venerates both Lord Ram and Lord Krishna, but from two different perspectives? What kind of mantra could achieve that? It's like two sides of the same coin—one that honors both avatars of Vishnu but in distinct ways. We need to figure this out, or everything we've done so far will be for nothing." Parashurama Ji agreed.

"This mantra isn't just a simple prayer; it's a riddle woven into the fabric of the divine. You'll need to see beyond the obvious, to understand the essence of both deities as they are individually and together."

Ananya added, "Maybe it's something hidden in plain sight—something we've heard before but never really understood in this context."

Manas took a deep breath, his resolve hardening. "We'll have to dig deep into the scriptures, study the ancient texts, and maybe even meditate on their meanings. This isn't just about reciting a few words—it's about connecting with the divine essence of both Lord Ram and Lord Krishna in a way that transcends the ordinary."

The descent from the Bijli Mahadev Temple had been steep, the rough path cutting through dense forests and sharp ridges. But now, as they moved quickly down the mountain, urgency gripped their every step. Raghav, who had seemed strong and invincible after his resurrection, suddenly stumbled, his body convulsing violently. His skin flushed an alarming shade of red, as if consumed by an internal fire. Ashwatthama rushed to his side, his heart pounding.

"What is happening to him?" he demanded, his voice filled with panic.

"Why is his body heating up like this?"

Shukracharya's face darkened, his brows knitting together with worry.

"We need to get him to a doctor, but there are none here. We must reach the valley below."

Without a moment's hesitation, Ashwatthama lifted Raghav's limp body onto his shoulders, his powerful arms flexing as he began to move swiftly down the rocky path. Akshay sprinted ahead, scouting the way for the fastest route down, his mind racing to find a solution.

After what felt like an eternity, they finally reached the base of the mountain. Akshay spotted a small clinic nestled in the shadows of the trees, a thin plume of smoke rising from its chimney.

"There!" he shouted. "A doctor—quickly!"

Bursting through the door, Ashwatthama laid Raghav down on a worn cot while Akshay spoke urgently to the doctor, a weary-looking man with spectacles perched on his nose.

"Please, help him!" Akshay pleaded. "His body is burning up!"

The doctor, initially taken aback by the intensity of the situation, composed himself and quickly approached Raghav, feeling his pulse and checking his temperature.

"Hmm," he mumbled, "it appears to be a severe fever. I'll give him something to reduce the temperature."

He prepared a concoction of some medicine and administered it to Raghav, who lay still, his breaths shallow and labored. Shukracharya watched closely, his eyes never leaving Raghav's face.

"Let's wait here for an hour," Shukracharya advised, his voice steady but tense. "We need to see if the medicine has any effect."

But as the minutes ticked by, it became painfully clear that Raghav's condition was not improving. His body continued to radiate an unnatural heat, and sweat poured from his brow. The doctor, now visibly worried, wiped his hands nervously on his apron.

"I… I don't understand," he stammered.

"The fever should have broken by now… this is no ordinary ailment."

Shukracharya stood up, his face a mask of grim determination.

"We are wasting time here," he said sharply. "This is beyond your understanding, Doctor. We need something much stronger. Only Ganga can help now."

Akshay blinked, confused. "Who is Ganga?" he asked, glancing at Ashwatthama.

Shukracharya turned to Akshay, his expression impatient.

"Not who, Akshay—the river. The Ganga at Prayagraj. We must reach it immediately."

Realization dawned on Akshay's face.

"Oh, the river… But why there?"

Shukracharya replied, "Because it's the only place where we can find the purity needed to counteract the energy of the Kundal. There, in the waters that once held the drops of Amrit. And soon, the Kumbh Mela will be upon us. At that time, the water will be at its purest."

Ashwatthama, still carrying Raghav, nodded. "Then we must go to Prayagraj now."

Akshay was already on his phone, making arrangements.

"We need to get to Delhi first," he said. "From there, I can charter a flight to Prayagraj."

As they hurried down the path, Ashwatthama asked, "What exactly is happening to Raghav? Why is his body reacting like this?"

Shukracharya kept pace, his mind racing with calculations.

"It is the Kundal," he explained.

"When Lord Indra deceived Karna and took the Kundal, he separated them for a reason. They were not meant to be apart. Now that we have one Kundal, its energy is causing a reaction in Raghav's body. It must be reunited with its counterpart—or his body will continue to burn from within."

Ashwatthama's face darkened with concern.

"But how do we fix this?"

Shukracharya's voice was firm.

"This was caused by something celestial—the Kundal is imbued with divine energy. Only a celestial remedy can counteract its effects. That is why we must go to the Ganga. The sacred waters there have been touched by the Amrit, making them the purest on earth. They hold the power to heal."

Akshay, still listening, asked, "But why specifically the river Ganga at Prayagraj?"

Shukracharya replied, "The Kumbh Mela is nearing, a time when the cosmic energies align, and the Ganga's waters are said to possess the highest spiritual potency. The very place where a drop of Amrit fell during the churning of the ocean. This is where the celestial and the terrestrial meet, where the veil between worlds is thinnest. If there is any hope of saving Raghav, it is there."

Ashwatthama's eyes hardened with determination. "Then we go now."

CHAPTER 22

The morning sun rose over the holy city of Prayagraj, bathing the landscape in a golden glow that shimmered on the waters of the sacred Ganga. The banks were alive with pilgrims, sadhus, and devotees, all gathered for the auspicious rituals of the day. The air was filled with the soft hum of prayers, the ringing of bells, and the distant echoes of sacred chants.

Parashurama Ji, Manas, and Ananya moved through the bustling crowd, their steps purposeful as they made their way to a secluded spot by the riverbank to offer their prayers. The energy around them was high, charged with the divine presence that seemed to envelop the city in a protective embrace.

Manas, still deep in thought, finally spoke up. "Guru Ji, I still can't figure out the mantra. The third part of the clue eludes me."

Parashurama Ji placed a reassuring hand on his shoulder. "Patience, Manas. The answer will reveal itself in time. The clue said that the mantra must be read from two different points of view. There must be a deeper meaning to this."

Manas pondered for a moment, then recited softly, "Hare Krishna Hare Krishna, Krishna Krishna Hare Hare; Hare Rama Hare Rama, Rama Rama Hare Hare. This chant venerates both Krishna and Rama, but I feel this isn't quite the answer we seek."

Parashurama Ji nodded thoughtfully. "The clue did suggest there's more to it... a mantra that, when read from two different views, glorifies both Lord Ram and Lord Krishna. But how?"

Just then, their conversation was interrupted by the laughter and shouts of children playing nearby. They watched as a group of kids ran around, calling out to each other. One boy shouted, "Naman!" and another replied, "Kanak!" A small girl ran up to Ananya, tugging on her sleeve with excitement.

"Didi, tell me a name!" she pleaded.

Ananya, a bit caught off guard, smiled and said, "Ananya."

The little girl thought for a moment, then scrunched her nose in concentration. "Ananya will be Aynana… no, that doesn't work!" she declared and ran over to Manas.

Bhaiya, what's your name? Manas replied, "Manas."

The boy's eyes lit up. "Manas is Sanam!" he shouted. "Oh no, this also doesn't work!"

Manas, perplexed, asked, "What are you kids playing?"

The boy grinned. "We are playing a game with names that sound the same when spoken backward, like Naman or Kanak!"

Parashurama Ji's eyes widened, and a sudden realization struck him. "Of course!" he exclaimed. "That's it! This is what the clue meant."

Manas and Ananya looked at him, still confused. "What do you mean, Guru Ji?" Ananya asked.

Parashurama Ji explained, "A mantra that, when spoken, glorifies Lord Ram, and when spoken backward, it glorifies Lord Krishna. That is the meaning of 'from two different views.' A shloka that can be read forward and backward, speaking of both gods."

Manas' face brightened with understanding.

"So this is the answer! But how do we find such a shloka, Guru Ji?"

Ananya, her eyes sparkling with inspiration, said, "I remember something! My father, Guru Vyas Ji, once taught me a verse that can be read both ways. Listen to this:

'तं भूसुतामुक्तिमुदारहासं वंदे यतो भव्यभवं दयाश्रीः।'

This verse glorifies Lord Rama when read normally…"

Manas interrupted excitedly, "And if you read it backward?"

Ananya continued,

"श्रीयादवं भव्यभतोयदेवं संहारदामुक्तिमुतासुभूतम्।"

Parashurama Ji's smile grew wider.

"And this verse, when read backward, glorifies Lord Krishna! It is the perfect balance of both divine forms. This is the mantra we need!"

Manas and Ananya exchanged a look of triumph. "So that's what the clue meant by *from two different views*," Manas said, his voice filled with awe.

Parashurama Ji nodded, his face calm but his eyes gleaming with pride.

"Yes, and now that we have the clue, we should perform the ritual at dawn tomorrow. The energy will be strongest at that time, and the alignment will be perfect."

Manas, feeling a surge of excitement, asked, "Guru Ji, what do we do now?"

Parashurama Ji replied, "We prepare. Rest well tonight, for tomorrow we will invoke the power of this mantra and use it to guide us to the next part of our quest." They bowed to the sacred river, their hearts filled with gratitude and anticipation for the journey ahead. The sun dipped low on the horizon, casting long shadows across the water, but there was a lightness in their steps, a renewed sense of purpose.

The journey to Prayagraj was fraught with tension. As they traveled, the air seemed to hum with unseen energies, the skies darkening with ominous clouds that seemed to mirror the urgency of their mission. Every second counted, for with each passing moment, Raghav's body grew hotter, his breaths more ragged.

Finally, after hours of relentless travel, they reached the holy city of Prayagraj. The banks of the Ganga were already crowded with pilgrims and sadhus, all gathering for the coming Kumbh Mela. The river flowed gently under the soft light of the evening, its waters reflecting the hues of the setting sun.

Shukracharya pointed toward the river.

"There," he said, "we must take him to the water's edge. Quickly, before it is too late."

Ashwatthama carried Raghav to the bank, his feet moving quickly over the soft sand. The cool breeze from the river washed over them, a stark contrast to the fever that consumed Raghav's body.

Shukracharya stood at the water's edge, his hands raised in invocation. "O Ganga, sacred river of life, bless these waters. Let the divine essence flow through and cleanse this soul. Bring balance where there is chaos. Bring calm where there is pain."

As Shukracharya chanted, the water seemed to shimmer with an inner light, as if responding to his call. With a deep breath, he motioned for Ashwatthama to lower Raghav into the river. The moment Raghav's body touched the water, a hiss like steam escaping filled the air, and the river seemed to swirl around him with a life of its own.

For a moment, there was silence, the world holding its breath. Then, slowly, the redness of Raghav's skin began to fade. His body, which had been tense with pain, seemed to relax as the fever's grip lessened. A cool, calming energy emanated from the water, enveloping him in its embrace.

Raghav's eyes fluttered open, and he gasped, taking in a deep breath of the cool air.

"What... what happened?" he whispered.

Ashwatthama grinned with relief. "You're going to be fine," he said. "You're safe now."

Shukracharya nodded, but his eyes were still serious. "For now. But we cannot rest. We need to find the next Kundal, and quickly. This is only the beginning of the trials ahead."

Akshay nodded in agreement. "Then let's not waste any more time."

Shukracharya Ji said, "Since we are already here, let us offer a prayer early tomorrow morning, and then we shall depart."

Shukracharya Ji said, "Let's arrange for some sleep, Akshay."

Akshay reached out to his phone and made the necessary arrangements. Shukracharya Ji added,

"The arrangements should be near the bank of the river."

Akshay agreed and soon arranged everything. All four of them set up a tent and settled down to sleep. Raghav was feeling somewhat better, but as soon as he drifted off, he found himself entering another world—a vivid dream that felt all too real.

In his vision, he saw Duryodhana, the mighty warrior and master of the mace. Duryodhana had decided to use a special technique he had

learned—a yogic exercise called Jalastambha. This ancient practice allowed him to control his breath and reduce his bodily functions to a bare minimum, enabling him to stay submerged in the water for an extended period without needing to surface for air. The cold water of the lake not only helped him soothe his battle-weary body but also kept him hidden from his enemies.

After the battle, the Pandavas, along with Lord Krishna, began searching for Duryodhana, knowing that the war would not truly be over until he was defeated. They combed the battlefield and eventually followed his trail to the lake.

When they arrived, there was no sign of Duryodhana on the surface, but Krishna, with his divine vision, knew exactly where he was hiding. Krishna advised Bhima to provoke Duryodhana with words that would challenge his pride and sense of duty as a Kshatriya (warrior).

Hearing Bhima's taunts, Duryodhana, unable to bear the insults, emerged from the water. Though he was exhausted and outnumbered, he was still determined to fight and restore his honor. He challenged Bhima to a mace duel, which Bhima accepted.

The duel between Bhima and Duryodhana was ferocious, as both were incredibly skilled with the mace. The battle raged on with tremendous intensity, but Bhima eventually gained the upper hand. Remembering his vow to break Duryodhana's thigh—a vow made after Duryodhana humiliated Draupadi in the Kaurava court— Bhima struck a devastating blow to Duryodhana's thigh, shattering it and bringing him down.

Raghav awoke with a loud cry, clutching his thigh in pain.

Ashwatthama, Shukracharya Ji, and Akshay woke up, alarmed, and asked what had happened.

Raghav, still shaken, said, "I had a dream... someone broke my thigh."

Shukracharya Ji, understanding the situation, said, "Since we used the soil where Duryodhana fell, you are experiencing his dream. You have his visions, and you must channel them. In doing so, you will also inherit his strength."

He continued, "Now relax. Tomorrow, you will take a dip in the river, and from then on, your fever will subside, and you will be alright."

The morning at Prayagraj was alive with a vibrant pulse, the air electric with divine energy. The banks of the Ganga were overflowing with devotees, their voices mingling in a powerful symphony of chants and hymns. The scent of marigolds and sandalwood incense filled the air, blending with the sacred smoke from the yajnas. Bells tolled from nearby temples, echoing through the crowd like a call from the heavens themselves.

Shukracharya, Ashwatthama, and Raghav moved quietly through the throng of worshippers. The expressions on their faces were tense, focused. They knew they had little time to spare.

Shukracharya leaned in close to Raghav, his voice barely a whisper amid the chaos. "Go quickly," he instructed.

"Take three dips as I've told you. Submerge completely each time, and don't draw attention to yourself."

Raghav nodded, his face set in a determined mask. He felt the eyes of his companions on his back as he waded into the river, the water rising to meet him like a cold, unyielding wall. The sacred river embraced him, its waters lapping around his waist, then his chest, as he moved deeper. The currents swirled around his legs with a strange, ancient force, as if testing his resolve.

With a deep breath, Raghav took his first dip beneath the surface, the icy water enveloping him completely. For a moment, everything went silent, and all he could hear was the faint, muted sound of his heartbeat, like a distant drumbeat in the depths of the river. When he surfaced, his hair hung over his face, obscuring his vision. He wiped it away quickly and blinked against the sunlight.

As his eyes adjusted, he saw a figure standing directly in front of him, no more than a few feet away. It was Manas.

For an instant, neither of them recognized the other. Raghav's face was hidden behind the wet strands of his hair, and Manas, oblivious to the proximity of his enemy, was focused on his own thoughts. But then, like a bolt of lightning, recognition struck. Raghav's mind began to race.

"Why is he here? Has he come for the second Kundal?

Could he have felt the radiation too? Or is he here searching for another clue?"

Raghav quickly composed himself, realizing he needed to stay calm and hidden. "I must remain here and discover what he is seeking."

Raghav shifted slightly, subtly signaling to Ashwatthama on the riverbank, pointing discreetly in Manas's direction. Ashwatthama's sharp eyes caught the signal, and he turned to Shukracharya, whispering urgently,

"Manas is here. If he's here, that means Parashurama and Ananya are not far behind."

Shukracharya's eyes narrowed as he considered the implications. "Akshay," he murmured, "prepare for a retreat. Keep yourself hidden. If things go wrong, we may need to disappear quickly."

Akshay nodded and melted into the crowd, moving toward a discreet hideout he had identified earlier. Meanwhile, Ashwatthama and Shukracharya slipped deeper into the shadows, their eyes scanning the crowd for any sign of Parashurama and Ananya.

Oblivious to their presence, Manas stepped into the water, his mind focused on the task at hand. He took a deep breath and began to chant the mantra with conviction:

"तं भूसुतामुक्तिमुदारहासं वंदे यतो भव्यभवं दयाश्रीः।"

"श्रीयादवं भव्यभतोयदेवं संहारदामुक्तिमुतासुभूतम्।"

He submerged himself beneath the surface, feeling the coolness of the water close over his head like a shroud. The river was calm, its currents steady. He waited, expecting something to happen, but as he surfaced and blinked the water from his eyes, he saw no change. The world around him remained as it was—the river shimmering in the morning light, the pilgrims moving around him, and the temple bells tolling in the distance.

Confused, he took another breath and tried again, repeating the mantra with greater intensity. But once more, as he emerged, the water remained still, and no divine sign appeared. Frustration crept into his heart.

"What am I missing?" he thought.

Manas thought back to the clue he read in the book: *"from two different views..."*

Suddenly, realization hit him. "Of course! Two different views... It must be the direction!"

He turned to face the rising sun in the east, chanting the first mantra with a clear, steady voice:

"तं भूसुतामुक्तिमुदारहासं वंदे यतो भव्यभवं दयाश्रीः।"

Then, he turned westward, toward the setting sun, and chanted the second mantra:

"श्रीयादवं भव्यभतोयदेवं संहारदामुक्तिमुतासुभूतम्।"

With each verse, he felt the air around him shift, as if it were suddenly charged with a strange, otherworldly energy. He took a deep breath, and with all his focus and intent, he dipped beneath the water once more.

This time, as Manas submerged, the river seemed to come alive. The water churned violently, as if caught in a whirlpool. The current swirled around him, faster and faster, pulling him deeper, and a low, vibrating hum filled the air, growing louder with each passing second. The river was no longer calm—it was a living, breathing entity, reacting to the power of the mantra.

A brilliant light burst forth from his folded hands, piercing through the water like a ray of sunlight breaking through a stormy sky. The glow grew brighter, pulsating with a golden intensity, illuminating the riverbed. The sacred waters seemed to dance around him, rippling outward as if responding to the ancient invocation.

Manas felt his heartbeat quicken, his entire body resonating with the energy of the river. He could feel something in his hands, something solid and warm. When he surfaced, he lifted his hands slowly and looked down. Resting in his palm was the second Kundal, its surface gleaming like a molten sun, radiating with divine light.

The Kundal felt alive in his grasp, humming with an ancient power. Its surface was etched with intricate symbols that seemed to shift and move, almost as if they were whispering secrets lost to time. The glow was mesmerizing, an otherworldly golden that seemed to pulse with every beat of his heart.

For a moment, Manas stood frozen, staring at the Kundal in awe. He felt a surge of emotions—exhilaration, triumph, and a hint of fear. The Kundal seemed to pulse with an inner light, as if it recognized him, responding to his touch with a warm, comforting glow. He could feel its energy coursing through him, filling him with a sense of strength and purpose.

But as quickly as the feeling came, it was replaced by a creeping sense of unease. He felt the weight of unseen eyes upon him, watching from the shadows.

He turned his gaze toward the riverbank, searching for Parashurama Ji and Ananya. Spotting them amidst the crowd, he raised the Kundal high above his head to signal them, a triumphant smile spreading across his face. But as he did, his expression faded.

Raghav watched intently, his eyes locked on the glowing object in Manas' hand. His heart raced with anticipation, and a flash of realization swept over him—the second Kundal was now in Manas's possession. He clenched his fists, his mind racing. He had to act quickly.

Manas raised the Kundal high, its golden surface reflecting the sunlight, casting a shimmering light across the sacred waters of the Ganga. Triumph was etched across his face as he looked for Parashurama Ji and Ananya. But as he caught sight of them, his eyes widened in horror. Behind them, moving like shadows against the vibrant backdrop of devotees, were Shukracharya and Ashwatthama.

"Guru Ji, behind you!" Manas shouted, his voice thick with urgency. Parashurama Ji, immediately sensed the danger and dropped into a crouch, just as Shukracharya lunged forward with a powerful thrust aimed at his back.

Shukracharya stumbled forward as his strike missed, his footing unsteady on the loose riverbank. Before he could recover, Ananya sprang into action. She leapt onto Parashurama Ji's back and launched herself into the air, her body twisting mid-flight, delivering a fierce spinning kick to Ashwatthama's chest. The impact sent Ashwatthama staggering back, his feet skidding across the wet stones.

Ashwatthama quickly regained his balance, his face a mask of rage. He charged at Ananya like a bull, his fists swinging in wide, powerful arcs. Ananya ducked beneath his first strike and countered with a rapid flurry of punches to his midsection. Her fists moved like lightning, each blow landing with precision. But Ashwatthama shrugged off the hits as if they were mere annoyances. He swung his arm in a brutal backhand, his knuckles grazing her temple. Ananya stumbled, but she recovered quickly, her eyes sharp with determination.

Meanwhile, Shukracharya regained his composure and circled around Parashurama Ji, his hands moving with rapid speed, striking out with open palms aimed at Parashurama Ji's head and torso. Parashurama Ji parried each blow, his arms moving in fluid, circular motions, deflecting Shukracharya's strikes with the precision of a master warrior. Shukracharya, sensing he was outmatched in speed, feigned a retreat, drawing Parashurama Ji forward.

In a blur of motion, Shukracharya twisted and delivered a spinning back kick aimed at Parashurama Ji's chest. Parashurama Ji caught the leg mid-kick, twisted sharply, and sent Shukracharya crashing into the ground with a resounding thud. Shukracharya rolled with the impact, coming up to his feet in one fluid motion, his eyes gleaming with dark amusement.

"Kill us, or save your disciples," Shukracharya taunted, a sinister smile spreading across his face.

Parashurama Ji's eyes darted toward the river. Manas was nowhere to be seen.

He asked Ananya, "Help him.". His heart pounded with dread. Without hesitation, he sprinted to the water's edge and dove in, his body cutting through the surface like a knife.

Below the surface, Manas was already submerged, his legs thrashing as he struggled against an unseen force. A powerful grip was wrapped around his ankle, dragging him deeper into the cold, murky depths. Manas tried to kick free, but the grip was relentless, pulling him further away from the light above.

He saw his attacker now—a dark silhouette with a face half-hidden in the shadows of the deep. The man's grip was ironclad, his strength unimaginable. Manas swung his free leg, aiming for the figure's midsection, but the attack was met with a counterstrike, a knee that knocked the breath from his lungs. His chest tightened, the cold water filling his nostrils as he fought to hold his breath.

Ananya, seeing the struggle from above, took a deep breath and dived in. The water stung her eyes as she plunged into the depths, her vision blurring momentarily before adjusting to the underwater gloom. She could see Manas now, struggling against the figure that held him. Without a moment's hesitation, she swam toward them, her arms slicing through the water with powerful strokes.

She reached Manas, grabbed his arm, and tried to pull him free, but the attacker's strength was overwhelming. She delivered a sharp kick to the side of the man's head, her foot connecting with his temple, but he didn't even flinch. Instead, he turned his gaze toward her—cold, unyielding eyes that seemed to burn with an unnatural energy. He released Manas' leg for a moment, only to grab Ananya by the wrist and twist it sharply, pulling her close.

Manas took the opportunity to aim a punch at the man's face, his fist moving through the water with surprising speed. The impact landed, causing the figure to recoil slightly, but it wasn't enough to break his grip. The man retaliated with a brutal elbow to Manas' chest, knocking the wind out of him. Bubbles escaped Manas' mouth as he gasped, his body instinctively trying to draw air.

Raghav, his form still obscured by the swirling waters, felt a surge of power coursing through him—a newfound strength that was growing with every passing second. He realized he could hold his breath far longer than any ordinary man, his body moving with an ease and fluidity he had never known. He felt invincible, like the river itself was lending him its strength.

With a burst of speed, Raghav twisted and yanked Manas' arm, spinning him around. He reached for the Kundal that Manas still clutched desperately, his fingers closing around the ancient relic. Manas tried to resist, but his grip was weakening. He felt the Kundal slipping from his grasp. Raghav gave one final, forceful pull and tore the Kundal from Manas' hand.

Above water, Parashurama Ji was handling Shukracharya and Ashwatthama with formidable skill. He blocked a series of rapid strikes from Ashwatthama, countering with a knee to his stomach, followed by a powerful chop to the back of his neck. Ashwatthama staggered back, growling in pain. Shukracharya came at him from the side, aiming a series of rapid-fire punches at Parashurama Ji's ribs.

Parashurama Ji parried the blows with quick, fluid movements, then grabbed Shukracharya's arm, twisting it behind his back and locking him in place.

"Enough of this," Parashurama Ji growled, tightening his grip.

Shukracharya, however, smiled through the pain.

"Choose, Parashurama," he sneered. "Defeat us… or save your disciples."

Parashurama Ji's eyes widened, realizing the stakes. He released Shukracharya and sprinted toward the river. He saw Manas' hand breaking the surface, struggling, then disappearing again. He dove into the water with a powerful thrust, cutting through the current like a blade.

Parashurama Ji descended into the murky depths, his sharp eyes quickly finding Manas, who was now floating unconscious, his body limp. Ananya was still grappling with the attacker, her strength fading. Parashurama's heart pounded as he propelled himself through the water. He reached Manas first, grabbing his disciple's arm and pulling him upward with a powerful kick of his legs.

As they neared the surface, he felt another surge of resistance. Ananya was being pulled down by the dark figure. Without hesitation, Parashurama Ji released a burst of energy from his body, sending a wave of force through the water that temporarily dazed the attacker. He reached out and grabbed Ananya by the waist, pulling her up with him.

They broke through the surface, gasping for air, their bodies soaked and shivering. Manas coughed violently, expelling water from his lungs. Ananya, still dazed, clung to Parashurama Ji's arm.

"Stay with me, Manas," Parashurama Ji urged, his voice calm but firm.

Manas' eyes fluttered open, red and irritated from the river water. "Guru Ji… the Kundal… he took it," Manas managed to say, his voice a mixture of despair and determination.

Parashurama Ji's face hardened. "Who was it?" he demanded.

"I don't know," Manas replied, shaking his head.

"But he was too strong… stronger than me and Ananya combined."

Ananya looked bewildered. "Could it have been Akshay, Raghav's grandfather?" she asked.

Manas shook his head again, his expression one of frustration and confusion.

"No, this was different. He was far stronger… like he was fueled by something else."

Parashurama Ji's eyes narrowed, piecing together the mystery. "Stronger than both of you… and he had the strength to hold his breath longer underwater…"

The trio looked at each other, realizing that this unknown enemy was someone unlike any they had faced before. The second Kundal was now lost to them, but their fight was far from over.

Raghav swam through the icy waters of the river, feeling an unearthly strength coursing through his veins. Each stroke cut through the current like a blade through water, propelling him faster and further than he ever imagined possible. He reached the opposite bank and climbed out, dripping and triumphant. A dark grin spread across his face as he saw Ashwatthama and Shukracharya approaching.

Ashwatthama rushed to him, his eyes filled with concern. "Raghav, are you alright?"

Raghav's grin widened, a strange light in his eyes. "Alright? I'm more than alright, *Dada Ji*," he replied, and with a dramatic flourish, he opened his fist to reveal the second Kundal, gleaming in his palm.

Shukracharya's eyes widened, a rare flicker of surprise crossing his otherwise composed face.

"What? How did you get this?"

Raghav chuckled, savoring the moment. "Manas found the second clue. He came here to seek it, and I saw him the moment he started chanting the Mantra. I signaled both of you, and as you engaged Parashurama Ji and Ananya in battle, I slipped under the water and grabbed Manas, dragging him down."

Ashwatthama looked bewildered. "But you were underwater for so long… How did you manage that?"

Raghav's smile grew even wider. "Do you remember, Dada Ji, the dream I had the night before?"

Shukracharya raised his hand, silencing Raghav mid-sentence. His eyes glinted with understanding.

"So, you are beginning to realize the depth of your new strength," he said, a knowing smile playing at his lips.

Raghav nodded eagerly. "Yes, Guru Ji. It seems Duryodhan was far stronger than I could have imagined. And he knew the secret Vidya of *Jalastambha*—the power to hold one's breath indefinitely and move with agility under water. Somehow, I channeled that knowledge, as if it was a part of me all along."

Shukracharya nodded thoughtfully. "Not just that, Raghav," he replied. "The Kundal you wear is no ordinary piece of armor. It holds power beyond mortal comprehension. The strength you feel now is not just from Duryodhan's essence but from the Kundal as well. One piece was already with you, amplifying your power. And when you took the second Kundal from Manas, it unlocked a new level of strength within you."

Raghav flexed his arms, feeling the surge of energy flowing through his veins.

"It's incredible, Guru Ji. I was able to fight both Ananya and Manas simultaneously, and it felt… easy. Like I had the power of ten men."

Ashwatthama, a flicker of pride in his eyes, nodded. "Good. You will need every bit of that strength for the battles to come."

Raghav clenched his fists, the glow of the Kundal on his wrist seeming to intensify.

"I can't wait to face them in open combat," he growled. "To see the fear in their eyes when they realize how powerful I've become."

Shukracharya placed a hand on Raghav's shoulder. "Patience, Raghav. You have Duryodhan's might within you, but it must be harnessed properly. The Kundal's energy will only continue to amplify your abilities, but if you lose control, it will consume you."

Raghav bowed his head respectfully. "Yes, Guru Ji. I understand. But what about the rest of the pieces? We have two now, but there are more to find."

Ashwatthama, his brow furrowed in thought, interjected, "Do we have any idea where the next piece might be?"

Shukracharya closed his eyes, deep in concentration. "Till now, I don't, but I will. I have my people who are still roaming this earth; maybe I can take their help."

"Your people?" Raghav asked, his curiosity piqued. "You mean Vibhishana Ji and Raja Bali?"

Shukracharya nodded, his expression unreadable.

"Yes. But remember, Raja Bali is in Patal Lok. He only walks upon the Earth once a year. It's unlikely he knows anything about the Kavach."

Ashwatthama's brow furrowed in thought. "Then we must find Vibhishana Ji. He may know something."

"Yes," Shukracharya agreed, his voice a soft rumble.

"Akshay, prepare for the journey. We are going to Lanka."

Akshay hesitated, his eyes flickering toward his guru for reassurance. "You mean... Sri Lanka?" he asked, seeking confirmation. Shukracharya nodded and spoke with quiet certainty. "Yes, Vibhishana may be found in two places. The first is the Kelaniya Raja Maha Vihara, a revered Buddhist temple near Colombo, where he was crowned the King of Lanka after Ravana's fall. The second, however, is the secluded Piduru Mountain. We must head there, for Vibhishana, now a saint, would have retreated far from the material world, seeking solitude amidst the heights."

Akshay nodded, understanding enough not to question further. He moved swiftly, reaching out to his contacts. Within moments, he returned with news.

"The helicopter will arrive in a few hours, Shukracharya Ji."

A thin smile appeared on Shukracharya's lips. "Ah, your helicopter... It brings to mind the *Pushpak Vimaan* that Ravana once possessed. That *Vimaan* was a marvel of the ancient world— far beyond anything your modern machines can fathom."

As they waited, the sky turned a deep crimson, and the sound of the approaching helicopter filled the air. The rotors whipped the grass into a frenzy as it touched down. They boarded swiftly, and the journey southward to Lanka began.

The helicopter cut through the clouds, rising above the earth like an arrow shot from the bow of a god. Below them, the land stretched out like an ancient tapestry, rich with history and myth. Raghav, seated by the window, was mesmerized by the shifting landscape.

First came the mighty Ganges, snaking through the plains of northern India like a silver serpent, glinting under the sun's gaze. They passed over vast fields, golden with ripening wheat, small villages clustered like islands in a sea of green, each a world unto itself. As the helicopter sped south, they crossed the Vindhya Mountains, their jagged peaks reaching skyward like the fingers of ancient giants.

Further south, the terrain grew more rugged, with the Deccan Plateau unfurling like a vast, undulating blanket, dotted with hill forts and the remains of ancient citadels. Rivers twisted through the landscape like veins of silver, and the dense forests of the Western Ghats appeared, their emerald canopy hiding untold secrets and mysteries of ages past.

As they neared the southern tip of India, the ocean came into view—a vast, endless expanse of blue, stretching toward the horizon. They flew over Rameswaram, a sacred place where the ocean whispered the legends of Lord Ram and his mighty vanara army. And then, there it was—the Ram Setu.

From the air, the bridge appeared like a mythical path carved by the gods themselves. Stones and sandbars created a trail over the water, a ghostly remnant of the great engineering feat that had once connected Bharat to Lanka. The rocks shimmered under the sun, as if still blessed by the touch of the vanaras who had placed them there eons ago.

Raghav leaned forward, his eyes wide with wonder.

"Is that… the bridge Lord Ram's army built?" he murmured, awe evident in his voice.

Shukracharya's gaze softened as he looked down at the ancient causeway.

"Yes, Ram Setu—the path forged by determination and divinity, built against all odds. It still carries the echoes of their chants, their faith strong enough to bridge an ocean."

Raghav closed his eyes for a moment, imagining the roar of battle, the thunderous march of the vanaras, and the mighty form of Hanuman leaping across the waves. The air seemed to hum with the energy of those ancient days, as if the bridge itself still held the memory of that epic journey.

Ten hours later, they arrived at the green shores of Lanka. The helicopter landed in a clearing surrounded by dense, verdant forests. The air was thick with the smell of salt and flowers, and unfamiliar birds called out from the treetops. Raghav stepped out, still mesmerized by the journey.

"Guru Ji," he asked, "How will we find Vibhishana Ji in a place like this?"

Shukracharya Ji turned toward the dense jungle, his eyes scanning the horizon.

"First things first," Shukracharya Ji said firmly, turning to Akshay. "I need you to come with me."

Before Akshay could respond, Shukracharya Ji leaned in and whispered something in his ear. Whatever it was, it made Akshay nod obediently. Without a word, he turned and headed back the way they had come.

Raghav watched him leave, then turned to Shukracharya Ji and said, "It's good that you sent him back. It wasn't safe for him to be here."

Shukracharya Ji simply smiled, a knowing expression on his face, but said nothing more.

"Vibhishana is a rakshasa by birth, but his heart is a devout temple of Lord Ram. Even in this land, his presence will be marked by a sanctified aura. Look for a place of prayer and devotion to Lord Ram—that is where we will begin."

They moved through the thick undergrowth, their footsteps careful and deliberate. Every shadow seemed to whisper a story, and every rustling leaf sounded like a breath from the past. They passed ancient ruins, once grand palaces now consumed by vines, their stone walls covered in moss and their arches broken by time. Here, a temple lay half-buried in the jungle.

They continued deeper into the forest, following an invisible trail, guided by Shukracharya's keen senses. The trees loomed overhead like towering giants, their branches weaving a dense canopy that blocked out the sun. The air grew cooler, and the light dimmed, the forest around them thick with the presence of spirits and forgotten myths.

At last, they came upon a small clearing where a lone temple stood, its walls ancient and weathered, overrun with wild vines and moss. Yet, from within, they could hear a soft, melodious chant—a hymn sung in praise of Lord Ram. Shukracharya's eyes sparkled with recognition.

"This is the place," he murmured, his voice filled with certainty. "Vibhishana is near."

They moved closer, each step careful and respectful. As they entered the temple, a wave of peace washed over them, a powerful aura of devotion filling the air. The scent of incense and fresh flowers surrounded them like a delicate veil. Inside, a solitary figure knelt before a small idol of Lord Ram, his hands folded in deep prayer.

This morning felt different for Manas. The usual sense of purpose and determination that fueled his spirit was overshadowed by a heavy feeling of failure. He couldn't shake off the thought that he had let down his Guru, Parashurama Ji. As he sat by himself, his eyes stared blankly at the distant horizon, yet his mind was far from the scenic view. His thoughts circled back to the lost Kundal, his inability to protect it, and the nagging feeling of defeat.

Parashurama Ji had been watching his disciple closely, noticing the furrow in his brows and the clenched fists by his sides. The weight of disappointment was evident in the way Manas carried himself, his shoulders drooping and his eyes cast downward. The guru sensed the turmoil within the young man, the self-blame that was beginning to take root.

"Come here, Manas," Parashurama Ji called out in a calm yet commanding voice, breaking the silence between them.

"Tell me what has happened to you."

Manas approached his guru, his steps heavy, his head still bowed low.

"Guru Ji," he began, his voice filled with frustration and regret, "I'm sorry… I failed you. I lost the Kundal."

Each word felt like a stone weighing on his tongue, his guilt almost palpable. Parashurama Ji listened carefully, his face a blend of patience and compassion. He waited for Manas to finish speaking before placing a reassuring hand on his shoulder.

"Manas," he said gently, "it was not in your hands, my child. Fate plays its own part, and sometimes, no matter how hard we try, the outcome is beyond our control. But rest assured, we have not lost hope."

Manas looked up, his eyes still clouded with doubt.

"How can you say that, Guru Ji?" he asked, his voice trembling slightly. "How can you still believe we have a chance when the Kundal is gone?"

Parashurama Ji's expression softened into a reassuring smile. "I just feel it," he replied simply, his words carrying a quiet conviction. "The path before us may have changed, but the journey is far from over. Sometimes, our greatest victories come after our greatest setbacks."

Ananya, who had been silently observing the exchange, stepped forward.

"But Guru Ji," she said, her brow furrowed with concern, "this time, we didn't get any clue to find the final piece—the Kavach itself. Without it, how will we complete our mission?"

Parashurama Ji said, "Believe in destiny, Ananya. Remember, we started with nothing, and then, because of the Ayodhya Mandir, we got the chance to meet Kaagbhusandi Ji, who gave us the first clue.

The second clue came to us when we decided to stay back and help the Pandit. Who knows where we would be if we had left earlier?

And now, the clue about the Mantra—Manas got an idea after seeing those kids playing. Everything is falling into place, so—"

Manas interrupted, "Only to lose the Kundal."

Parashurama Ji gently replied, "You must rest. Go back to sleep and calm your mind."

CHAPTER 23

Shukracharya sat cross-legged under the shade of a banyan tree, his eyes closed in deep meditation.

"I will stay here," he said, his voice low and resonant, "and seek guidance through my inner vision. You two—go, search the forests, the temples, anywhere you might find a trace of Vibhishana. Look for any sign of devotion to Lord Ram. He is bound to reveal himself."

Ashwatthama and Raghav nodded and set off into the dense jungles of Lanka. Hours passed as they moved through narrow paths and climbed rocky outcrops, their senses alert to every sound and movement. The air was thick with humidity, and the shadows seemed to stretch and coil around them like living things.

They returned after several hours, empty-handed and frustrated. Ashwatthama's face was set in a grim expression, his patience wearing thin, while Raghav's brows were furrowed in deep thought.

Suddenly, a sound caught Raghav's ears—a faint voice carried in the wind, chanting, *"Jai Shree Ram."* The words pierced through the air like a sacred bell, clear and unwavering. Raghav's eyes narrowed, and he turned toward the direction of the voice.

"Jai Shree Ram," he murmured to himself. "Could it be Vibhishana?"

He quickened his pace, pushing through the dense undergrowth until he came upon an elderly man, seated beneath a large tree, his eyes closed in prayer, his lips moving softly with the chant.

Without a moment's hesitation, Raghav strode over to him, his shadow falling across the old man's face.

"You!" he barked, his voice harsh. "Are you Vibhishana?"

The elderly man opened his eyes, confusion and fear flashing across his weathered face. "No, my son… I am but a humble devotee of Lord Ram."

Raghav wasn't convinced. "A humble devotee, are you?" he sneered. "Then you must know where Vibhishana is hiding."

Before the man could respond, Raghav grabbed him by the collar and lifted him effortlessly, his newfound strength pulsing through his veins. The man gasped, struggling against Raghav's iron grip.

"Tell me where Vibhishana is, or I will crush you!" Raghav growled, his voice menacingly low. The old man whimpered, his hands trembling, but remained silent. Frustrated, Raghav threw him to the ground and bound his hands tightly with a sturdy vine, torn from the mountainside, its rough texture biting into the man's skin.

"You're coming with me," he muttered. "Shukracharya Ji will know how to deal with you."

Meanwhile, on the other side of the jungle, Ashwatthama moved silently through the underbrush, his senses keen and alert. He, too, was searching for any sign, any clue. As he rounded a bend in the path, he saw a small child sitting by a stream, humming a tune to himself while splashing water with his feet. The tune was familiar—a hymn in praise of Lord Ram.

Curious, Ashwatthama approached the boy.

"Hey, kid!" he called out. "What's your name?"

The boy looked up, smiling fearlessly. "People call me Selva," he replied in a clear, unwavering voice.

Ashwatthama raised an eyebrow. "Aren't you afraid of me?" he asked, intrigued by the boy's calm demeanor.

Selva shook his head. "No, why should I be? We are a devotee of Hanuman Ji, and he protects our tribe from all evil."

"Really?" Ashwatthama said, a slight smile playing on his lips. "And what is your tribe called?"

"We are the *Mahatang Tribe*," Selva replied proudly.

Ashwatthama felt a flicker of something—perhaps respect, perhaps nostalgia. He nodded and let the boy go, thinking to himself,

"This child is nothing but a worshiper… but I must return to see if Raghav had any luck."

As Ashwatthama made his way back to the banyan tree, he saw Raghav had already returned, dragging an elderly man behind him, his hands bound.

"Guru Ji!" Raghav called out triumphantly.

"I found this man chanting 'Jai Shree Ram.' I thought he might be Vibhishana."

Shukracharya opened his eyes slowly, his gaze falling upon the terrified man before him. He sighed and shook his head. "This is not Vibhishana."

Raghav frowned, his pride wounded. "How can you be so sure, Guru Ji?"

A faint smile played on Shukracharya's lips.

"If this man were Vibhishana, you would not have captured him so easily, my overconfident disciple. Vibhishana is far more powerful and clever than you imagine."

Raghav's face flushed with anger and embarrassment. "But how could you know?" he pressed.

Shukracharya's expression grew stern. "You are becoming arrogant with your newfound strength, Raghav. Hear me well—Vibhishana is older than even Ashwatthama, older and far stronger. His wisdom surpasses yours by millennia."

Ashwatthama, standing nearby, spoke up. "Then why did you send us out to search?"

Shukracharya's smile returned, enigmatic and knowing.

"Because I wanted the word to spread," he explained.

"I knew that if two strangers were seen searching for Vibhishana, the news would spread through the land faster than any message I could send. And once Vibhishana hears of it, he will come to us."

The elder man, Sanga, looked up, bewildered but unharmed. Shukracharya turned to him, his voice calm but commanding. "Go now. Return to your people and tell them what you have seen."

Sanga nodded, his eyes wide with relief, and hurried away, disappearing into the dense foliage.

Raghav watched him go, his face still etched with frustration. "So, we wait?" he asked, his voice laced with impatience.

Shukracharya chuckled softly.

"Patience, Raghav. We have set the bait. Now, we wait for the fish to take it." His eyes gleamed with a cunning light.

Ashwatthama nodded, understanding at last.

Manas was utterly exhausted after spending so much time underwater. As soon as he lay down on the flat bank of the river, he fell asleep instantly.

In his dream, he found himself locked in a fierce battle with the unknown man who had dragged him down. The scene replayed over and over, but this time, something caught his attention—a beam of light emanating from the depths of the river, not too deep below the surface.

As he tried to make sense of it, he heard someone calling his name, "Manas, Manas!" Suddenly, he jolted awake, gasping for breath. It was Parashurama Ji.

"There's something down there," Manas said, breathing heavily. "I have a strong feeling... something useful."

Ananya tried to calm him, "Manas, you've been through a lot. Maybe it was just a dream."

But Manas shook his head, "No, it wasn't just a dream. It felt... real."

Parashurama Ji leaned in, "Tell me exactly what you saw."

Manas recounted, "I saw myself fighting that person, but something was different this time. I also saw a beam of light at the bottom of the river."

Ananya's eyes widened, "Maybe it was the Kundal."

Manas considered this, "Maybe, or maybe not."

After a moment of silence, Manas spoke again, "What other options do we have? Can't we go take a look?"

Parashurama Ji nodded thoughtfully, "Alright, we will go."

They all descended into the water once more. Parashurama Ji led the way, with Manas guiding them through the depths. As they reached the bottom, they spotted a statue of Lord Ganesh. But this was no ordinary idol—it was glowing, as if imbued with life itself.

They all bowed down to Lord Ganesha, seeking his blessings and guidance. They carefully lifted the statue and brought it back to the shore. Water dripped from their faces as they stared at the idol, scrutinizing every detail.

Ananya speculated, "Maybe it came here from a Ganpati Visharjan."

Manas shook his head, "No, look at the material. This isn't ordinary clay or metal. It's something else entirely."

They examined the idol closely. The statue of Lord Ganesh had a unique form—two hands, one open and the other clenched into a fist. His trunk was straight and pointed directly at the ground. The open hand appeared as though it had only recently unfurled, with faint marks and a slight discoloration indicating that it had been closed for eons. The fist, though still clenched, bore subtle signs—tiny cracks along the knuckles, a shift in color—that hinted it had once held something within.

Parashurama Ji's eyes narrowed as he observed these details.

"Look at his hand," he said, pointing to the open one.

"It seems like it just opened. The lines in the palm are fresh, and there's a faint imprint, almost as if the fist was closed around something... something that radiated heat."

Manas examined it closely and said,

"This fist that just opened—it seems like it was holding the Kundal. The palm is more red than the rest of the statue, as if it had absorbed the heat from the Kundal over centuries."

Parashurama Ji said, "Ananya, you were looking for a sign, and I believe we've found one."

Manas, still studying the statue, spoke with resolve, "If the first fist has opened, revealing the Kundal, then maybe we need to open the second fist. It might hold the next clue."

With that, they all looked at the still-clenched fist of the idol, wondering what secrets it held within.

They attempted to open the fist of the statue, but it remained closed, as if bound by some divine force.

Manas pondered, "Is this also bound to some mantras?"

Ananya replied, "There's no harm in trying. Let's see if the right mantra might unlock it."

They began chanting:

वक्रतुण्ड महाकाय सूर्यकोटि समप्रभः।

निर्विघ्नं कुरु मे देव सर्वकार्येषु सर्वदा।।

But nothing happened.

सुमुखश्चैकदन्तश्च कपिलो गजकर्णकः।

लम्बोदरश्च विकटो विघ्ननाशो गणाधिपः।।

Again, nothing happened.

गजाननं भूतगणादिसेवितं कपित्थजम्बूफलचारुभक्षणम्।

उमासुतं शोकविनाशकारकं नमामि विघ्नेश्वरपादपङ्कजम्।।

Still, there was no response from the statue.

Parashurama Ji, observing the statue with intense focus, said, "We need to pay closer attention to the details."

Manas, almost in a trance, murmured, "Ganesha Ji, sitting on his vāhana, with one hand open and the other in a fist..."

Ananya suddenly suggested, "Parashurama Ji, perhaps you could try using your axe."

Parashurama Ji hesitated, "I can try, but I must be gentle. I cannot risk damaging the statue." He carefully placed his divine axe against the fist and applied a slight force. But still, nothing happened.

Just as they were about to lose hope, Manas noticed something. "Guru Ji, look!"

The trunk of Lord Ganesha, which was pointing downward, seemed out of place. Manas, with a sudden insight, said, "Isn't Ganpati Ji's trunk usually facing upwards?"

Parashurama Ji, thoughtful, replied, "Yes, it usually faces upward, symbolizing the rise of consciousness and success. When Ganesha's trunk is raised, it signifies a blessing."

Manas, filled with reverence, approached the statue. He folded his hands in respect and slowly began to move the trunk upwards. As he did, a soft, squeaky sound filled the air. When the trunk was fully raised, they all watched in awe as the tightly closed fist began to open slowly, as if responding to some long-forgotten command.

As the fist opened fully, they saw, inscribed within, a single word glowing with divine light:

"राम"(Raam).

The word glowed softly in the palm of Lord Ganesha's statue. Everyone stood in silence. The air around them seemed to hum with the power of that sacred name.

Parashurama Ji, breaking the silence, folded his hands and chanted with deep reverence,

"*Jai Shree Ram.*" Manas and Ananya, caught in the moment, echoed,

"*Jai Shree Ram.*"

Manas, his mind racing, said, "It seems like the third clue is linked to Prabhu Shree Ram."

Parashurama Ji nodded thoughtfully, "And what could be more closely linked to Lord Ram during this age than..."

Manas, his eyes widening with realization, exclaimed, "Bajrang Bali, Lord Hanuman!"

Ananya, her voice steady but filled with conviction, said, "Exactly. Bajrang Bali, the eternal devotee of Lord Ram. The connection is undeniable."

Parashurama Ji said, "Lord Hanuman's devotion to Lord Ram is legendary. Perhaps He holds the final piece of this puzzle."

Manas, with renewed determination, said, "Then our path is clear. We must seek out Lord Hanuman's presence. He will guide us to the next clue, and perhaps, the Kavach itself."

Parashurama Ji agreed, "Yes, but remember, Hanuman Ji appears to those who are true in heart and spirit. We must approach this with humility and faith."

Manas asked hesitantly, "But… is there a way to find him, Guru Ji? He is Chiranjivi, just like you. How do we even begin to look for him?"

Parashurama Ji nodded, acknowledging the challenge ahead. "Yes, Manas, but there is a way, but before that, let me take you back to where it all began."

After the great war of the Ramayana ended and Prabhu Shree Ram ascended to Vaikunth Lok, Lord Hanuman found himself wandering the vast lands of Earth. His heart was filled with the duty to continue spreading righteousness across the mortal realm. His journeys took him to many places, but one day, his path led him south.

Hanuman Ji wandered through the thick jungles of Lanka, a place that still echoed with the memories of the great battle fought there. As he moved deeper into the forest, he came upon a small, secluded village, hidden among towering trees and winding rivers. The locals there, a tribe, immediately recognized the divine presence of the mighty Vanara. Their hearts swelled with reverence, for the tales of Hanuman's valor and devotion to Lord Ram were well known even in these remote lands.

They were, humble and devoted, welcomed Hanuman Ji with open arms, becoming his eager hosts. They treated him with the utmost hospitality, offering him fruits and water, and singing songs of his great deeds. Their humility and deep respect for dharma touched Hanuman Ji's heart.

Moved by their sincerity and devotion, Hanuman Ji decided to impart to them the sacred knowledge of Aatm Gyan—the highest spiritual wisdom that leads to the realization of the Supreme Self. For days, he taught them about the nature of the soul, the essence of truth, and the path to moksha. His voice, filled with divine authority and love, resounded through the jungle, reaching every corner of the village. The people listened with rapt attention, absorbing every word with devotion.

After the teachings were complete, the eldest of the tribe, a wise and gentle man, approached Hanuman Ji with folded hands.

"Prabhu," he said with a tone of deep respect, "You have blessed us with the Aatm Gyan, but what about our future generations? How will they receive this sacred opportunity to learn from you?"

Hanuman Ji smiled and replied, "I promise to visit this place every 41 years. I shall return to your tribe and share the sacred knowledge with all who are willing to learn."

The elder voiced another concern. "Prabhu, what if something unforeseen happens, and we need your guidance or help before those 41 years pass?

How will we call upon you?"

Hanuman Ji, understanding the depth of their devotion, decided to grant them a special boon.

"I will give you a mantra," he said, "a sacred chant that will invoke my presence whenever you are in need. Recite this mantra with a pure heart, and I will come to you with all my speed." And with that, he shared the mantra with them:

"कालतंतु कारेचरन्ति

एनर मरिष्णु,

निर्मुक्तेर कालेत्वम

अमरिष्णु."

The tribe listened intently, their faces lit with a mixture of awe and gratitude. But the elder, always cautious, voiced another concern.

"Prabhu," he asked, "What if this mantra falls into the wrong hands, into the hands of evil people? Would they not misuse it to summon you?"

Hanuman Ji, with a reassuring smile, replied, "Do not worry. This mantra will work only under two conditions."

He continued, "Firstly, the person reciting this mantra must have a pure heart, filled with goodness and free from malice. They must have attained Aatm Gyan, the highest knowledge of the self. Only then will the mantra bear fruit."

The tribe listened with keen interest as Hanuman Ji went on,

"Secondly, if there is anyone within a 900-meter radius who does not fulfill the first condition—who harbors ill intentions or lacks purity—the mantra will lose its power. Even if the one reciting the mantra is virtuous, my presence will not be summoned if those around them are not."

Hearing this, the elder and the tribe felt a wave of relief.

"This is a great idea, Prabhu," the elder said, his voice filled with gratitude. "We are forever indebted to you for your blessings."

Hanuman Ji blessed them with a radiant smile and spoke one final word, "May the Mahatang Tribe stay forever blessed." With a mighty leap, he soared into the sky, flying towards the Himalayas, leaving the Mahatang tribe with a sense of divine security and a promise that their protector would always be near.

Manas continued reciting the mantras, almost as if they had become a rhythm in his mind, a way to focus on the task ahead.

Ananya, noticing his concentration, chuckled softly and said, "Manas, didn't you hear the two conditions that Guru Ji mentioned?"

Manas stopped momentarily and laughed. "Haha, of course, I heard them. I was just repeating the mantra. But I have to admit, the two conditions set by Bajrang Bali are ironclad."

Parashurama Ji nodded, acknowledging the weight of Manas's words. "Yes, those conditions are indeed formidable," he said. "Even with all the Aatm Gyan I possess, I am bound by those conditions as well. The power cannot be wielded by just anyone."

Manas, always eager to find a solution, thought aloud, "But if we can reach Lanka and find the Mahatang Tribe, perhaps they can guide us."

Ananya agreed, her eyes lighting up with the possibility. "That's a good plan, Guru Ji. The Mahatang Tribe has a history deeply connected with Hanuman Ji."

Parashurama Ji stroked his beard thoughtfully. "Yes, finding the Mahatang Tribe could be our best chance. However, traveling to Lanka will not be an easy journey. It will take time, and we must be prepared for whatever lies ahead."

Manas furrowed his brow, thinking of the long journey. "Time… Yes, the journey will take time, and we cannot afford delays. But if this is the only way, then we must proceed. We need to find a way to expedite our travel."

Finally, Parashurama Ji broke the silence. "We'll start our journey to Lanka, but not before ensuring we're fully prepared. This is not just a physical journey; it's a spiritual one. The Mahatang Tribe holds the key, but we must unlock it with wisdom, faith, and determination."

Manas decided to gather information from the locals. Ananya, eager to help, joined him in the search. They split up to cover more ground, each hoping to find a faster way to reach Lanka. After a while, Ananya returned with some promising news.

"Guru Ji, I didn't find anything," she said, her voice filled with frustration. "All I've figured out is that to reach Sri Lanka, we'll need to take a flight. Manas can arrange the tickets—he's wealthy enough to handle that."

Parashurama nodded thoughtfully, then added, "I must travel in disguise." With that, he began chanting, his voice steady and firm:

"अस्त्रं मम गूढं भवतु अदृश्यं, लयमेति पवनोपमं।"

("Let my weapon be hidden, unseen, fading like the wind.")

As the mantra left his lips, his mighty axe shimmered for a moment and then vanished into thin air.

"Before we start our journey," Parashurama Ji said, "we must return this statue to its rightful place. It has served its purpose here."

CHAPTER 24

There was no sign of Vibhishana, and frustration began to creep into the camp. Shukracharya, seated in meditation, finally opened his eyes, the glint of determination hardening in his gaze.

"Raghav, Ashwatthama," he called, "it's time to change our approach. Start terrorizing them. But listen carefully—only target the forest dwellers. The modern people will spread news too quickly, bringing us unwanted attention. Vibhishana holds no sentiment for them. The key lies with those who are closest to the land, who still remember the old ways."

With swift nods, Raghav and Ashwatthama set off, their expressions grim with intent. The next few days were filled with the echoes of fear in the deep woods. The forest dwellers whispered of strange shadows moving through the trees, of unseen terrors lurking just out of sight. Children cried, and elders prayed, but still, there was no sign of Vibhishana.

After days of effort, Shukracharya called them back. "Expand your terror," he commanded, his voice cold as steel. "Drive them out of their hiding places."

Another day passed, and they returned, faces etched with frustration but carrying news.

"Tell me in detail," Shukracharya demanded.

Ashwatthama spoke first.

"I found a group of children in the woods. I tried to scare them, but… they weren't afraid. I asked where they were from, and they said they belong to a small local tribe"

Shukracharya's eyes narrowed, but he remained silent, listening as Raghav began to speak.

"I encountered a few elderly men. I injured them, but it was strange… they didn't show fear, not even a hint of it. They were from a local tribe. But something else—" Raghav paused, his brow furrowing. "There was one man, I hurt him badly yesterday. His hand was bleeding; it looked broken. Today, I saw him again, and he was perfectly fine, as if nothing had happened. He showed no sign of injury, no pain, no fear."

Ashwatthama interjected, "Perhaps they have access to the Sanjeevani Booti, scattered around these parts. That might explain the sudden healing."

Shukracharya's face darkened, and a slow smile crept across his lips.

"Or… perhaps that man was Vibhishana himself."

The words hung in the air like a curse. Ashwatthama and Raghav exchanged a glance, suddenly seeing the possibility.

"Tell me where this tribe is," Shukracharya demanded.

Ashwatthama replied, "We haven't seen the tribe itself, only a few scattered people."

Shukracharya's eyes gleamed with renewed focus. "Then let's find this tribe. And if Vibhishana is hiding among them, we will flush him out."

He rose, his dark robes flowing around him like shadows. "These forest dwellers… They are not ordinary. If they are not afraid, it is because they have the protection of someone powerful. But no one can hide from me for long."

With a commanding wave of his hand, he signaled them to spread out.

"Lets' comb the forest, every inch of it. Speak to every villager, every child, every elder. Find this tribe. And when you do, we shall confront Vibhishana himself."

The three of them roamed the dense, shadowy forest for hours, their frustration mounting with each step. The jungle seemed to conspire against them, twisting its paths and masking its secrets. Leaves rustled underfoot, and the canopy above blotted out the sun, casting strange, shifting shadows around them. Ashwatthama, his senses sharp, suddenly halted, his eyes narrowing as he caught sight of a familiar figure in the distance.

"There!" Ashwatthama pointed. "That old man…Sanga. He's the one I injured yesterday. How is he walking without any sign of pain?"

Shukracharya's eyes gleamed with interest. "Bring him to me."

Ashwatthama moved with the stealth of a predator, closing the distance quickly. The old man tried to back away, but Ashwatthama's hand was swift, his grip unyielding. He dragged the man back to where Shukracharya waited, a grin on his lips.

"Where is your home, old man? Take us there," Shukracharya demanded.

The elderly man, his face lined with age but his eyes bright with defiance, shook his head.

"No outsider is allowed. None can enter—not even the sunlight touches our sacred grounds."

Shukracharya smirked. "Leave that to me. Take him and return to our location," he instructed, gesturing for Raghav and Ashwatthama to move.

Raghav frowned, sensing something more. "What will you do, Guru Ji?"

"My old trick," Shukracharya replied with a dark smile. "I will hypnotize him. No one can resist my will."

As they led the old man away, a sudden rustling noise broke through the silence. Ashwatthama's head whipped around, his eyes scanning the trees. He moved silently toward the sound, slipping through the shadows like a panther stalking its prey. His gaze fell on a group of young boys perched on a branch—Selva, the child who had confronted him before.

"Ah, you," Ashwatthama sneered, "Selva, was it? You said you were not afraid of me. Let's see if that's still true."

He reached up, grabbing the boy by his ankle and pulling him down with a swift yank. The boy kicked and flailed, but Ashwatthama's grip was like iron. He lifted Selva effortlessly, slinging him over his shoulder despite the child's struggles, and carried him back to the small temple where they had been staying. The rest of the kid ran.

Inside the dimly lit temple, Shukracharya sat cross-legged, his eyes closed in concentration. He gestured for Ashwatthama to place the old man and the boy before him.

"Sit," Shukracharya commanded. The old man sat calmly, but Selva was defiant, his young face twisted in a mix of fear and fury.

Shukracharya leaned closer, his voice a low hiss, "Let me into your mind, old man. Show me the way."

He began to chant softly, his words laced with hypnotic power. The air grew colder, and the temple seemed to darken. The old man's eyes fluttered, but his expression remained resolute. Shukracharya's brow furrowed as he felt a resistance—a barrier, like a wall of iron around the man's thoughts.

"What is this?" Shukracharya muttered, pushing harder, his eyes narrowing. He felt the mental block, a strange strength he hadn't anticipated.

"You have attained Aatm Gyan," he realized.

Sanga smiled, his voice calm. "Yes. You will find no entrance into my mind."

Shukracharya's frustration was evident, but he quickly masked it with a mocking laugh. "Perhaps. But the boy…"

He turned his gaze to Selva, who looked between the two men with wide eyes. The old man's face paled.

"No," Sanga, the old man, pleaded. "Please, don't hurt him. He is just a child."

"Then take me to your tribe," Shukracharya demanded, his voice sharp as a knife. "Or the boy will suffer."

Sanga hesitated, his hands trembling. "I… I will take you, but you must promise—"

"What am I looking for?" Shukracharya interrupted, his patience thin. "I'm not interested in your tribe, old man. I seek one person."

"Who?" Sanga asked, his voice a whisper.

"Vibhishana," Shukracharya replied, his eyes gleaming with determination.

Sanga's face tightened, a mixture of fear and resignation. "There is no Vibhishana in our tribe," he repeated, but his voice lacked conviction.

Shukracharya's eyes narrowed, sensing the hesitation. "Your tribe… there is something mystical about it. Don't deny it."

Sanga tried to steady his breathing. "There is nothing specific," he lied, "just that our tribe remains hidden from the world."

Ashwatthama, his patience waning, leaned in closer. "Then explain how you heal so quickly," he demanded, his voice like a growl.

Sanga's eyes flickered, betraying a sliver of the truth. "Our tribe is powered by energy," he replied cautiously. "A mystical energy. No one knows how old it is… some say it's more than a Yuga old."

"A Yuga old?" Raghav's eyebrows shot up. "Are you saying your tribe has existed for more than a Yuga?"

"Yes," Sanga admitted, his voice softening, "and Lord Hanuman is the one who gave us the Aatm Gyan."

"Hanuman?" Shukracharya's curiosity was piqued. "What is the name of your tribe?"

Sanga hesitated again, glancing nervously at the child in Ashwatthama's grip. Sensing the elder's reluctance, Shukracharya nodded at Ashwatthama, who tightened his hold around the boy's neck.

"Stop, please… Our tribe is called Mahatang," Sanga whispered, his face etched with worry.

Shukracharya's eyes widened, the recognition lighting up his face.

Raghav caught the change in Shukracharya's expression. "What's so special about this tribe?" he asked.

Shukracharya's voice was thoughtful, almost reverent. "As this man said, Hanuman has blessed them."

"That's why they kept chanting Jai Bajrang Bali," Raghav noted. Ashwatthama's curiosity flared. "But there's something else. What is this energy that you speak of?"

Shukracharya's tone was firm. "Tell me about this energy," he demanded.

Sanga hesitated, casting a glance at the child. "The energy… we have it because…" he faltered, fear creeping into his voice.

"Continue, or else the boy dies," Shukracharya warned, his patience fraying. Ashwatthama's grip around the child's neck tightened further, the boy's face reddening.

Sanga's resistance crumbled. "Alright, I'll tell you. Our ancestors say that many thousands of years ago, Lord Hanuman promised us to come every 41 years to visit us, but once, around 5,000 years ago, he came early… and he gifted us with armor. An armor that gives us constant energy, that keeps our tribe strong."

Shukracharya's eyes glinted with realization. He turned to Raghav. "Remove your hood."

Raghav pulled back his hood, revealing the glowing Kundal, which shimmered like molten gold against his skin. Its radiant light illuminated the dark corners of the small temple.

Shukracharya pointed at Raghav. "Is the energy you speak of… something like that?"

Sanga's eyes widened in shock, his mouth falling open. "Yes… it is! It is exactly like that! How did it come to you?"

Shukracharya's sinister smile deepened. They had come searching for Vibhishana, but had stumbled upon something far more valuable—the Kavach itself. Fortune, it seemed, was on their side.

"Now," Shukracharya's voice dripped with confidence, "take us to your tribe."

Sanga shook his head, panic setting in. "Even if you reach us, you won't be able to claim it. The Kavach is protected by powerful mantras. No one can touch it."

Raghav, feeling the pulsating strength of the Kundal coursing through his veins, stepped forward. "Leave that to me," he said with a grin, his voice brimming with newfound confidence. "If there are any barriers, I'll break through them."

Shukracharya nodded, his face alight with malicious intent. "Lead the way, Sanga," he ordered, knowing they were on the verge of seizing a prize beyond their wildest dreams.

CHAPTER 25

Children ran through the dense foliage, their screams were echoing through the jungle. The smallest among them, eyes wide with fear, darted through the thick underbrush, not looking where he was going. He collided head-on with a towering figure, stumbling backward.

"Get up, be careful," Ananya said, stepping forward and helping the child to his feet.

Parashurama Ji, sensing something was off, bent down to meet the child's gaze. "Why are you running, little one?" he asked, his voice gentle but probing.

The child hesitated, glancing back over his shoulder. "We... we are just playing," he stammered, trying to hide his fear.

Manas, noticing a trickle of blood on the child's foot, knelt beside him. "You're hurt," he said softly. "Don't worry, we can help you." He tore a strip from his cloth and quickly bandaged the wound.

Parashurama Ji leaned closer, his expression warm. "Trust us," he coaxed, his eyes scanning the boy's face for any sign of deception.

The child looked around nervously before whispering, "There were three of them... they're looking for our tribe. They want to invade our home."

Manas exchanged a quick glance with Parashurama Ji. "Three of them?" he repeated.

"That means Shukracharya is here. But how did they find out?" His brow furrowed. "We were the ones who discovered the clue… how do they know?"

The child, overhearing, spoke up, "They were looking for someone named Vibhishana."

Parashurama Ji's eyes narrowed thoughtfully. "Ah… clever Shukracharya. He's picked the right person to ask about the Kavach," he murmured.

"Kavach? What is that?" the child asked, his face scrunched in confusion.

"Kavach is something we are looking for. It glows like gold," replied Manas, hoping to make the child understand.

The child's eyes widened with understanding. "Oh, you mean the energy! In our tribe, we call it 'The Energy' or 'The Shakti.'"

Parashurama Ji's eyes widened. He glanced at Manas and Ananya, realizing the significance. "The third piece... the Kavach itself," he whispered, almost in awe.

"Which tribe are you from?" Parashurama Ji asked quickly.

"Mahatang," the child replied.

Parashurama Ji looked up at the sky, then back at his companions.

"The gods are on our side," he said, a spark of hope igniting in his eyes. "Jai Shree Raam!"

The child's face brightened at the sound of the chant, his fear replaced with a newfound trust. "Jai Shree Raam!" he echoed, smiling.

"Will you take us to your tribe, little one?" Parashurama Ji asked gently.

The child nodded, his resolve strengthened by the familiar cry of devotion. "Follow me," he said, turning and leading the way deeper into the jungle.

Raghav paused, his steps slowing as a strange sensation washed over him.

"I feel… something different," he murmured, his brow furrowed in concentration.

Shukracharya turned to him, a keen glint in his eyes.

"What happened, Raghav?" he asked, sensing the shift in the young warrior's demeanor.

"It's like… something is calling me," Raghav replied, his voice almost distant, as though he were hearing a whisper carried in the wind. "The deeper we move into the jungle, the stronger it feels."

Shukracharya's eyes narrowed thoughtfully. "Ah, it must be the Kavach," he said, nodding slowly. "The energy within it is resonating with your Kundal. They share a bond, a force that pulls them together."

Raghav's face grew more serious. "But there's more, Guru Ji… I feel like something is chasing us."

Shukracharya closed his eyes. His breathing slowed, and a faint aura began to shimmer around him, as if he was tapping into a source of ancient knowledge. Silence enveloped the group, each of them watching with bated breath, waiting for Shukracharya to speak, to reveal what his mystical senses had uncovered.

Shukracharya's expression darkened. "You're right," he said, his voice low. "I sense it too—a powerful presence. I think Parashurama Ji has arrived."

Raghav glanced sharply at Shukracharya.

"How do you know?" he asked, his eyes scanning the dense foliage around them.

Shukracharya gave a faint smile. "Parashurama radiates a strong, positive energy—one that stands out even in this jungle."

Shukracharya continued, "We need to be prepared for anything. If Parashurama is here, it means he knows about the Kavach too. We must not underestimate him." Ashwatthama adjusted his stance, his hand resting on his weapon. "What's the plan, Guru Ji?" he asked, his eyes never leaving the surrounding trees.

Shukracharya's gaze sharpened. "We wait," he said again, "but not for long. We must hurry, and if they strike, then we strike back harder."

Ashwatthama turned to Raghav. "Hide, they still don't know about you."

Shukracharya, however, countered, "No. He is our secret weapon, yes, but also our strongest warrior. With the might of Duryodhana and the combined power of the two Kundals, Raghav is more formidable than we realize. Raghav, move ahead and secure the Kavach. Ashwatthama and I will hold them off."

They pushed forward until they arrived at a seeming dead end — a sheer rock face blocking their path.

Raghav frowned. "Guru Ji, this man fooled us. There's nothing here."

Shukracharya's eyes narrowed, a dangerous gleam flashing within them. "You are a fool to doubt," he said coldly, before signaling Ashwatthama to finish the job and eliminate the kid…Selva.

Just then, Sanga, sensing his imminent demise, shouted, "Wait! There is a reason no one could ever find our tribe. It is hidden… in plain sight."

He moved forward, placing himself directly in front of the mountain wall. There, he stood still, hands raised, and began to chant softly, words reverberating through the cave like a deep hum:

ॐ ऐं भीम हनुमते, श्री राम दूताय नमः।

As the mantra echoed in the cavern, the rock shifted, sliding away to reveal a hidden hallway carved into the mountain itself. A passageway opened up before them, leading into the unknown depths of the mountain.

Everyone stood stunned at the sight of this hidden entrance, the way into the secret world of the tribe. As they stepped inside, the narrow hallway quickly gave way to a vast, cavernous space. Raghav's eyes widened.

"This... this can't be a mountain."

Sanga turned to him, a faint smile on his lips. "It is a mountain… but a hollow one. And within it lies our tribe."

Raghav's curiosity sharpened. "Sanga, this energy you keep talking about… where is it?"

Sanga gestured upward. "Look at your shadows, can you see that?" he said.

They all glanced at their feet, confused. "Yes," Ashwatthama muttered. "What kind of question is that?"

Sanga's smile broadened. "If we are inside a mountain, then how are shadows being cast?"

Realization dawned on them all. Shukracharya, Ashwatthama, and Raghav looked up, and there it was — suspended high in the air, glowing with an otherworldly brilliance: the Kavach. It hung as if in defiance of gravity, radiating light in every direction, casting their shadows below.

"So, when you said no sunlight enters your tribe, you meant it literally," Ashwatthama murmured.

Sanga nodded. "Yes," he replied, his smile never wavering.

Shukracharya's voice turned cold and threatening. "Why are you smiling, old man? Do you not fear us? Do you think we cannot take this energy of yours?"

Sanga met his gaze evenly. "Fear? No," he said softly. "The Kavach is protected by powerful mantras — mantras bestowed by Lord Hanuman himself. You can harm us, but that energy will not be yours."

Shukracharya's eyes glinted with malice. "Leave that to us," he sneered.

With a swift motion, he closed his eyes and began to chant a mantra, his words flowing in a dark, guttural cadence. He dipped his fingers into the *kamandal*, pulling out water that shimmered with an eerie light. With a forceful flick of his wrist, he hurled the water at the Kavach. The water formed a ball of light as it flew through the air, propelled not by strength but by the sheer force of the incantation itself.

As the ball of light approached the Kavach, it collided with an invisible barrier. The protective layer surrounding the Kavach shimmered momentarily before repelling the attack with twice the power. The energy blasted back toward Shukracharya, striking him in the chest and sending him stumbling back, his robes singed by the power of his own spell.

Sanga's laughter rang out again, echoing off the cavern walls. "Do you think you can break the protective shield placed by Lord Hanuman himself?" he taunted.

Shukracharya's expression darkened with anger and determination. "Raghav!" he barked. "Go up and see if you can reach it. Use the Kundals to counteract the protective barrier!"

Raghav nodded and began to climb, his fingers finding grips in the rock face as he ascended. The glow of the Kundals on him intensified, their energy resonating with the Kavach above.

The commotion from Shukracharya's failed attempt had drawn more of the tribe members to the cavern. Seeing the growing crowd, Shukracharya knew he needed to act swiftly. "Ashwatthama," he ordered, his voice like a whip crack, "bring havoc."

Ashwatthama, with a roar, charged into the crowd. His massive frame plowed through the tribe members like a force of nature, sending them flying with every blow. His fists swung like hammers, smashing anyone who came too close. The ground trembled beneath his feet as he rampaged, his shouts filling the cavern with a terrifying echo.

"You will remember this day," Ashwatthama shouted, "the day Mahawatthsa brought havoc upon you!" He moved with a deadly grace, his every motion designed to inflict maximum damage.

But then, a powerful voice cut through the chaos like a blade. "Ashwatthama!" It was Manas, his voice filled with fury and resolve. He sprinted forward, eyes locked onto Ashwatthama, his expression fierce. Beside him, Ananya moved with equal determination, her eyes burning with a warrior's focus.

The two forces collided, and a new battle erupted amidst the madness. Meanwhile, the children who had been with Parashurama moments before rushed back to their parents. At the cave's entrance, Parashurama stood tall, his silhouette framed by the dim light. His hand gripped the handle of his axe, and he raised it high, ready for the confrontation ahead.

His gaze was locked onto Shukracharya.

"Shukracharya," he murmured, his voice carrying across the cavern, "today, this ends."

Ashwatthama's eyes locked onto Manas and Ananya, a fierce grin spreading across his face. His muscles rippled beneath his skin like coiled serpents, his body charged with primal energy. He lunged forward with a roar that reverberated through the cavern, his fist swinging like a sledgehammer aimed straight at Manas' head.

Manas ducked just in time, feeling the rush of wind as Ashwatthama's blow passed mere inches from his skull. The force of the strike smashed into the rock wall behind him, shattering it into fragments. Manas rolled to the side and sprang to his feet, his eyes never leaving his opponent. Ananya moved with him, their years of training allowing them to anticipate each other's moves without a word.

Ashwatthama pivoted quickly, his footwork surprisingly light for someone of his massive size. He charged again, this time feinting to his left before swinging his right leg in a powerful roundhouse kick. Manas leaped back, but Ashwatthama anticipated his movement, closing the gap with a swift jab aimed at Manas' ribs.

The blow connected, and Manas staggered back, pain shooting through his side. But Ananya was already there, striking at Ashwatthama exposed back with a series of rapid kicks. Ashwatthama grunted, feeling the sting of each hit, but he swung his arm back, catching Ananya by the shoulder and tossing her away like a rag doll.

Ananya twisted in midair, landing gracefully on her feet. She regrouped with Manas, nodding slightly—acknowledging the challenge before them. They had faced him before, but this time he was a different beast. He was relentless, his movements charged with the fury of centuries of warfare.

Manas charged forward again, his fists raised, feigning a right hook before spinning into a left uppercut aimed at Ashwatthama's jaw. Ashwatthama parried the blow, but Ananya was already moving in, her hand chopping down at his shoulder. He blocked it effortlessly, his eyes flashing with irritation, and retaliated with a swift backhanded slap that sent Ananya sprawling to the ground.

"You're both children compared to me!" Ashwatthama roared, his voice booming in the confined space. He brought his fists down like twin hammers, but Manas and Ananya dodged in unison, their movements fluid and synchronized. They darted around him, launching coordinated strikes at his legs, his ribs, his face—each hit designed to wear him down.

For a moment, Ashwatthama seemed to falter under the combined assault, his defenses weakening. Manas saw his chance. He leaped into the air, spinning into a powerful kick aimed at Ashwatthama's temple. But Ashwatthama, with reflexes honed over thousands of battles, caught Manas's ankle in mid-air and flung him across the cave. Manas crashed into the cavern wall, stones crumbling around him as he slumped to the ground, dazed.

Ananya seized the moment, leaping onto Ashwatthama's back, her arms snaking around his neck in a chokehold. Ashwatthama staggered backward, reaching up to grab her, but she held on tight, squeezing with all her strength. He thrashed wildly, slamming her into the walls, trying to break her grip. Manas, shaking off the dizziness, sprang to his feet and lunged forward again, fists flying in a rapid barrage.

Ashwatthama roared, breaking free from Ananya's grip with a mighty shrug. He swung his arm, catching Manas squarely in the chest with a blow that sent him skidding back across the floor. Blood trickled from the corner of Manas' mouth, but his eyes remained fierce and determined.

Ashwatthama, breathing heavily, paused to catch his breath. "I was born for war," he spat, "while you two are merely players in a game you cannot comprehend."

Manas wiped the blood from his lip, his resolve unwavering. "We may be outmatched in strength," he panted, "but we fight for something greater than ourselves. You fight for nothing but your own vengeance."

Ananya, back on her feet, nodded in agreement, her gaze locked onto Ashwatthama. "And that makes all the difference."

Ashwatthama snarled and charged again, his fists swinging with renewed fury, and the battle raged on.

Parashurama and Shukracharya stood apart, their eyes locked in a silent exchange of power and intent. The air between them crackled with unseen energy, as if the very atmosphere had become charged with the electricity of their ancient conflict.

Shukracharya raised his hands, his fingers weaving intricate patterns in the air as he began to chant a powerful mantra. His voice was deep and resonant, filled with dark authority:

"ॐ नमो भगवते रुद्राय। अग्निसंयोगे शत्रुविनाशिनी स्फुरः।"

As the words left his lips, a surge of fiery energy erupted from his palms, spiraling toward Parashurama like a coiled serpent made of flame.

Parashurama stood firm, his eyes narrowing as he prepared his counter. He raised his axe, his voice calm but commanding, resonating with the authority of a true warrior:

"ॐ भूर्भुवः स्वः। त्रिनेत्राय महादेवाय नमः।"

The air around him shimmered, and a translucent shield formed, deflecting Shukracharya's fiery attack. The flames dissipated against the barrier, leaving nothing but a faint smell of smoke in the air.

Shukracharya's lips curled into a sneer. "You've grown weaker, Parashurama," he taunted, "The years have dulled your edge."

Parashurama's eyes blazed with determination. "Age has not dimmed my strength, Shukracharya. You forget, I have been chosen by Lord Shiva himself!"

With a swift movement, Parashurama twirled his axe, summoning a gale of wind that whipped around the cave, the very air turning into a weapon in his hands. The gusts funneled into a single point and burst toward Shukracharya with the force of a raging storm.

But Shukracharya was ready. He uttered another incantation, his hands glowing with a dark blue light:

"ॐ कालिकायै नमः।"

The darkness from his hands spread outward, swallowing the wind, and for a moment, the entire cave seemed to darken as if night had descended. The winds ceased, absorbed by the inky blackness that now filled the space between them.

Parashurama's jaw tightened. He could feel the weight of Shukracharya's spells pressing against him. He closed his eyes briefly and began to chant.

With each syllable, the ground beneath his feet began to pulse, the rocks vibrating with ancient energy. The dark shroud surrounding Shukracharya wavered and then shattered, light bursting through it like the rays of the sun piercing a storm cloud.

Shukracharya staggered back, momentarily stunned by the force of Parashurama's counter. But his lips twisted into a grin. "You still have your strength, Parashurama, but I have grown wiser. And today, wisdom will triumph over strength!"

He drew a small vial from his robes and smashed it against the ground. A thick mist erupted, covering the cave floor, tendrils of smoke curling upward like the fingers of a hungry spirit.

Parashurama could feel the mist clawing at his consciousness, attempting to dull his senses. He knew he had to act quickly. Summoning his inner strength, he thrust his axe into the ground with a mighty cry, channeling his divine energy through the weapon.

The cave walls vibrated with the power of his words, and a surge of divine light blasted from his axe, cutting through the mist, dispelling it like a sunbeam piercing morning fog.

The air was thick with tension as Manas and Ananya watched Ashwatthama stumble back, clutching his shoulder, blood seeping through his fingers. They had managed to wound the great warrior, but they knew it wouldn't be long before he regained his strength. Ashwatthama snarled, his eyes wild with fury, and lunged toward them once more, swinging his fists with brute force.

Manas dodged to the side, narrowly avoiding a punch that could have shattered his jaw. Ananya, quick on her feet, moved in with a swift kick to Ashwatthama's side, sending him reeling backward. For a moment, it seemed they had the upper hand again. Ashwatthama staggered, disoriented, his movements slowing as blood flowed freely from the cut.

Sanga, who had been observing the battle closely, raised his hand and pointed upwards. "Look up!" he shouted to Parashuraam Ji, his voice strained with urgency.

Parashuraam Ji, his senses always alert, immediately shifted his gaze. Manas and Ananya followed his line of sight, their eyes narrowing as they tried to pierce through the blinding light that surrounded the Kavach. The glow was too intense, its golden brilliance almost unbearable, like a sun radiating within the cavern. They shielded their eyes with their hands, squinting against the dazzling light.

Without a moment's hesitation, Parashuraam Ji hurled his mighty axe. It cut through the air like a blazing streak, its divine edge sharp and true. But the target wasn't easy to hit. The axe missed its mark, narrowly avoiding the heart of the figure clinging to the wall, but it did not miss entirely. The blade sliced through the man's leg, leaving a deep gash. He let out a grunt of pain and lost his grip, tumbling from the height.

The man crashed to the ground with a heavy thud, his body limp, and for a moment, he seemed completely lifeless. The glow from the Kavach flickered slightly, then returned to its full brilliance. Manas and Ananya rushed forward cautiously, their hearts pounding in their chests.

Manas reached the fallen figure first, his breaths quick and shallow. The man lay face down, his long hair tangled, and the angle of his fall had hidden his face. Manas bent down, his hands trembling slightly, and moved to turn the man over. His eyes caught a glimpse of something familiar—earrings, gleaming in the dim light. The Kundals. They were unmistakable, glowing with a soft, otherworldly light.

"Could it be…?" Manas muttered to himself, his mind racing.

He leaned closer, reaching for the Kundal. But as soon as his fingers touched the kundal, the figure beneath him sprang to life. In a blur of motion, the man's hand shot up, grabbing Manas' wrist with an iron grip. The pressure was immediate and excruciating. Manas gasped in pain, and before he could react, the man twisted his wrist violently. A sickening crack filled the air.

Ananya, standing just a few steps away, froze as she heard the sound. Her eyes widened in horror, recognizing that awful sound— the sound of bones snapping under immense pressure. "Manas!" she screamed, rushing forward.

But it was too late. The man who had been lying motionless a second ago was now fully alert, his face illuminated by the dim light. It was Raghav. Alive. His eyes were filled with a cold, calculating intensity that sent chills down Ananya's spine. He looked nothing like the friend Manas once knew.

Manas's scream caught in his throat as he stared into Raghav's eyes. "Raghav… how?" His voice was strained, filled with pain and confusion.

Raghav's lips curled into a mocking smile. "Surprised?" he sneered, his voice a low, menacing growl. "Yes, I was dead, but I have been revived," he said. Manas looked bewildered. Observing this, Parashurama Ji turned to Shukracharya and remarked, "You have misused your knowledge of the *Mrit Sanjeevni*."

Before Manas could muster a response, Raghav tightened his grip, twisting Manas' wrist even further, making him cry out in agony. Ananya, her instincts kicking in, ran toward them, desperate to free Manas from Raghav's grip. But Raghav, moving with a speed and strength they had never seen before, lifted Manas effortlessly and swung him like a rag doll, hurling him through the air toward Ananya.

The impact was brutal. Manas crashed into Ananya, and they both fell to the ground, rolling over in a heap. Manas clutched his arm, pain coursing through his body, while Ananya tried to push herself up, dazed from the collision. Her vision blurred for a moment, but she forced herself to focus.

Raghav stood over them, towering like a dark specter, his eyes blazing with a new, dangerous energy. Ananya noticed the Kundals glowing even brighter than before, pulsing with power. She glanced at Manas, whose face was contorted with pain, his hand twisted at an unnatural angle.

"How… how did you survive?" Ananya whispered, her voice barely more than a breath.

Raghav's smile grew wider. "I have been reborn," he replied, his voice thick with pride. "And now, with the power of the Kundals, I am unstoppable."

Manas, fighting through the pain, managed to sit up slightly. "Raghav, this isn't you."

Raghav's expression hardened. "No, Manas," he hissed, "this is who I truly am."

Ananya, her mind racing, knew they had to act fast. If Raghav had become as powerful as he seemed, they were in more danger than ever before. She caught Manas' eye, and a silent understanding passed between them. They would not give up, not yet.

Manas and Ananya lay on the cold ground, their breaths shallow and pained. Ananya clutched her side where she had taken the brunt of Manas' fall, feeling the bruises already forming under her skin. Beside her, Manas' face was twisted in agony, his broken wrist cradled against his chest. Their bodies ached, but they knew there was no time to rest. They could hear the clamor of battle growing around them.

Ashwatthama, recovering from his wounds, stood tall beside Raghav, their eyes fixed on Parashurama Ji, who was moving swiftly towards them with a fierce determination in his gaze. His axe gleamed with divine energy, its edge sharp and ready, reflecting the light of the glowing Kavach above. Every step he took seemed to make the earth beneath him tremble.

Parashurama Ji's voice was steady, calm amidst the chaos.

"Ananya, take a moment. The Somras in your and Manas' veins will help you guys recover faster. Heal yourself and tend to Manas."

Ananya nodded, closing her eyes, focusing her breath as she felt the mystical Somras working its way through her wounds, knitting tissues together and numbing the pain. She moved quickly to Manas's side, her hands glowing faintly as she began to help him heal.

Meanwhile, Parashurama Ji's attention was fully on the enemies standing before him. "Ashwatthama! Raghav! If you wish to fight me, then come forward!" His voice was like a command, echoing through the cavern.

Ashwatthama, with a roar that could shake the heavens, charged at Parashurama Ji, his bare hands clenched into fists, his eyes filled with fury. Raghav followed closely behind, his muscles bulging with newfound strength, ready to strike. Shukracharya stood back, his lips moving silently, preparing a mantra with a sly smile on his face.

Parashurama Ji swung his axe with blinding speed, aiming for Ashwatthama's torso. Ashwatthama narrowly dodged, feeling the wind of the blade's swing brush past him. Raghav moved in from the side, his fist raised to strike. Parashurama Ji twisted his body just in time, deflecting the punch with the shaft of his axe, using it like a staff. The impact was strong, but Parashurama Ji was stronger. He pushed Raghav back, his feet sliding on the ground from the force.

Ashwatthama, taking advantage of the moment, came in from behind with a powerful kick aimed at Parashurama Ji's back. But Parashurama, with the agility of a young warrior, turned and caught Ashwatthama's leg mid-air, twisting it with a force that sent Ashwatthama spinning to the ground. Before Ashwatthama could recover, Parashurama brought his axe down, but Ashwatthama rolled away just in time, feeling the blade carve into the earth where he had been moments before.

Raghav, seeing his comrade in danger, charged again, this time with more ferocity. He leapt into the air, his fists clenched, aiming a double-handed strike at Parashurama Ji's head. Parashurama Ji raised his axe horizontally, blocking the blow, but the sheer force of Raghav's attack sent a shockwave through his arms. He staggered back a step, his feet digging into the ground to find balance.

Parashurama Ji did not hesitate. He swung the axe again, this time with a horizontal slash that caught Raghav off guard. The blade scraped against Raghav's arm, drawing blood. Raghav winced but did not falter. He gritted his teeth and launched another attack, this time going low, sweeping his leg to knock Parashurama off his feet.

Parashurama jumped, evading the sweep, and came down with the blunt end of his axe, aiming for Raghav's shoulder. But before the blow could connect, Shukracharya intervened, his voice rising in a chant. The air around them shimmered, and suddenly, a force field appeared, blocking Parashurama Ji's strike. The axe bounced back with a sharp clang, as if hitting a wall of iron.

Parashurama Ji's eyes flickered with anger as he turned his gaze to Shukracharya. "So, you choose to meddle in our fight with your mantras, Shukracharya?" he growled.

Shukracharya smirked, his hands glowing with a dark energy. "You may be powerful, Parashurama, but let's see how you fare against the magic of the Asuras!" He clapped his hands together, and a wave of black mist shot forth, aiming directly at Parashurama Ji.

Parashurama Ji swung his axe in a wide arc, the divine weapon cutting through the mist like a blade through water, dispersing it into nothingness. But Shukracharya was relentless; he began chanting another mantra, the ground beneath him glowing with dark runes, ready to unleash another attack.

Ashwatthama, now back on his feet, rushed forward, trying to grab Parashurama from behind, his massive hands reaching for his neck. But Parashurama, sensing the movement, spun around and delivered a powerful knee strike to Ashwatthama's chest, sending him stumbling backward, gasping for breath. He followed up with a quick, upward strike of his axe, aiming for Ashwatthama's head. Ashwatthama barely managed to dodge, feeling the axe graze his cheek, leaving a deep, bleeding cut.

Raghav seized this moment to attack, his movements swift and brutal. He moved in close, too close for Parashurama to use his axe effectively. He grabbed Parashurama's arm, twisting it, trying to disarm him. Parashurama responded with a headbutt, stunning Raghav momentarily, and freed his arm with a powerful jerk. He stepped back, regaining his stance, the axe poised for the next strike.

Shukracharya, seeing the battle turning, unleashed his mantra. The ground beneath Parashurama Ji began to crack, and dark vines erupted, reaching out like serpents, trying to entangle his legs. Parashurama Ji jumped back, swinging his axe to cut through the vines, but more kept coming, faster and more aggressive.

"Enough of this!" Parashurama Ji roared, slamming the butt of his axe into the ground. A burst of divine light exploded from the point of impact, burning the vines to ash and sending a shockwave toward Shukracharya. Shukracharya shielded himself with a barrier, but the force of the shockwave pushed him back several steps.

Ashwatthama, seizing the moment, lunged at Parashurama Ji again, his fists like hammers, but Parashurama met him head-on. The two collided with a thundering impact, their strength evenly matched, their muscles straining, veins bulging as they pushed against each other, testing who would yield first.

Raghav, seeing Ashwatthama locked in a struggle with Parashurama Ji, tried to flank him from the side, but Parashurama Ji was too quick. He sidestepped, bringing the blunt end of his axe crashing into Raghav's side, knocking the wind out of him. Raghav fell to one knee, gasping for breath, but still glaring with defiance.

Parashurama Ji, panting but unyielding, stood his ground, his axe gleaming in the dim light. "Is this all you have, Shukracharya? You will not win this battle with your tricks and treachery."

Shukracharya, undeterred, began chanting again, his hands weaving complex patterns in the air, preparing another spell. Ashwatthama, fueled by rage, charged once more, and Raghav slowly rose, his eyes burning with determination.

Shukracharya's lips twisted in frustration as he completed the freezing mantra. Parashurama Ji's muscles locked up, his body stiffening mid-motion. He felt a cold paralysis grip his limbs. His divine axe, held aloft, hung suspended in the air, powerless. His eyes blazed with fury, but he could not move.

Seeing their chance, Raghav and Ashwatthama exchanged a glance, a silent understanding passing between them. With a battle cry, they surged forward, both kicking Parashurama Ji with all their might. The impact was brutal. Parashurama Ji's body staggered backward, stumbling, and he fell heavily onto the ground beside Ananya and Manas.

Ananya and Manas tried to move, but before they could react, Shukracharya turned his attention to them, chanting the freezing mantra once more. The air around Ananya and Manas seemed to thicken like cold molasses, and they too were frozen in place, their eyes wide with fear and anger. Their limbs were locked, bodies unable to move despite their best efforts.

Shukracharya's voice dripped with malice as he gave his command, "Raghav, Ashwatthama, do you see those boulders? Lift them and crush all three of them. Ananya and Manas will perish, and Parashurama, though a Chiranjivi, will suffer greatly from the blow."

Raghav and Ashwatthama nodded, their eyes narrowing in determination. They moved toward the boulders — massive, heavy rocks that towered above them, each easily weighing a ton. Their muscles flexed as they bent low, gripping the stones with their powerful hands, veins bulging with the strain. Slowly, they lifted the rocks above their heads, their faces contorted with effort.

Parashurama Ji, Ananya, and Manas watched in horror, struggling against their unseen bonds, their bodies shaking with the effort to break free. But the freezing mantra held them tight, their movements reduced to mere trembles.

With a synchronized heave, Raghav and Ashwatthama positioned the boulders directly above the helpless trio. The rocks loomed ominously, casting long shadows over their

prone bodies. The air was thick with tension, and every second stretched into eternity.

Just as Raghav and Ashwatthama prepared to bring the boulders crashing down, a sudden sound sliced through the air — a deep, resonant hum that grew louder, a whistling roar approaching with incredible speed.

THWACK!

A golden blur streaked through the cavern with a thunderous impact. It struck the rocks with the force of a meteor, shattering them into thousands of pieces. The fragments exploded outward like shrapnel, striking Shukracharya, who stumbled backward, clutching his face as blood trickled from a gash on his forehead. Raghav and Ashwatthama were also thrown off balance, crashing to the ground as they lost their grip on the boulders.

The air was filled with the echoing sound of the shattered rocks scattering across the cavern floor. The mysterious object that had caused the devastation landed with a heavy thud, embedding itself in the ground between Parashurama Ji, Ananya, and Manas. It glowed with a radiant golden light, humming with a divine energy that seemed to shake the very air around it.

It was a Mace — a Golden Mace.

Ananya's eyes widened in recognition, her mind racing as she beheld the weapon before her. "Could it be...?"

To be continued...

ABOUT THE AUTHOR

My life story is a tapestry woven from the threads of technology, chess, and the written word. I am Aman Shekhar, a Mobile App Developer by profession, a Chess Player by heart, and an Aspiring Author by ambition.

The inception of my journey occurred in the captivating realm of technology. As a Mobile App Developer, I've had the privilege of witnessing and contributing to the ever-evolving landscape of mobile applications. Yet, beyond the digital confines, there's another realm where I thrive—the chessboard. The intricate dance of chess pieces, the strategic manoeuvres, and the constant pursuit of improvement have always drawn me in. My journey as a Chess Player has been both challenging and rewarding, a testament to the power of intellectual pursuit. In the quieter moments of my life, I turn to the world of words. Writing isn't just a hobby; it's a lifelong dream. The aspiration to become a great author fuels my creative spirit. With every stroke of the keyboard or scratch of the pen, I embark on new literary adventures, seeking to inspire and connect with readers. But my life is more than just work and writing. It's enriched by a medley of hobbies. Reading opens doors to realms of knowledge and imagination, while travel provides the canvas for new experiences, cultures, and flavours. These activities are the colours that paint the tapestry of my life.

If you would like to connect, you may reach me via email at *aman.shekhar4@gmail.com*. Additionally, you can find me on Instagram at "*amanshekhar1403*." I look forward to potential collaboration and meaningful discussions.

Thank you for joining me on this remarkable journey of self-discovery and ambition.

Manas' Legacy:

Guardian of the Saraswati River

Coming Soon